Fracture

Other Frankie MacFarlane Mysteries
Death Assemblage
Detachment Fault
Quarry
Hoodoo

Fracture

Susan Cummins Miller

Texas Tech University Press

This book is typeset in Sabon. The paper used in this book meets the minimum requirements of ANSI/NISO Z39.48-1992 (R1997). ∞

Library of Congress Cataloging-in-Publication Data
Miller, Susan Cummins, 1949–
    Fracture / Susan Cummins Miller.
        p. cm. — (Frankie MacFarlane mysteries)
    Summary: "Now reunited, Frankie MacFarlane and Philo Dain attempt to recover the Dain coin collection stolen by Philo's murdered aunt. As they follow the trail, Frankie and Philo unearth secrets from Philo's past and discover a treasure hidden from the world for nearly two hundred years"—Provided by publisher.
    ISBN 978-0-89672-685-7 (hardcover : alk. paper) 1. MacFarlane, Frankie (Fictitious character)—Fiction. 2. Women geologists—Fiction. 3. Treasure troves—Fiction. I. Title.
        PS3613.I555F73 2011
        813'.6—dc22   2010048818

Printed in the United States of America
11 12 13 14 15 16 17 18 19 / 9 8 7 6 5 4 3 2 1

Texas Tech University Press
Box 41037
Lubbock, Texas 79409-1037 USA
800.832.4042
ttup@ttu.edu
www.ttupress.org

In memory of Molcie Lou Halsell Rodenberger
and Diane Wood Middlebrook, who wrote about
and mentored women's journeys.

Fracture:

[mineralogy] The breaking of a mineral other than along planes of cleavage; *[structural geology]* a general term for any break in a rock, whether or not it causes displacement, due to mechanical failure by stress. Fracture includes cracks, joints, and faults.

—R. L. Bates and J. A. Jackson, eds.,
Glossary of Geology, 2nd ed., 1980

Part I

The Call
'Tis all a Checkerboard of Nights and Days
Where Destiny with Men for Pieces plays:
Hither and thither moves, and mates, and slays . . .

—Edward FitzGerald, *The Rubáiyát of Omar Khayyám* (trans.
1859)

1

Tuesday, May 16
5:10 p.m.

The fluorescent light directly above the man's car flickered once, twice, then went dark. He looked up from his travel chessboard and noticed that his cigar had died, too. Cursing, he relit it, puffing the smoke through the open driver's window.

The blue-white glow from the other ceiling lights in the parking garage turned the concrete pillars into bas-relief sculptures. Every few seconds a car drove past his rear bumper. None slowed to check him out. It was rush hour. The drivers just wanted to get home or find their motel as quickly as possible.

The man's cell phone sounded the opening bars of "Zorba's Dance." He flipped open the cell and said, "You're thirty minutes late. I was beginning to worry."

"The connecting flight was delayed in L.A." A woman's voice, tinged with sardonic humor. "All set?"

"Yes. Everything went smoothly?"

"Except the usual hassle at security. Otherwise the items didn't leave my side."

"Good. I'll be there in ten."

"You're not at home, then."

The man paused, choosing his words carefully. "I made a preliminary pass—to make sure things go without a hitch."

"You're such an old woman."

"That's not what you said last time."

Her deep laugh resonated in his ear. "Touché." Her voice sobered. "The codes worked?"

"Perfectly."

"Didn't I tell you? Nothing will go wrong. See you out front."

The man held the silent phone for a moment, then slipped it into his breast pocket. Tucking the cigar into the ashtray, he backed the car out of its slot and joined the queue exiting the parking garage. He'd arrived at the airport early, not wanting to chance rush-hour traffic delays. As the queue inched forward, he lifted the travel chessboard from his lap, studying the positions of the pieces.

Nothing will go wrong, he repeated to himself. *The plan's solid, the players are in position, and I control the center of the board.*

The kiosk attendant was a gray-haired Latina. The man didn't waste a smile on her as he handed over his ticket and a twenty. While she rang it up, he moved the white queen into position on the chessboard.

Checkmate, you son of a bitch.

2

Tuesday, May 16, Tucson, AZ
10:15 p.m.

The muted ring of the bedside phone interrupted my private party with Philo Dain. We'd been making up for lost time since his return from Afghanistan.

"Ignore it," said Philo.

"No one in my family calls after nine." I rolled off him. "Unless it's an emergency."

"Could be a wrong number."

"That's why I'm letting it go to the answering machine."

Philo kissed my shoulder, slid out of bed, and padded to the guesthouse kitchen. I heard water running, a glass being filled, as the phone rang a fourth time. The machine clicked on. My anonymous voice gave the phone number and said I was unavailable. An understatement.

"I hope I've reached Frankie MacFarlane's house," said a male voice. "This is Derek Dain, Philo's uncle. It's urgent—"

I picked up. "This is Frankie. If you hold a minute, I'll see if Philo's available."

Philo was standing at the foot of the king-size bed, holding two glasses of water. I covered the receiver and said, "Well?"

He walked slowly to the bedside table, set down the glasses, took the phone. Sitting on the edge of the bed, he said, "How'd you know I was home, Derek?"

Philo had returned two days ago. Except for his debriefing yesterday and a MacFarlane family party on Mother's Day, we hadn't ventured off my property. To be more exact, we hadn't left my guesthouse, where I was living while I remodeled the main house. To be still more precise, we'd hardly been out of the bedroom.

A shaft of moonlight fell across Philo's back, highlighting an assortment of small circular burn marks and fine knife scars—physical reminders of time spent as a prisoner in the Colombian jungle. I'd written Philo off for dead when he went missing that time. But he was a survivor. One more thing we had in common.

The muscles of his back and neck were tense. I reached up to massage them, but Philo leaned away from my touch, leaving my hands holding nothing more substantial than desire. I didn't push it. After seventeen months apart, we were still finding our footing with each other.

"We said all we had to say to each other years ago, Derek." The OFF button beeped. Philo sat for a moment, staring down at the cordless receiver. I didn't see his arm come up, but a moment later the phone smacked against the brick wall.

Philo looked at his hand, then turned to me. I heard his indrawn breath.

Putting a finger over his lips, I said, "My sentiments, exactly." I felt the smile beneath my finger, and took it away. "Though it might have been more satisfying if Derek had still been on the line."

His smile turned to a grin. He picked up the water glasses and handed me one. "I owe you a phone."

I drained the glass and handed it back. "You owe me more than that."

"Debts I don't mind paying—with interest." He slid in beside me. "Now, where were we?"

"Rounding third," I said. This time he didn't pull away when my hands slid down his back. "The coach was waving us in."

"I want another turn at bat."

"Now you're talking."

3

Wednesday, May 17, Tucson, AZ

7:30 a.m.

I sat in a leafy corner of my guesthouse patio, watching Philo sleep on the chaise lounge pad he'd tossed onto the patio floor. His face, lean and tan under close-cropped hair, seemed no less alert than when he was awake. Every time the old porch timbers creaked or snapped, adjusting to the rapidly rising temperature, muscles flicked under his skin.

He murmured something in a foreign language. Dari, perhaps. Or Pashto. A smile touched his lips, deepening the vertical clefts that scored each cheek. His face relaxed.

I wasn't concerned that Philo had left my bed in the middle of the night. He'd been unable to sleep easily indoors for years. At his home in central Tucson, he'd designed a rooftop aerie where he slept in all seasons. He'd be there now, except that his business partner, E. J. Killeen, and his family had been house-sitting while Philo was overseas. He was giving them time to finish moving into their new place.

Philo muttered again and shifted on the pad. His arms and legs were damp with sweat, as was the flowered cotton sheet covering his torso. The thermometer on the guest-house wall showed eighty. The forecast was for triple digits. No rain in sight.

A fly landed on Philo's right hand, moving from one scraped knuckle to another. Though I'd braced myself for the worst, Philo had arrived home uninjured—except for those abrasions. Mentally and emotionally he seemed as strong as ever. But then, he knew how to compartmentalize. He'd had years of practice. Yet somehow Derek

Dain had slipped through Philo's carefully constructed defenses.

I knew little of what had caused the strain in Philo's relationship with his uncle. Philo was an only child, orphaned at thirteen when his parents died in a light-plane crash in the Sierras. Derek and his first wife, Margaret, became Philo's guardians. There were no other relatives. But if either guardian had a nurturing bone in their bodies, I'd never seen it.

Philo had enrolled in my brother Kit's class. They shared a love of baseball and had played on the same teams from middle school through college. In all that time I'd seen Derek Dain only twice, the first time soon after Philo came to Arizona. I was eight, and my mother was picking Philo up for a baseball game. Derek and Margaret happened to be standing in their driveway, loading the car for a weekend trip—a trip that would leave Philo alone. On the spur of the moment, my mother asked if Philo could spend the weekend with us. Derek shrugged. Margaret said, "Thank you, yes." Then they both turned away.

My parents, aware of the emotional desert of the Dain home, absorbed Philo into our noisy, active MacFarlane household. The estrangement between Philo and his uncle deepened until, on his eighteenth birthday, Philo moved into the bunkhouse with my four brothers. He stayed there for his last quarter of high school. Derek, by then divorced from Margaret and courting wife number two, didn't object. But when he turned up at his nephew's graduation—accompanied by a girl no older than Philo—they had words. That was the last time I saw Derek, or heard Philo mention his name.

Now Derek was back. I couldn't help wondering what he wanted, and why he'd contacted Philo so soon after his return. Despite Philo's rejection, I doubted Derek would just let it go.

I stood and walked over to the sleeping soldier. As I knelt to straighten the sheet that covered him, he shouted something—one word, over and over, in a voice filled with anguish. And then body and voice stilled.

Inside the main house, a phone began to ring. I scrambled to my feet and ran to answer it.

4

Philo's watch vibrated against his wrist. Time to go.

He pushed back from the table at the rear of the wedding hall and stood, half a foot taller than every man in the place. The bride and groom sat on the dais, laughing together, clapping in time to the music. Nasrullah danced between lines of men. Happy faces, happy music, despite the never-ending war beyond the festooned walls.

Smiling, Philo made his way around the back of the crowd. No one noticed him. Hours ago, after a flurry of glances and murmurs, the other guests had welcomed him as Nasrullah's friend. It helped that Philo spoke passable Dari.

Outside, he stood for a moment by the garden wall, collecting his thoughts. The sharp winds of early spring bit through his borrowed finery. The scents of lamb kabobs, rice, and Afghan bread lingered in the air, rich and heavy against the odors of dust and smog that clung to Kabul even at midnight. Philo pulled the Afghan cell phone from his pocket. Sensed someone behind him—Nasrullah, downing a citrus drink. Festive strings of lights reflected from his pale eyes and caught the sheen of sweat on his face. He set his glass aside, put a hand on Philo's shoulder, and said, "You need to leave?"

"As soon as I make one phone call."

"To your Frankie?"

"Who else?"

"Then I shall dance some more. Come find me when you are finished." Nasrullah squeezed Philo's shoulder and turned back to the hall.

From the front of the house came popping sounds. Firecrackers, Philo thought. But gunfire, too. He'd witnessed it *before at Afghan celebrations, and elsewhere in the Middle East.*

He moved quickly to the shelter of the patio. Crouching in a corner to avoid spent bullets falling from the sky, he punched Frankie's number into his cell. Her dissertation defense had been scheduled for earlier this morning, California time. If all went well, there'd be double cause for celebration—her achievement, his birthday. He knew she'd be thinking of him, as he was thinking of her.

"Hello?" Frankie's voice sounded tentative. She'd have seen that the call came from Afghanistan, and might leap to conclusions. He should have thought of that.

"It's Philo. I only have a minute."

"Are you at a party?"

He laughed. "A wedding."

"As long as it isn't yours," she said.

"Not a chance. Is it over?"

"Signed, sealed, and soon to be delivered."

"Good. We'll celebrate when I get home. How does a trip to Grand Canyon sound?"

"Sounds perfect. When?"

"Late summer, maybe early fall. Depends on the Boss." When she didn't say anything, he added, "Don't worry if you don't hear from me."

The firecrackers had stopped, but the gunfire was moving closer. "I love you," said Philo.

"I love—"

The hall exploded with a deafening sound. The back wall blew outwards, taking the patio roof with it. The sky hailed shards of glass, flaming wood, lumps of brick, and human remains down on his corner. Smoke and screams poured from the breached walls. Flames lit the night.

Philo lay on his back. Cushions had broken his fall. A length of cloth twisted around his torso. He checked to see if his limbs were functional. Carefully wiggled fingers and toes. All working. Oddly enough, he now wore boxers and nothing else, except the field watch, circling his left wrist.

Yelling Nasrullah's name, Philo crawled toward the heat and smoke pouring through the hole where the door had been. Nasrullah didn't answer. But somewhere, far away, a phone rang. A voice answered, speaking English . . .

English? The hair on Philo's arms stood up.

Struggling to pull himself from the dream, Philo reached instinctively for the gun that wasn't on his hip, the knife that wasn't on his shin. He had no weapons but his hands, feet, and what lay within reach. His right hand touched an empty flowerpot, a plastic watering can, a rusted weight. His hand closed around it. He heard the whisper of bare feet on stone.

"I wouldn't," said a woman's voice, rich and throaty.

Frankie's voice.

5

"I really wouldn't," I repeated, keeping my voice easy. I was standing in the middle of the flagstone courtyard, a few feet from Philo's makeshift bed on the covered patio. The phone call had been from Derek. Again. But that could wait.

Philo's eyes went from confused and dreamy to focused and sharp. He took his hand away from the rusty ten-pound weight, saying, "Would have made a decent discus."

"No doubt," I agreed. Moving closer, I touched Philo's cheek. "You okay?"

"Didn't know where I was for a minute." Philo rolled to a crouch. His face held the impressions of the cushion he'd used as a pillow. His eyes had a haunted look. I didn't know where his dreams had taken him, but it hadn't been a pleasant journey.

I smiled and held out my hands. "How about some breakfast?"

Philo let me pull him up. Opening the guesthouse door he said, "Did I hear the phone?"

"Derek. He said he really needs to see you."

"Tough for him." Philo followed me into the dim, cool house.

I opened the refrigerator and began handing Philo the ingredients for an omelet. "He insisted on coming here at nine. I countered, suggesting he meet you at the office, but he thought that was too public."

"Sounds like Derek."

"Sorry, I couldn't put him off," I said. "But we could leave before he arrives."

"That would only postpone the inevitable." Philo set

the eggs and cheese and salsa on the counter and put his arms around me. "Don't worry. I'll handle him."

I kissed him and handed him a bowl and the omelet pan. We were quiet while we worked. I didn't know what Philo was thinking, but I pondered what Derek wanted that was so urgent. Had his fourth wife left him? If so, Heather had lasted longer than the two women who'd preceded her. She'd shown remarkable staying power, considering the thirty-year difference in their ages. Maybe she no longer wanted a father figure. Maybe age had slowed Derek down. Maybe he didn't have the same stamina in bed, or he'd lost interest in open marriages. Whatever. None of that would matter to Philo. He hadn't said goodbye to his uncle before he'd gone to Afghanistan. He hadn't called him when he returned. As relationships go, theirs had no proof of life.

We took our breakfast outside, where we ate as if we hadn't eaten in a year. Stacking the empty plates, I said, "Derek'll be here in thirty minutes."

Philo stood, stripped off baseball cap and dark glasses and dropped them on the deck. He took a running dive into the pool, swam five lengths under water, surfaced at the shallow end. He sat on the bottom step, eyes closed, motionless. He must have sensed me standing beside him. He opened his eyes and said, "Nice suit, by the way."

I was wearing an electric-blue bikini. It was too hot for anything else. "Thanks," I said, offering him a gaudily striped beach towel.

He took the towel and tossed it onto the pool deck. Slipping an arm behind my knees, he tugged, toppling me into the water. I surfaced, sputtering, my hair a wet curtain over my face. Philo leaned back on his elbows, smiling. Retrieving my hair clip from the bottom of the pool, I combed my black mane with my fingers and twisted it back up.

I sat next to him on the step, curving into his side, staring at the light patterns refracting on the bottom and sides of the pool. The water was warm as blood. I wished Derek would call and cancel his visit. I wanted to protect this private world Philo and I had created.

He kissed the top of my head, put a finger under my chin, and tilted it till our eyes met. "What's the matter?"

"In your sleep you were, shall we say, speaking in tongues."

"Speaking, or shouting?"

"Shouting, at the end. Just one word. It sounded like 'Nasrullah.'"

He turned away from me and snagged the towel from the deck, passing it roughly over his hair and face. *Let it go,* I decided, as he left the pool. No need to press him so soon.

Stretching his six-four frame, Philo grabbed my yoga mat and started his morning exercise routine, a mix of calisthenics, martial arts moves, and qigong. The routine was his form of meditation. But the moves also eased the stiffness in his right leg, the lingering effect of a combat wound.

I climbed out of the pool, toweled off, and went back to my chair in the shade. Picking up my notepad, I began to list the things I still had to do before Teresa Black's bachelorette party. She was marrying my brother Jamie a week from Saturday, and I was the maid of honor. The prenuptial party would be here, at my home, the night before the wedding.

I looked up from my list a few minutes later to watch Philo, silent and focused, gliding through the final moves of his sequence. His limp had almost disappeared. Turning, he jumped back into the pool to rinse the sweat from his body. Seconds later he was walking toward me, slowly toweling off. He halted next to my frayed lawn chair.

Beyond the picket fence, a car maneuvered up the dirt-and-gravel drive. It circled the island of desert vegetation, coming to a stop on the far side, by a palo verde.

Philo gave a low whistle. "A Mercedes SLR McLaren. Half a mil, easy."

I grinned. "You planning to receive Uncle Derek in your skivvies?"

6

I slipped a cotton shift over my almost-dry bikini and ran a comb through my hair. Standing in the shadows of the guesthouse porch I watched a silver-haired man lever himself gracefully from the Mercedes. Midsixties, maybe six two, he had a tennis player's lean torso and a swimmer's shoulders. He went with the car—cool, tailored, and expensive in a blue knit shirt, sand-colored pants, dark loafers. Every inch the wealthy power player.

Stepping away from the car, Derek Dain surveyed the scene. The rutted driveway. My white Toyota Tacoma parked under the carport. Philo's green Sierra pickup in the sparse shade of a mesquite. The sixty-year-old, one-story, brick-and-glass main house and guesthouse, enclosed by a sagging, brown-painted picket fence. The ladders, paint supplies, and buckets of roof sealant stored next to the back door . . .

Derek took his time. His expression suggested he was calculating to the penny the value of the property and all it contained: suburban ranch. Two and a half acres. Great views of the Santa Catalina and Rincon mountains. Close to Saguaro National Park East. Prime site for a shitload of condos. The zoning regs wouldn't be a problem . . .

I could have saved him from all the mental gymnastics. My property, inherited last year from my maternal grandmother, wasn't for sale.

Behind me the glass door to the sitting room slid open with a scraping sound. Philo was at my elbow as Derek turned. Philo stepped to the gate and pushed it open. Derek closed the car door and sauntered to meet him. The two men stood three feet apart, gazes locked. They didn't touch.

"You look thinner," Derek said.

"War does that," said Philo.

Without another word, they turned and walked, side by side, toward the guesthouse. I met them at the gate.

"Frankie, you remember my uncle, Derek Dain. Derek, Frankie MacFarlane."

Up close, I could see a family resemblance—ear and nose shapes, hairlines, rangy, athletic build. Philo was a couple of inches taller. But whereas conventionally handsome Derek Dain had unlined fair skin, no tan, and streaks of black in his silver hair, Philo's dark blonde hair had touches of gray only at the sides. And his tanned, angular face, scored by lines of laughter and pain, had settled into a comfortable cragginess—an aging warrior, though he was only thirty-six. Derek's face looked bland by comparison. Plastic surgery can have that effect.

Derek's gaze met mine, then slid downward, lingering on the places where cotton sundress touched bikini. I wanted to wrap myself in a beach towel, but instead I held out my hand.

Derek smiled and shook it. "Of course," he said. "Mac and Emily's daughter."

"Amy," I said. "My mother's name is Amy."

"That's right. Amy. Been a long time." Then to Philo, "I need to talk to you. Alone."

"We can speak in front of Frankie." Philo sent me a warning glance, just a casual flicker, but I fielded it. "She works with me from time to time." Which was almost the truth. I'd been peripherally involved in a couple of investigations before he left for Afghanistan.

Derek shook his head. "Alone."

"It's a deal breaker, Derek." Philo opened the gate.

"Okay. She can stay." Derek turned his back and walked with a smooth, easy gait to the umbrella-shaded table where Philo and I'd eaten breakfast. Derek chose the chair facing the pool.

Philo shrugged, closed the gate again, and took the chair directly across from Derek. I formed the apex of the tense little triangle. The two men studied each other silently. Derek caved first. "May I have a glass of water, Frankie?"

I smiled, acknowledging his move to get me out of the way, even for a moment. "Of course. Ice?"

"Please."

As I walked the short distance to the guesthouse, I heard Philo say, "Is this business or personal, Derek?"

"Business for you, personal for me."

"Ahh . . . How *is* Auntie Heather?"

"We're separated," said Derek. "As of yesterday."

I stopped at the guesthouse door, wanting to catch Philo's reaction. "I'm sorry to hear that," he said, sounding not at all sorry. "Any hope of reconciliation?"

"None whatsoever."

"Is there a new Auntie Tiffany on the horizon?"

I swallowed a laugh and went inside, where I loaded a tray with a pitcher of filtered water and three plastic glasses, one with ice. When I returned to the wrought-iron table, Derek's eyes had narrowed to slits. "It took a lot for me to come here, Philo. I need your help."

"There are other private investigators in town."

"I need someone I can trust implicitly."

"Bullshit."

Whereas I was slow to trust anyone, Philo lived by a different, more cut-and-dried code. He offered trust and left it in place until it was broken. Philo didn't believe in do-overs.

A tiny jumping spider crawled along the arm of my chair and hopped onto the table. Derek saw the movement and raised his hand. Before he could smash the spider, I blew it off the table. Derek's eyes darkened.

Philo looked at me and winked. "Frankie and I are going to take some time off," he said. "But I'd be happy to have my partner set up—"

"No." Derek slapped the table, making the glasses jump. "This is a delicate situation, and you're the only investigator who would recognize Heather, even in disguise."

"My partner's good."

"I'm sure he is, but . . ."

Philo smiled. "But he hasn't seen Heather naked?"

"To put it crudely."

"I didn't sleep with her, Derek."

"It didn't matter then. It matters less now."

"It matters to me."

"Okay. She tried to seduce you—" Derek seemed to remember I was there. "Do we have to go into that?" he said to Philo.

Yes, I wanted to say. *We're just getting to the good part.* But I left the decision to Philo, who was studying the grazed knuckles of his right hand. His twisting and turning this morning had rubbed off some of the fresh scabs, revealing the healing tissue beneath. I sensed that he wanted to plant that pink skin in Derek's face.

But instead, Philo shrugged and said, "You're right. No use rehashing old issues. Won't change anything." His eyes glittered. "Let's cut to the chase. Why are you here?"

Derek's eyes shifted to me for a second before he said, "Heather stole my coin collection."

"Surprise, surprise. Coins are portable, easily converted. She could cross any border with them in her purse."

"Exactly."

"When did you start collecting coins?"

Derek frowned. The muscles barely moved, but his color was returning to normal. "You don't remember?"

"No."

"My grandfather—your great-grandfather, Philo—began collecting coins as a hobby. Dad and I inherited the passion. Your father didn't care much about them, one way or another."

Derek spoke the truth. I knew that Philo's parents, KC and Ann, had had little interest in material wealth. They'd met in Cairo, at the end of their respective Peace Corps tours—KC in Afghanistan for three years, Ann in India for two. Kindred spirits, they'd traveled up the Nile together, falling in love. Philo hadn't come along until much later, when they were living in a commune in Oregon.

"You had the coins appraised?" Philo said.

Derek nodded. "I was executor of your grandparents' estate."

"Convenient."

"What are you insinuating?"

Philo opened his mouth to say something, then shook his head. "It doesn't matter. It was all a long time ago."

Derek looked disconcerted. "Okay then. Let's get back to the coin collection. At today's prices, at auction, the coins would go for roughly ten million dollars. Maybe eleven."

Philo had been rocking in his chair. He stopped. The swamp cooler on the guesthouse roof hummed. At the top of a mesquite a mockingbird sang without pause.

"How many coins, exactly, are we talking about?" Philo said.

"Sixty-odd. I added to the collection and then trimmed the holdings—fewer coins, but greater value. My agreement with KC was that if I ever decided to sell, I'd give KC half the current market value of the collection. If I didn't sell, then the collection would be owned jointly by our respective offspring. Since I have none, the coins will go to you when I die. You already own half of the original collection."

Philo's fingers tightened on my hand. "Why have you waited till now to tell me about the joint ownership, Derek?"

"I tried to interest you in the collection when you first came to live with us. You wanted to play sports. I figured I'd wait till you were an adult."

"I've been an adult for years. Those coins could have paid my way through college."

"That would have been short-sighted."

"Says you."

"Eighteen-year-olds have no understanding of money."

"And you do? By the time I graduated from high school, you'd lost the rest of my inheritance in some development scheme."

Derek leaned forward. "We're digressing." He took a folded paper from his pocket and handed it to Philo. "Anticipating your next question," he said, then fell silent.

I scooted my chair close enough that I could read the typed page, a copy of a prenuptial agreement. Derek had highlighted in yellow the relevant passage. All Dain family property—including, but not limited to, art objects, the coin collection, and a place called Foggy Gulch Ranch—was controlled by the Dain Trust. Should Derek and Heather divorce, he would retain his portion of the Dain Trust property. If he should predecease Heather, she could not sue the Dain Trust for Derek's share.

"The Dain Trust," Derek said, "was established by your great-grandfather. Your grandfather added items to it. The trust says, in effect, that no part may be sold, given away, or disposed of without the consent of all male heirs in the direct line." I must have reacted because Derek said to me, "Old-fashioned, I grant you, but legal." He turned back to Philo. "Though the language is fireproof, I made sure I had a prenup so the trust wouldn't be contested. Why waste all that money on litigation?"

"You had prenups for all your marriages?" Philo said.

"Except with Margaret. We worked things out."

"What about my parents?"

"KC didn't bother with a prenup. He couldn't have cared less about the trust. But it's moot anyway. At the moment, you and I are the only male heirs—unless you have offspring I don't know about."

"We haven't had time." Philo smiled at me.

"Ah, so that's the way the wind blows," Derek said.

Philo didn't respond, silently posting a no-trespassing sign on our relationship. Refolding the paper Derek had given us, I handed it back. "You're saying you want Philo to track down Heather and recover his inheritance."

Derek sat back. "In a nutshell."

"Do you know where she is?"

"She called me last night from her sister's house in Menlo Park. A real slanging match." Derek wrinkled his nose in distaste. "She said she was leaving there and slammed down the phone. She hasn't shown up at any of our vacation homes, so I'm guessing she's still in the Bay Area."

"Foggy Gulch Ranch?" Philo said. To me he added, "My grandparents' place on the ocean side of the Penin-sula—Woodside."

"Heather hates that house," Derek said. "Too foggy, even for someone who grew up on the coast. No neighbors. Just twelve hundred acres of solitude. She's not big on solitude. But I asked the ranch manager to call me if she showed up." He stared at a windfall lemon, rotting on the flagstones. "It's more likely she'd head for Daly City, where she was raised."

"You've contacted her parents?" Philo said.

Derek shook his head. "Russ Helmsley died last fall, and I didn't want to upset Gabrielle. She's not in the best of health."

"Does Heather have her own bank and credit accounts, separate from your business ones?"

"Checking and retirement accounts. A couple of department store credit cards. Everything else was joint. I checked last night. No activity."

"Really?" Philo said.

"She didn't need them yet. In addition to the coins, she took $500,000 in cash from the safe. I don't care about the money. She can have it. She earned it."

Philo drank more water, then refilled the glass. "What proof can you offer that Heather's still alive?"

Derek's face flushed. He struggled for control. "You think I murdered her? Disposed of the body somewhere?"

"People kill for a lot less than half a mil in cash and a coin collection."

Derek took a cell phone from his pocket and handed it to Philo. "She called me this morning."

Scrolling back through the call log, Philo saw my home phone number, and then a call from Heather. Local Arizona number. It must be her cell.

I got up and grabbed my notebook and pen from the table on the porch. While I wrote down the number, Philo went to his truck, returning moments later with a small recording device that plugged into the phone. He walked to the edge of the pool. I followed. Derek didn't move.

Heather answered the call on the fifth ring. Philo punched SPEAKER. "Do we have an agreement, Derek?" A woman's voice, surprisingly sweet, despite the harsh words.

Philo stared at the ripples of light breaking on the bottom of the pool. The knuckles of the hand holding the phone turned white.

The sweet voice sharpened. "Derek, are you there?"

Philo took a deep breath, gathered himself. "It's Philo."

"Ah. Welcome home. Glad you didn't come back in a body bag." She could have been discussing the weather. "Are we on SPEAKER?"

"Yes. Derek wants me retrieve the coin collection."

I expected Heather to pause and consider the implications of her answer, but she jumped in with both feet. "He came to you despite our, um, history?"

"We have no history."

"There's still time. I'll be a free woman soon—a free, *rich* woman."

Philo ignored the invitation. "You remember that night I came home from the hospital—after Colombia?"

"Like it was yesterday."

"What were you wearing?"

"A green silk robe. Short. Nothing else."

Philo nodded and said, "You signed a prenup. If you give the coins back, Derek says you can keep the five hundred grand."

"He voids the prenup and I'll deliver the coins."

"That's blackmail."

"Barter's a nicer word. A simple trade."

"Doesn't work that way."

"Sure it does. Derek's not going to have me arrested. The publicity wouldn't be good for business."

"How do I know you two aren't in this together—that this isn't some scheme to defraud the insurance company?"

Heather's laugh was harsh, strident. "The coins aren't insured."

Philo turned and looked at Derek. He nodded. Philo said, "Well, that was short-sighted of him."

"His loss, my gain."

"You want him to contact you at this number?"

"No, I'm getting rid of this cell. When he wants to deal, he can leave a message at my sister Gwen's house in Menlo Park. I won't be there—I'll access it remotely." Another laugh. "But, Philo? Tell Derek he'll have to be quick. I've lined up a buyer."

"How quick?"

"I'm comfortable for now. Let's say three days. And don't bother to come after me. You won't find me."

The line went dead. Philo took off the recording device, walked back to the table, and handed the phone to his uncle. "Satisfied?" said Derek.

"Not remotely. But I know Heather's alive and well. I doubt that even *you* would remember what she was wearing nine years ago."

"On the contrary. I remember exactly what she was wearing that night. I made her burn it the next day, after you left."

Philo ignored him, seemingly transfixed by a pyrrhuloxia chirruping in a palo verde. A faint breeze fluttered the edges of the umbrella.

"I thought you didn't care what Philo did or didn't do with Heather," I said to Derek.

"Don't you have fieldwork to organize or papers to grade?"

So he'd checked me out. That meant he probably knew, before arriving here, that Philo and I were a couple. What was he up to?

"Semester's over," I said. "I have all the time in the world."

Philo laughed. Derek scowled. Their eyes locked. Two alpha males marking their territories. Derek's territory included large parts of southern Arizona and God knows what else. But next to Philo, Derek seemed like a synthetic sapphire in a gold-plated setting. All form, little substance.

The West has always been a place of false fronts. Two-story faces on one-story buildings. Fast-talking land developers spouting plans for limitless growth. Get in, build, sell out, move on before the problems surface—ground fissures linked to water table drawdown, local plumes of subsurface contamination from factories long gone, and too little water to support an exploding population.

Observing their silent duel, I sensed that underneath his smooth facade, Derek was strung tight as a new guitar. He said, "Well, are you going to help me or not?"

"You don't need me. Heather told you exactly how to reach her—through her sister. That means Heather's in the Bay Area, as you suspected. You can rendezvous wherever she chooses and make the exchange. Better yet, why don't you just go to the police? Theft is theft."

Derek ignored Philo's second suggestion. "I can't leave just now. I have something big going down this week."

"Worth more than ten million?"

"Worth five times that much."

If Derek thought that would impress Philo, he'd misread his nephew, who rocked casually in his chair.

"You really don't care if Heather takes the coin collection?" Derek prodded. "What about the sons you'll have some day?"

"I live in the present, Derek. Besides, you're lying to me."

Derek shoved back his heavy chair, walked to the picket fence, and gazed over it toward the Mercedes. His hands were in his pockets, jingling keys and change like worry beads.

Philo watched him, as if memorizing and cataloguing each move. I slid my hand into his. His eyes softened. "Don't worry," he murmured.

Derek, back in his chair, assessed his only blood kin. "Okay, son."

"I was never your son." Philo's voice was low and soft. "Just tell me the truth."

"I can't go to the police for the same reason the collection isn't insured—I can't legally own one of the gold coins."

"You'll have to do better than that, Uncle D. We've been able to own gold in this country for more than thirty years."

"Not the 1933 Saint-Gaudens Gold Double Eagle. The last person who tried to sell it in the U.S. was arrested and jailed. That was in 1996. The seller was a Brit who said he'd bought the coin legally."

"What's so special about that coin?" I said.

"It was the only 1933 Double Eagle legally exported, and it originally went to King Farouk. Egypt must have sold it quietly." Derek's fingers drummed the table. "The Brit brought the coin back into the U.S. to sell, and the FBI set up a sting. There were suits and countersuits. Finally, because the government couldn't prove the coin *wasn't* the Farouk Double Eagle, they settled for part of the proceeds of a special auction. An anonymous buyer paid nearly eight million dollars for it. They call it the most expensive coin in the world."

"Impressive," I said. "But what I meant was, why is our government obsessing about the *1933* Double Eagle?"

"It was issued during the Depression. People started to hoard gold, so President Roosevelt signed an order making it illegal to own gold bullion or coins. Problem was, the 1933 Gold Eagle and Double Eagle were available for three weeks before Roosevelt halted sales and melted down the remaining stock. My grandfather was in the East on business when the coin was released. He ordered one as a gift for my grandmother."

"Sounds perfectly legal," Philo said.

"The purchase was, but citizens were required to sell their coins back to the government—at a low rate, of course. The government even went so far as to remove gold from safe deposit boxes."

"The government went into the banks?" I said.

"They did. Roosevelt declared a long bank holiday. Closed some banks permanently. Removed bullion from others. It was a desperate time, but still . . ."

"Did Great-grandpa Dain defy the order to sell back his coin?" Philo said.

"Not exactly. When he'd gone to pick up his order, he bought a second coin—spur of the moment. There was a bit of confusion at the window, and though he paid for both, only one was marked down on his receipt. That's what the government went by. Grandpa dutifully turned his in, but Grandma stored hers in her jewelry box. She could be . . . intractable. Dad inherited it and kept the secret. And I found the coin and an explanatory letter when I handled the estate."

"So," I said, "did the ten million dollar appraisal you mentioned include the Double Eagle?"

Derek smiled. "The appraiser never saw that coin. The rest of the collection is only worth between one and two million. That's all Heather thinks it's worth."

"What happens if Heather's caught with the Double Eagle?" Philo said.

"The Secret Service will confiscate it, and perhaps arrest her. Then they'll come after me for holding onto it all these years."

"Yet, knowing that, you kept it," I said.

Derek shrugged. "I hoped Treasury would eventually rescind the clause about this coin. Hell, they lifted the ban on bullion back in 1974."

"Our family's played the odds," Philo said, "but they just ran out. Maybe it's time to give the damn thing back."

"You sound like your father."

"KC knew about it?"

"Of course. He's just as guilty as I am. As *you* are, Philo. Technically, as KC's heir, you're part owner. You can't now cite ignorance as a defense."

"Very clever, Derek."

Derek couldn't hide his satisfaction. "But look," he said, opening his arms in a magnanimous gesture, "if you agree to get the coins back from Heather, I'll go along with whatever you decide to do with the Double Eagle."

Philo shook his head. "I'll take my chances with the law. The answer's no."

"If it's money you want," Derek's voice was taut, "I'll sell one of my houses."

"I'll wait for the payout when you're dead," Philo said. "If there's anything left."

7

I watched the Mercedes drive off, tires crunching on gravel. Philo didn't. He'd ushered his uncle through the gate and then gone into the guesthouse. I found him crouched in the sitting room, rifling through his briefcase.

"We *work together sometimes?*" I said with a smile. "Exactly when did you hire me?"

Philo handed me a standard employment contract. I crossed out everything but the first line: "I, [blank], agree to the terms of employment stated below." I printed *Francisca Coltrane MacFarlane* in the space provided, signed and dated the bottom. "We can negotiate my salary and benefits later."

Philo laughed. "Especially the benefits."

I handed him the form. "I'm no lawyer, but what you're intimating has to be illegal."

"So sue me. At least this will cover you if I ever do need you on a case."

"Such as, helping Derek?"

"Unlikely," Philo said, "but I might agree to recover the collection just to turn in the Double Eagle."

"Which would lead to an investigation as to where it's been hiding—and to possible criminal charges for Derek and Heather. Is that what you want?"

"I don't care either way." Philo stuffed the contract in his briefcase and stood up, rubbing his gimpy leg. It was a constant reminder of how close he'd come to dying.

He disappeared into the laundry room and came back with a basket of clean clothes. I followed him into the bedroom, closed the door, and leaned against it.

He dumped the clothes on the bed and said, "I once promised you a trip to the Grand Canyon. How quickly can you pack?"

I moved to the bed, pushed his clean clothes aside, and sat. I smiled brightly—or my interpretation of brightly. I don't do winsome.

He stopped searching for the mate to a gym sock. "You aren't packing."

"Observant of you."

"The Grand Canyon awaits."

"The rocks have been there for hundreds of millions of years. They're not going anywhere."

"Ah, this is one of those Mars versus Venus moments."

"More like Mars versus Mars. You might as well acquiesce." I patted the spot beside me. "So, where shall we begin?"

Philo sat on the edge of the bed and gave me a cautious smile. "You tell me."

"How about Derek's larcenous trophy wife?"

"Don't underestimate Heather. I did . . . once."

"Then start there."

I knew the first part of the story, about the abortive mission in Colombia, the helicopter crash, Philo's capture in the jungle by a sadist named Morongo—a man with a sharp knife and an endless supply of cigarettes and time. I knew the story because I'd met Morongo and witnessed the reckoning. Philo had been rescued by a team led by Toni Navarro's husband—the same Toni who co-owned Philo's fixer-upper in central Tucson.

I now surmised that Derek and Heather had offered their house while Philo recuperated from his South American adventure. But, feeling as he did about Derek, why had Philo accepted?

"Derek came to visit me at the hospital," Philo said. "He apologized for the way he'd treated me when I was younger, and wanted to make amends. He overheard the doctor telling me that she would release me only if I had help at home. But I didn't even have an apartment then— I'd let it go and put my stuff in storage when I went to Colombia. And I balked at going to a care facility . . . Your parents offered their place, but I knew they both had full teaching schedules and no live-in help. I didn't want to impose."

"That's when Derek volunteered?"

"Without even blinking. Derek said he and Heather had more than enough room for me—and a housekeeper to handle the cooking, cleaning, and running me to rehab appointments."

"You *really* must have wanted to get out of that hospital."

"In the worst way. I couldn't sleep. I needed to be outside. I asked Derek if his house had a patio or sunroof. He said they had both, plus a guesthouse and pool house. They'd set me up wherever I chose. I think that was the deciding factor."

"And your first mistake. The second, I take it, was putting yourself within reach of Heather?"

Philo nodded. "That first night she brought juice to the guesthouse patio. They'd moved the bed outdoors for me. She shed that silk robe and skinny-dipped in the pool, then offered her body. No conditions." He stared at the wall, painted the soft color of desert sand. "When I turned her down, she thumped my wounded leg as she left."

I winced, feeling it in my own leg. But there had to be more to the story. I said, "That's it? She tried to seduce you, you refused, she departed?"

"More or less. Derek was awake when she returned to their room. I could hear the shouts over the noise of the waterfall and pool motor. I decided I wasn't going to stick around for Act II. I called your father. He and your brothers retrieved me and took me home—to the patio outside your old room, in fact. I hired a live-in caregiver for the next month or so. He slept in your bed."

I hadn't known that last bit. I lived in California back then, and was out in the field for months at a stretch. Sometimes I wouldn't call home for six weeks—longer, if my parents were out on research junkets of their own. We loved each other. It was a given. We didn't live in each other's pockets.

Philo gave a wry smile. "That was the last time I tried to normalize relations with Derek."

I was quiet, trying to make sense of this morning's visit. "Did you catch Derek's tone when he said he'd made Heather burn the robe? Despite what he claims, he still has feelings for her."

"Maybe you're right. I always thought those two were made for each other. But then, I thought that about each of Derek's wives." Philo stood, and began folding his clothes.

"Not so fast," I said.

"What did I leave out?"

"Nasrullah."

Philo's eyes seemed to focus on a point over my head. "You said, once—I'll never forget it—you said that even your scars had scars."

"I remember."

He sat closer this time, and laced his fingers with mine. Our hands fit together as if they'd been carved from the same block of ironwood. I could feel his blood pulsing faster than normal. Perhaps he feared my reaction more than he feared confronting his memories.

"Two years ago, I discovered I had family after all. Nasrullah was my half brother. He was a professor of Near Eastern studies in Geneva."

"Was?"

"He's dead."

Philo, who'd always wanted siblings and a large, caring extended family, had found a brother, only to lose him again. I, who'd always had what he wanted most, couldn't begin to imagine his pain. I said, "He was KC's son?"

"Yes. His mother, Yasmin, was going to school in Switzerland. KC had just finished an extra year with the Peace Corps. They met at a ski resort and fell into a brief relationship. He left, went south to tour Egypt. That's where he met my mother."

"And took the fateful trip up the Nile."

Philo nodded. "KC sent Yasmin a farewell letter from the Valley of the Kings."

"Ouch." I could guess the rest. Yasmin discovered she was pregnant, but didn't tell KC.

"She went back to Afghanistan and promptly married her fiancé. Apparently no one suspected anything. Quite a trick, considering she would have had to prove her virginity on her wedding night."

"Resourceful women have always found a way," I said. "When did Yasmin tell Nasrullah?"

"After his father died. Out of respect for her, my

brother waited until after her death to start searching for KC. As luck would have it, Nasrullah contacted me first, instead of Derek. I checked Nasrullah out, then flew to Switzerland to meet him."

"This was two years ago?" I was remembering where I'd been and what I'd been doing then. "The summer I was finishing up my work in Nevada."

"And six months before I shipped out to Afghanistan. I didn't tell you then because I had to be careful. So did Nasrullah. He still had family and friends in Afghanistan, and I have a high security clearance from the government. We had decided to keep the relationship a secret for a while. I was planning to introduce you to him after I returned from Afghanistan."

"But fate intervened."

"Yes." He looked down at our intertwined fingers, but his thoughts were far away.

I waited a while, then said, "Did he have any children?"

"A boy and a girl—Azim and Ziba." A smile chased the shadows from his face. "They're at school in England. And they're in on the secret."

"The relationship can't be hidden forever. Azim's a male heir, and therefore in line for the Dain Trust."

"I know—Derek will fight it. But I'll cross that bridge later, after I figure out what he's really up to."

"Would it be legal for Azim to own the Double Eagle?"

"I'll have to check, but I shouldn't think so. Derek said the coin can't be exported."

"Did Nasrullah go back to Afghanistan while you were there?"

"Yes. I requested him as my interpreter. The government needed me badly enough to agree to the deal." Philo let go of my hand. Turning, he picked up the gym sock again and found its mate in the pile of clothes. Carefully folding them together, he set them aside, saying. "Nasrullah had been back to Afghanistan a number of times as part of his work. And to visit relatives. There was a wedding he wanted to attend that coincided with my posting. That three-month tour would give us a chance to get to know each other without anyone being the wiser."

"But something happened."

"You remember that phone call? The day you defended your dissertation and handed it in?"

"It was the day before your thirty-fifth birthday. There was noise in the background. A wedding, you said. Then the connection was lost."

Standing abruptly, Philo walked to the window and stared into the heat waves rising from the flagstone courtyard.

"Philo?"

He kept his back to me. "It was the beginning of spring, an auspicious time for a wedding. I was on the outskirts of Kabul, standing just inside a garden wall, talking to Nasrullah. He had my green eyes, Frankie. Our father's eyes. He was holding worry beads that caught the lights from the wedding hall. He was laughing over a story I told him about living with my parents on the commune. I said I had to call you, that I'd see him in a minute. He clapped me on the shoulder, and went into the house . . . I reached you at school. I was thinking how much I loved you, how proud I was of what you'd accomplished. For the first time, I'd begun to think about the future, instead of living in the moment. I was the happiest I've been since I was a child." A long pause. "And then the world exploded."

Suddenly, the room seemed dark and confining. I needed sunlight. Taking Philo's hand, I pulled him outside. The scorching sun was high overhead. The shadows had withdrawn under rocks and tree roots and the rafters of the porch roof. But a palm threw a swath of shade over the pool steps. I tossed off my yellow shift. He shed his shirt and pants. We stretched out in the water, our heads on a step. It felt like a womb must feel—safe and warm.

Philo said, "They came in through the front door, opened fire, tossed grenades, and disappeared into the night. By the time I called in the attack and got inside . . . eleven of them were dead. Nasrullah was dying. On the way to the hospital, he told me he loved me, asked me to track down who'd done this to his family, asked me to take the news to his children."

"And you did."

"I called them. As soon as he was buried, I took leave,

flew to England, and escorted the kids back to Switzerland. Their mother had died the year before, but her relatives took over. They thought I was just a good friend of Nasrullah's who happened to be with him when he died. Only the children and I know the truth."

"If you could call me from Kabul, why not from Switzerland or England?"

He lifted a handful of water and let it dribble through his fingers. "I'm not sure I can make you understand. The operation required complete secrecy. We'd been betrayed once, and it had resulted in my brother's death. The bomb had been meant to stop me, not him. He was collateral damage. I'd gotten too close. So, when I went back to Afghanistan, I was in deep cover. It was the only way I could protect myself, my contacts—even you."

"Did you find the men who killed Nasrullah?"

"Eventually. They were responsible for many of the bombings over there. That's why I was assigned to track them down. The trail led to some pretty isolated country." He paused, massaged his forehead.

"And when you reached the end of the trail?"

"That's another story." His tone was shuttered.

It struck me then that I'd been sharing my bed with any number of ghosts.

Philo read my face. "Having second thoughts?"

"Not exactly. I was thinking that I don't really know you at all. We've spent only a couple of months together, max, since I moved back to Tucson. If these are examples of your secrets—a murdered half brother, an unacknowledged niece and nephew, and participation in a search-and-destroy mission—then . . ."

He put his feet down on the bottom of the pool and his forehead against mine. "Then what, Frankie MacFarlane? You know there are secrets I'll never be able to share, even after an operation's over. It's the nature of my work, of my life."

"Then we may have to lay down a few ground rules."

It was his turn to put space between us. "Such as?"

My hands were on his shoulders. I felt the muscles bunch under my fingertips.

"Such as, the past stays in the past. I won't ask questions unless it intrudes on our present. If you want or need to tell me something, then that's your decision."

His muscles relaxed. "That sounds pretty one-sided. The benefit's all mine. I'm not complaining, mind you."

"Who said I was finished?"

"And the axe falls." But he was smiling now. "What else?"

"No more disappearing for long stretches—at least, without warning. I know you do undercover work from time to time, but . . . but limbo doesn't suit me."

"Understood. That it?"

"For now. But I'm keeping my options open."

8

Wednesday, May 17
Noon

The chess player's personal trainer stood with thick arms bent and hands positioned to catch the barbell in the unlikely event his client faltered. Quiet, circumspect Richard—never Rick or Rich or Dick—was the only person the man trusted to stand that close to his head while he worked out. Close enough to kill him, if he wanted.

The man had let his trainer guide the workouts for eighteen months—except for the weight bench. Last week was the first time they'd used it. Even then, the memory of that high school prank—of being pinned under a barbell for thirty minutes—made the man's muscles tense. He hadn't squealed on his wrestling teammates. He'd said he'd been alone, tried to bench-press too much weight . . . Hadn't fooled the coaches. Hazing wasn't tolerated. Team practices had been brutal for a week. The man—the boy, then—had finished the season, placed second in his weight class at regionals, then quit. It was the last time he'd quit anything.

"One more," said Richard. "Give me just one more."

The man grasped the bar, lifted it cleanly from the holders, lowered it to his chest, pressed—

The phone rang, the sound echoing in that modern room of concrete, stainless steel, and large bright windows. The man ignored it, extending the bar once, twice—

The message machine clicked on. A nervous male voice said, "It didn't go exactly as planned. It wasn't—"

The man dropped the bar in the holder. The frame shook. Richard steadied the sliding bar as the man rolled off the bench and grabbed the phone on the wall, cutting off the recording.

"What do you mean? What happened? . . . Shit. I gave you a simple goddamn job . . . No, let me think." The man sighed with frustration. Sweat dripped from his dark hair, following the lines and grooves of his face. Richard handed him a towel. The man took it and absently mopped his face. "Okay, find the second name on the list. And don't lose him. Let me know when phase two starts."

The man hung up, threw the towel on the floor, and went to the punching bag in the corner. Richard helped him slide his hands into gloves, then held the bag while the man hit it and hit it and hit it . . .

9

Derek called while Philo and I were packing a cooler for our Grand Canyon trip.

"Can you come up to the house right away?" Derek's measured tones carried to where I stood at the end of the kitchen counter. "It's important, Philo . . . Please."

Please? This was a different Derek Dain—less confident, almost pleading. Philo frowned, looked at me, gave a little half shrug. "Why?"

"It's—you'll understand when you get here. Remember where it is?"

"Yes. Give me an hour."

"Us," I whispered. "Give *us* an hour."

"That'll be too late," Derek said.

"Twenty minutes, then." Philo ended the call. "I have to go, Frankie. I shouldn't be too long."

"*We,*" I said, closing the lid of the cooler. "I'm on your payroll, don't forget. And for the next few days, at least, I plan on sticking to you like cholla spines."

Derek Dain's starter mansion was in a gated community in the northeast foothills of the Santa Catalinas. We stopped on the street below the Mediterranean-revival house that dwarfed its neighbors. The two-story monstrosity, as cold and aloof as its owner, faced east, with 270-degree views and a saguaro-dotted ridge out back.

"I don't remember this place," I said.

"You wouldn't. Derek and Heather built it. He needed lots of garages, so he could tinker with his vintage cars. She wanted a house big enough for entertaining." Philo studied the changes the years had wrought to the house. "I was here for only that one night . . . It seems so long ago now, as if it happened to another person." He lifted my chin and kissed me quickly. "Thank you for coming with me. I didn't realize how much I hated this place."

"Anytime."

"If you don't mind, I'd like to park here and walk the rest of the way."

"I could use the exercise."

Hand in hand we started up the long, curving drive. Derek had clear-cut the land before building, and he hadn't bothered to replant mesquite and palo verde for shade. My cotton camp shirt was sticking to me by the time we'd gone fifty feet. Philo's, too. He said, "I hope the air-conditioning's on high."

The bright, flat light of afternoon reflected in shimmering waves from the crushed granite gravel covering the terraced hillside. Desert broom, buffel grass, and other invading plant species crowded among agave and Santa Rosa prickly pear. The pebbled-concrete driveway had potholes. The entire house needed painting.

I wondered about all those houses Derek claimed to own, and that new Mercedes. How was he keeping it all afloat?

The ground bucked under my feet. I lurched into Philo. We steadied each other as the earth settled down. He smiled at me and said, "Earthquake?"

"Probably another Mexican one." I looked north to where Thimble Peak rose above Sabino Canyon. Back in 1887, an estimated 7.4-magnitude quake in Sonora had sent rocks tumbling from the canyon walls. Tucson might not be on the margin of a tectonic plate, but it could still shake, rattle, and roll.

Philo took my hand and tugged. "You can check it out on the computer once we finish with Derek."

"Deal."

A jutting portico threw the porch and front steps into shadow. The finish on the door had crackled and was peeling away in long strips. We climbed the stairs, and pushed the doorbell. Footsteps echoed in the house. The door opened, loosing a rush of cool air. Derek looked at me, disconcerted for a moment, then opened the door wider. "Thanks for coming."

In the distance I heard sirens scream, harsh on the desert air.

"Hurry," Derek said. "We don't have much time."

"What have you done, Derek?" said Philo.

"Nothing."

We followed him into a foyer floored with Italian tile. The entryway fed into a great room with areas for formal dining on the right, entertainment on the left, grand staircase in the center. The cathedral ceiling went up to a slanted roof. Dust motes danced in the light from tall windows and French doors. No window coverings. We were above the city, and higher than Derek's nearest neighbor. No one could peer in his windows or infringe on this splendid isolation.

A hallway beyond the staircase led past an office and a half bath. I smelled urine, as if a toilet had backed up. But the smell wasn't coming from the half bath on our left. It was emanating from the rear of the house. Philo frowned. Catching my look, he squeezed my hand. His uncle kept walking, without comment. I wondered if he'd lost his sense of smell.

Derek paused in the doorway to a massive kitchen, then stepped aside. I saw gneissic granite countertops with large pink crystals of orthoclase feldspar and swirling clusters of red garnets. Distressed oak cabinets and kitchen table. Black-and-white tile floor. No clutter anywhere. No newspapers or mail or dirty coffee cups in the sink. The stainless steel appliances looked as if they'd never been used. The pans hanging from a rack above the center island looked as if they'd just come out of boxes.

Here the smell of urine was stronger, the ammonia overlain with a sweet, coppery odor.

I heard the buzzing of flies as I entered the kitchen. I started toward the back door. I think I planned to open it. I don't know. But I heard Philo say, "What?" at the same time Derek said "Don't—" just as I rounded the counter and saw a shoe on the floor. A woman's black leather pump, lying on its side.

And next to it was a woman's body, duct-taped to a kitchen chair.

10

Blood had pooled on the tile under the victim's head and spattered the chair and cupboard doors of the island. And some of those "red garnets" I saw in the countertop . . . weren't garnets.

Philo didn't touch the body. He knew she was gone. We all knew.

Philo's gaze shifted from the corpse to his uncle. "Heather?" he said softly.

Derek's skin was the color of an oyster shell bleached by the sun. Sweat dripped from his forehead when he nodded.

Although I'd never met Heather, I'd heard her voice on the phone less than two hours ago. It didn't seem possible that she was dead.

Philo pulled out his cell. Derek said, "I just called 911. They're on their way."

"You *waited?*" Philo said.

"I wanted a little time with you before they got here."

Philo opened his mouth, then shut it. In the distance, the keening sirens grew louder, closer.

I forced myself to look again at the body. She'd fallen on her left side. She'd been shot in the back of the head, just behind her right ear. The entry wound looked small. I was glad her blonde hair covered her face, or what was left of it.

Her clothes were simple—charcoal slacks paired with an incongruously cheerful bubblegum-pink linen shell. Her right hand, the only one I could see, was small, smooth-skinned, and dimpled, her ankle fine-boned. No ring or bracelet, but a gold earring, shaped like a knot, poked through her hair and reflected light from the window. I heard a watch, probably on her hidden left arm, moving in time with the big kitchen clock on the wall. *Tick, tick, tick.* The sounds were loud in the silence. I could almost see the wheel of time turning.

I looked at that right hand again. The fingers were bent at odd angles. She'd been tortured first, then shot. "Jesus," I whispered. "Philo, look at that."

He crouched down beside the body, leaning as far forward as he could without tipping over. "Christ, Derek, what have you done?"

Derek seemed to draw himself together, one muscle at a time. "Nothing. I told you that. I went out for breakfast. Talked to you at Frankie's house. Ran errands. Came home . . . to this."

"I thought she was in the Bay Area," I said.

"She must have caught a flight back to Tucson." Derek kneaded the muscles at the back of his neck.

Philo interrupted his perusal of the crime scene. "So she was here when we talked on the phone this morning . . . I wonder where she spent the night?"

"Not with me," said Derek. "That's all I know, except, well, the police will naturally assume I killed her."

"Did you?" My thought slipped into speech. But once spoken, I needed to hear Derek's answer—for Philo's sake, as much as my own.

Derek's glare was meant to reduce me to ashes. It didn't work. I said, "Well, did you?"

"And torture her? What kind of monster do you think I am?" Derek looked to Philo for help.

Philo gave a noncommittal shrug and scanned the room. "I don't see a gun."

"I haven't touched anything—other than to see if she was still breathing . . . and if she was, um, carrying anything." He waved a hand in the general direction of an oversized black leather handbag standing open on a counter.

"You looked for the damn coins while your wife lay dead on the floor?" Philo said.

"Yes." Derek met Philo's eyes without flinching. "And if she had the coins with her, they were taken. Or she stashed them somewhere."

"You have bigger problems than lost coins."

"My lawyer's on his way."

Outside, the sirens advanced up the long driveway.

"Philo, you have to find the coins. I—" Derek's voice broke. He cleared his throat and gave a defeated half shrug.

I said, "Who else knew she had them?"

"No one. Unless she told Gwen."

Without a word, Philo circled around the counter to the other side of the kitchen, aiming for the purse. He took a clean handkerchief from his pocket, used it to hold the purse while he searched the contents. In the parking area out front, the sirens died midscream. A moment later, the doorbell rang, accompanied by a loud knock. Derek ignored it.

Philo turned to me, said, "Please." The magic word. "And take your time."

I nodded and went slowly to answer the insistent knocking.

The patrol officer looked like he was just out of high school. But his eyes were old, as if he'd done a tour or two in Iraq. Another officer was standing by their patrol car, which sat squarely in the middle of the paved parking area. He had the car radio mic in his hand. Both officers turned to watch a fire-and-rescue truck lumber up the driveway. It started to pull into the same area, then stopped.

The young officer turned back to me, then checked his notes. "A Mr. Derek Dain reported finding the body of his wife."

"In the kitchen," I said. "At the rear of the house. There's more parking out back, if the fire truck wants to pull around."

I spoke slowly to give Philo and Derek more time. But questions swirled in my head. I wanted to write them down. I wanted ten minutes alone with Derek. I wasn't going to get either wish.

The officer signaled the fire truck, and then he and his buddy followed me through the house. Philo and Derek were standing in the hallway, by the kitchen door, conversing in low tones. As we approached, they turned to face us, effectively blocking the doorway. We stopped.

Four large males, sizing each other up, made the hallway seem small.

Finally, Philo stepped aside. With a last glance at his nephew, Derek led the officers into the kitchen.

I made my way back to the great room and wandered the perimeter. I couldn't talk to Derek, but I might be able to answer some of the questions racing through my brain.

One area of the great room flowed harmoniously into another. Dust lay thick on the surfaces. In the den or TV area, I swatted a pillow on an overstuffed armchair, raising a choking cloud. The half-empty bookshelves contained an eclectic selection of reading material, purchased in bulk from a Friends of the Library sale last year. I found the receipt sticking out of a Danielle Steele novel. Danielle had been shelved between the *Complete Poems of Robert Frost* and *The Da Vinci Code*. Derek and Heather had paid ten bucks for the lot.

Turning my back to the bookshelves, I looked for clues to the woman lying dead in the kitchen and the man who'd be the prime suspect. The great room was barren of personal information. No family pictures on the side tables or on the mantel over a fireplace large enough to heat a pueblo. I crossed to the coffee table centered in a grouping of tan microsuede furniture. Using a tissue from my purse, I picked up the magazine on top. *Tucson Lifestyle,* also from a year ago. Underneath I found a *Golf Digest* and *Tennis World,* same vintage, both sent to Derek's business address. I fished a pen and paper from my purse, copied down the address, and replaced the magazines as I'd found them.

I crossed to the U-shaped bar set off in one corner of the room. The mirrored cupboards above it were empty of glasses and bottles. I stepped behind the granite counter. On a shelf underneath I found a realtor's lockbox, Derek's and Heather's business cards, and a stack of fliers advertising the home's assets. The listing price was just under two mil. I whistled silently. Tucking their business cards and a flier into my purse, I began to fit the pieces together.

The resulting picture had gaping holes in it. Where had Derek and Heather been living for the past year? Had the mansion been on the market that long? Probably. Nothing moved quickly these days, especially not a property this expensive. If this wasn't her residence, why was Heather murdered here? Had she come here to sleep after her secret flight home, knowing that the house was empty? Had she met a lover, a lover who killed her? And where was *Derek* last night?

I thought back to what Heather was wearing. Linen pants and top, good quality. Black leather pumps on her feet. Or rather, on one foot. The other shoe had fallen off . . . She looked like a realtor who'd been surprised while showing the house this morning. And if she'd traveled here last night, where was her luggage?

I crossed the room to the grand staircase. My ascent would be screened from the officers in the rear of the house. One officer, taking Derek's statement in the kitchen doorway, had his back to me. His partner must be outside, cordoning off the crime scene. I hadn't a clue where Philo was, but I could hear voices coming from farther away, beyond the kitchen door. The firefighters? Or had the medical examiner arrived?

No matter. They'd forgotten all about me. I tiptoed up the stairs. I was at the top, out of sight, when I heard two more vehicles climbing the hill. They continued toward the rear of the property. I looked out a window in the upper landing. The detectives had arrived, followed by the forensics minivan. I shed my sandals and moved swiftly from room to room, trying to make no noise.

Four suites to the right of the landing, three to the left. The master suite was larger than my entire house. The walk-in closets, his and hers, would have held my guesthouse. And the sunken master bath could have accommodated six adults. Philo wasn't kidding about fun and games at his uncle's house. Except no games had been played here in a very long time. The entire upstairs was vacant of furniture or any sign of occupation, temporary or otherwise, including Heather's things.

On a whim, I went back into the master closets to check for a safe. I found it, under a flap of carpet. Using the edge of my top as a glove, I tugged the handle. The safe opened easily. Empty. No coin collection worth millions.

Only a slip of paper with the combination for the safe. I checked to see that it worked. Smooth as soft-serve yogurt.

"Find what you're looking for?" Pima County Sheriff's detective Toni Navarro stood in the closet doorway, observing the scene with wry blue eyes.

"Shit, Toni. You scared the hell out of me."

"I should think. You're not supposed to be up here."

"Nobody directed me to stay in a certain place. Besides, I was curious."

"So, what's new?"

I knew Toni was referring to my recent spot of trouble in the Chiricahuas. I'd had to resort to using her name to shore up my bona fides with Paul Cruz, the detective in charge of the case. I hadn't had a chance to thank Toni. I did now.

"I'm not sure I helped your cause." She chuckled, tucking an errant strand of short, sandy hair behind her ear. A bullet scar traversed the back of her right wrist—a narrow miss I'd never asked about. We'd both collected our share of scars, emotional and physical, since high school. Toni had joined the marines, been an MP. Her first husband had been killed in a skirmish not long after he led the operation to rescue Philo in Colombia. When both Toni's tour and her second marriage expired, she'd come back to Tucson, joined the sheriff's department, and bought the fixer-upper with Philo. Philo lived in the house. Toni occupied the remodeled guesthouse. For Toni, today's murder would create circles upon circles of conflicting interest.

"I got the impression you and Paul Cruz might have a thing going," I said.

"If you call a shared training workshop and two dates a 'thing,' then yes. But our schedules are incompatible. With Paul in Bisbee and me here, I'm not sure it'll go anywhere."

"Invite him to Sunday dinner at your mother's," I said. "He'll decide to transfer to Pima County." Marielena Navarro, in addition to managing Philo and Killeen's office, wrote cookbooks. Lena was always trying out Sonoran recipes on friends and colleagues, her extended family.

I dropped the slip of paper with the combination into the safe, closed the door, and twitched the carpet into place. "Is it coincidence you're on the case?"

"Munger and I were in the area. You remember Scott?"

I nodded. Scott Munger and I had met a year and a half ago, when one of my students had been murdered. The case had brought both Philo and Toni back into my life after a dozen years.

"Soon as I heard Derek's name, I recused myself," Toni said. "Munger will be lead detective. I'll second until someone can replace me."

I felt awkward, caught between wanting to share with Toni what I'd noticed downstairs and wanting to protect Philo and his uncle.

Toni took in the size of the room, the closet, the master bath. "You checked all the rooms?"

I couldn't very well avoid a direct question. "Yup. They're all like this. Looks like they were professionally cleaned and painted a while back." I ran a finger over a closet shelf and showed her the dust on my fingertip. "A *long* while back."

She nodded and led the way to the hall. "The furnishings downstairs are from secondhand stores. Purely for show. Did you see a for-sale sign outside?"

"Nope."

"I can't see the Dains footing the bill for cooling the place while it's on the market. Was the air-conditioning on when you got here?"

"Yes, thank God . . . I thought you'd recused yourself from the case?"

"Just pro forma. I'll help Munger any way I can."

What she was saying, between the lines, was that I'd better be very careful of what I said to anyone, including Toni.

"Do I need a lawyer?" I said.

"Depends on how deeply you're involved."

"I'm not—"

"Stop right there. Save it for Munger."

We'd paused on the landing, halfway down the grand staircase. "Philo looks good," Toni said. I heard a question in her voice. She hadn't seen Philo since he'd returned.

"He's relishing the peace and quiet."

"I can imagine," she said. "Look, Frankie, I can't be your friend today—or Philo's."

"Got it."

"Good. And, by the way, private investigators aren't protected by privilege unless they're working for a lawyer."

"Philo doesn't need protecting."

"We all need it from time to time," she said, as we reached the foot of the stairs. But I thought I heard relief in her tone.

11

Detective Navarro preceded me out the front door. On the street below, a few neighbors clustered in a tight circle. Two local news vans pulled to the curb, fore and aft of Philo's truck, just as another patrol car arrived, lights flashing but no siren. A deputy parked, got out, and walked over to stand at the foot of the driveway. A high-profile murder drew gawkers and reporters like bees to a blooming palo verde tree.

Toni and I hurried out of camera range, circling the house to the backyard. The forensics van had pulled into the parking space left by the departing fire truck. Toni's partner stood talking with the crime scene unit and first-responding officers.

"You can sit with Philo or his uncle, as long as you don't talk about the case," Toni said, joining Scott Munger and the others by the kitchen door. "We'll be with you in a minute."

"Thanks," I said, hoping she hadn't noticed that I had neither agreed nor disagreed with her request.

Derek occupied a deck chair in the farthest corner of the patio. His eyes were closed, as if in meditation. Philo sat in a patch of shade at the edge of the spa, his legs dangling in the water, his back to the milling crime-scene workers. He turned and held up a bottle of water he'd conjured from somewhere.

I walked around the far end of the pool, a huge, free-form, pebble-bottom special. Like Philo, I wore shorts, so I kicked off my sandals and plunked my feet into the spa. The water was lukewarm, but cooler than the air. The rock waterfall beside us would cover any murmurings we might make.

"Let me guess," Philo said, a whisper of sound. We

were both staring at the water, our backs to Toni and Scott. "Derek doesn't live in the main house anymore."

"Not for a long time." I took a sip from the water bottle, then drained it. "It's empty upstairs."

"For sale?"

"I found the lockbox."

"Shit." It was more sigh than word. "Some of their things are in the guest house. The rest must be in storage."

"Well, it explains why the pool and spa are so well kept when no money's been spent on maintaining the house." I scooped water in my hands, spread it on my thighs, and watched it evaporate. "The officers let you just wander around?"

"I said I needed a bathroom. They sent me to the pool house. I checked the garages and guesthouse on the way back. Derek's classic cars are still there. So's the Mercedes. And there's a rental car in the last bay. Heather's overnight bag is in the backseat. Not much in it."

Scott and Toni walked toward Derek, calling to us at the same time. "We're on," Philo said, giving me a hand up. Fingers laced, we joined the trio.

"Detectives Munger and Navarro, this is my uncle, Derek Dain." Philo's voice was businesslike, a civilized patina on a surreal situation.

"And the victim?" Scott Munger said, wanting Derek to confirm what he already knew.

Derek's face seemed to have aged ten years in the past hour. "My wife," he said. "Heather Dain." No mention of a separation. "I found her when I came back from running errands. I'll wait for my attorneys before I answer your questions. They should be here any minute."

Toni and Scott jotted notes, paused. Derek didn't add anything. Scott beckoned the young officer I'd met at the door. He double-timed it over. "Would you escort Mr. Dain," Scott pointed to Derek, "into the pool house to wait for his lawyer? And stay with him." He didn't add please.

Derek opened his mouth as if to respond, then closed it in a firm line. His color was improving. He turned smartly and led the officer toward the small separate building at the end of the pool. Scott and Toni looked at each other for a moment, then nodded. Unvoiced questions, asked and answered.

Scott said, "Do you two also want to wait for your lawyers?"

"No," I said. Philo shook his head.

"Okay, we'll question you separately. The entire house is a crime scene, so we'll have to stay outside. Mr. Dain, Detective Navarro and I will take your statement first. Dr. MacFarlane, please don't speak to anyone, by phone or otherwise, while you wait."

I turned off my cell as I retraced my steps to the shady patch on the lip of the spa. The shade had moved with the sun, but was still large enough to cover me. I took out my notebook and jotted down what I'd seen and heard since Derek's phone call. I didn't mention the coin collection or our earlier conversation with Derek. I hoped Philo would be as reticent. If not, my interview would be awkward.

Someone tapped me on the shoulder. Startled, I nearly fell into the spa. Philo grabbed my left arm. "You move like a bloody ghost," I said.

"Occupational requirement." He nodded toward Toni and Scott. "You're on."

I picked up my sandals and walked back around the pool. My damp footprints on the blistering-hot concrete evaporated within seconds. Someone had turned on a large fan, mounted from the patio rafters. The moving air felt a blessed degree or two cooler.

I handed my notes to Scott Munger. His preliminary who-what-where-when questions didn't take long. He looked at Toni, to see if she had anything. She said, "Had you ever met Heather Dain?"

"No."

As they finished with me, Derek's lawyer arrived, a man cast from the same physical mold as his client. But this man's hair was pure white, except for a charcoal stripe waving back from his widow's peak. I was betting he was senior partner in whatever law firm bore his name on its shingle. And he wasn't alone. He'd brought along a striking brunette in a short-sleeved navy suit. She sported impossibly red lips and matching nail polish.

Derek, followed by his keeper, emerged from the pool house to meet them. His attorney introduced the woman as a specialist in criminal law. Of course. Derek's regular lawyer would specialize in corporate law. He'd be out of his element in a murder case.

"You need us to stick around?" Philo said to his uncle.

Derek shook his head. "I'm in good hands. Nothing more you can do here."

Did I imagine a slight emphasis on the last word?

Scott Munger released us after advising us not to leave town.

"That's a problem," Philo said. "Frankie and I have booked seats to the Bay Area." He squeezed my hand to keep me from reacting. "We leave this afternoon."

"When are you scheduled to return?" Scott said.

"Monday. Frankie has to be back for her brother's wedding."

Scott looked at Toni. She nodded. "Okay," Scott said. "But keep in touch."

"Will do."

With a last glance at the kitchen door, Philo and I walked down the potholed driveway toward his truck, now hidden by a milling crowd of reporters and onlookers.

"Derek seemed pretty shaken," I said.

"At Stanford, Derek's major was business. His minor was theater." Philo stopped, looked back over his shoulder. "Today, this was his stage."

12

2:45 p.m.

Wading through the media throng on the street, Philo and I ignored the microphones thrust in our faces, the yelled questions. When we reached the truck, we found it firmly wedged between the two news vans.

Philo handed me the keys. "I'll clear an exit."

While he had a few quiet words with the officer handling crowd control at the bottom of the driveway, I climbed into the truck. It felt like a convection oven, but the air-conditioning and engine hums muted the noise beyond the windows. Seconds later, the news van in front moved forward, and the crowd parted like the Red Sea. Passing through, I drove halfway up the block and stopped. In my rearview mirror, I saw a reporter noting Philo's license plate.

"I'm glad I'm not a Hollywood celebrity," I said, as Philo climbed into the passenger seat and closed the door. "Can you imagine going through this every time you leave your house?"

"I've handled security details. It can be a nightmare." Philo glanced up at Derek's mansion on the hill. "Would you drive? I need to make some calls."

"Right. Plane reservations?"

"Among other things. Thanks for going along with that, by the way."

"You've decided to help Derek recover the coins?"

"I told him I'd see what I could do. No promises."

I put the truck in gear and started rolling. "What direction?"

"South, to the bottom of the hill." Working his iPhone,

Philo pulled up directories and maps as I drove toward the empty hut and gate guarding the entrance to the neighborhood. "Now west," Philo said as the truck cleared the gate. "She's still at the old address."

"Who?"

"Margaret."

Good old Aunt Margaret. Derek's first wife.

"If anyone knows what the hell's going on, she does," Philo said, then grimaced. "She still moves in the same circles, just with different partners."

I turned right, heading across the foothills. The sun beat into the windshield. The air conditioner chugged and whirred as Philo pressed more numbers. "It's Philo," he said. "Yes—last weekend. Could I stop by? It's important . . . No, Derek . . . I know. I'll explain when I get there. Ten minutes . . . Okay—any brand? . . . Got it. Make that fifteen minutes, then."

We stopped for a red light. I took my hand from the gearshift and set it gently on his thigh.

"Don't feel sorry for me, Frankie. Living with Derek and Margaret, I learned a lot about people."

I left my hand where it was. I felt sorry for the orphaned boy. But I didn't say it.

Philo speed-dialed a number. While he waited for the call to be answered, he said, "We need to make a stop. There's a drugstore at Swan and Sunrise."

"No problem." The light changed. I transferred my hand back to the gearshift.

"Lena?" he said into the phone. It was Toni's mother, Philo's office manager—one more reason why Toni couldn't be lead investigator on Heather's homicide. My thoughts flashed to the body on Derek's kitchen floor. Something bothered me about the scene. What was it?

"Frankie and I need tickets to SFO," Philo said. "This evening. One stop . . . No, it's business. Well, mostly. Frankie's working for us as of today . . . Yes, round-trip. Whatever airline can get us there in the shortest time. Coming back Monday."

Philo covered the mouthpiece and touched my shoulder. "Will that give you enough time before the bachelorette party?"

"Yes. I've already sent out the invitations. But can Derek wait till Monday if we find the coins?"

"I'll return them by courier. I don't want either of us associated with them."

"Monday's fine, then," I said.

Philo relayed the decision, listened for a moment, looked at his watch, and said, "We should be able to make that. Book it, please, and print out our boarding passes. We'll pick them up on the way to the airport. Is Killeen there?"

I pulled into a parking space in front of the drugstore. "What do we need?" I said.

"A liter of Absolut—make that two."

"That all?"

"Better get a couple of bottles of orange juice. You and I will be working, not drinking."

When I came out five minutes later, Philo was in the driver's seat, engine running. I waited till we were under way, then said, "Do you think they'll arrest Derek?"

"Doubt it. He was with us, or at the hardware store, when Heather was killed. I'm sure they have security cameras that can verify his story. He showed me a store receipt for charcoal lighter fluid and a multipurpose lighter."

"No briquettes?"

"No, but he may already have a bag."

"I saw only a huge gas grill. It wouldn't need either briquettes *or* lighter fluid."

Philo shrugged. "He might have a little hibachi hidden away. I'll ask him next time we talk."

"When did he give you his alibi?" I said, thinking that there hadn't been much time to talk while I was answering the door.

"Right after I went through Heather's purse and found her plane ticket and a motel receipt. She flew into Phoenix late last night, rented a car, and slept at a motel near the airport."

"Where she met her killer?"

"Maybe, but he must have had his own car here. Her rental's still in the garage."

"With her overnight bag," I said. "Why didn't she carry it into the house?"

"Because she couldn't stay here. No furniture, food, or amenities. And she couldn't use the guesthouse because she'd walked out on Derek. My guess is that this was just a quick trip to pick up something she'd forgotten."

Philo turned left on Pontatoc Road, then right a few streets down. He pulled into a circular gravel drive in front of an earth-toned, one-story house. "I talked to Killeen while you were in the store. He said I should leave you home."

"Killeen's a worrywart."

"He predicted you'd say that." Philo picked up my hand and kissed the tips of my fingers, an oddly gentle gesture in stark contrast to what we'd seen and heard today. I felt my eyes tear up as Philo added, "He also said that Derek and Heather sold all their Tucson properties in the last year or two."

"All but the mansion."

"Yep."

"What about their other properties?"

"Derek offloaded his interests in at least some of the developments and all of their vacation homes."

"You think Derek's getting ready to walk?"

"Killeen says Derek and Heather stashed money in the Grand Caymans and Costa Rica. They even bought a house down there."

"And just how did Killeen find this out?"

"I didn't ask."

"Makes me wonder if Derek wanted to walk away from Heather, too" I said. "Permanently."

"Let's ask Margaret, shall we?"

13

Wednesday, May 17

2:45 p.m.

Sitting in the Jacuzzi, the man who played chess smoked and sipped his drink. A cool wind coursed down the grassy hillside behind him, whipping the smoke away. If the phone didn't ring soon, he'd have to find someone else.

In the distance, gunmetal-gray water stretched to the horizon. Being close to water both soothed and energized him. The limitless expanse reminded him of his Uncle Plato's house near Lake Michigan. Life was good there. At night they played chess and talked about the building trade. People would always need houses, Plato said. And when times were tough, there was smuggling to fall back on. Weapons, people, drugs, cigarettes, whatever. If you lived near water, it made everything easier. What his uncle hadn't told him was that you could lose your shirt on the development side of the business.

The man ground out his cigar in an abalone shell. Climbing out of the Jacuzzi, he wrapped a white towel around his naked body and picked up his glass and cell phone. He drank retsina today. He always drank retsina when things went wrong.

The pool area and recreation center were deserted. So was the street. Nothing moved except the line of cars and trucks on the highway. Their constant hum irritated him. Everything irritated him lately. What had seemed so easy in the planning stage had been well and truly bungled in the operation. He wished he had his uncle's counsel right now.

He crossed the concrete deck to a game table, inlaid

with black-and-white onyx squares. Sitting on a leather chair, he considered possible opening moves. But everything depended on his opponent.

His cell rang.

"You need me?" The voice had the soft rhythm and accent of a man who'd been raised in a barrio.

"Can you get to Tucson by tonight?"

"How many targets?"

"Just one stupid motherfucker."

"What did he do?"

"Does it matter?" When the voice didn't answer, the man said, "He screwed up—tortured and killed someone. It wasn't necessary."

"Torture is never necessary. I will take care of it."

"Tonight," the man repeated. He heard the sound of computer keys clicking in the background.

"I can get there by midnight."

"I'll set up a meeting for 3:00 a.m. There are a couple of other things he's doing before then—if he can pull himself together."

"*A las tres de la mañana. Buena.* The usual price, half up front."

"Agreed. I've put his photo and the particulars on the Web site."

"Understood. You want him found?"

"Doesn't matter. Just make it clean."

"Of course." There was more typing, then the voice said, "New game?"

"Of course," said the man, mimicking the accent.

The voice said only, "I believe it is my turn to play White. Pawn to g4."

"But—"

The line went dead. The man refilled his glass from the retsina bottle on the bar and sat again. His hand shifted the white pawn. *Why did you cede the advantage to Black on the first move? The power plays are in the center.*

He studied the board, his hand hovering over one pawn, then another. Should he block or take the center? He went into the building, pulled de Firmian's *Modern Chess Openings* off the shelf in the office, took it back outside. Found the opening at the very end of the book. Grob's Attack. The "Spike." He didn't like the sound of that.

Fuck you. If you won't take the center, I will. He moved his black pawn to d5, then sat back, more relaxed than he'd been in hours.

"Things might just work out after all," he said aloud. With a last glance at the board, he went into the empty rec center.

PART II

The Keys

The mythological hero, setting forth from his common-day hut or castle, is lured, carried away, or else voluntarily proceeds to the threshold of adventure. There he encounters a shadow presence that guards the passage.

—Joseph Campbell, *The Hero with a Thousand Faces* (1949)

14

Margaret Dain still lived in the southwestern-style home I associated with Philo's teen years. I'd never been inside, but I recognized the stained-glass window above the front door. Rays of green and turquoise glass spread from a transparent center. It seemed to say that within lay a cheerful household. For Philo, it had been anything but.

Margaret opened the door with her left hand. A freshly lit cigarette dangled from her right. She stubbed the cigarette out in a night-blooming cereus on the stoop, then patted her hair.

"Philo, I'm so glad you—" She caught sight of me standing off to the side. Her expression morphed from gushing welcome to cold accusation. "You didn't say you were bringing a friend."

Philo drew me in front of him like a shield. "You remember Frankie MacFarlane, Kit's sister."

Margaret stared up at me from hostile brown eyes. I countered with what I hoped was a neutral expression, considering that I now remembered why I'd instinctively mistrusted this woman. Margaret came first. Margaret came last. There was no in-between.

She hadn't changed much. Still petite, toned, tan, and dressed in white. Today it was a sundress. Makeup carefully applied. White-blonde hair scraped back into a pony-tail, tied with a silk scarf in primary colors. Pearl jewelry, except for a diamond ring on her left hand. White thong sandals studded with a rainbow of glass cabochons.

"Well, don't just stand there," she said. "You're letting in the hot air." She stepped aside to give us room to enter.

"Nice to see you, too, Margaret." Philo didn't kiss her hello.

The foyer led to a combination living-dining area. The house reeked of cigarette smoke. The originally off-white walls, curtains, carpet, and furniture were a dingy tan. The southwestern paintings on the walls—detailed studies of cowboy boots, blanket-wrapped Navajo women, and big-eyed Ted DeGrazia children—looked as if they'd been stained with tea. My throat and eyes started to sting. I wanted to hold my breath.

"Before I forget, dear boy, I found a box of your stuff when I was cleaning out the garage last month. Trophies, and such. A few things your parents left. I put the box in your old room."

Philo glanced to his right, toward the dark red-tiled hallway that led, I guessed, to bedrooms and baths. He thrust the grocery bag into Margaret's arms, saying, "I'll just put the box in the truck."

Margaret peeked into the bag and then handed it to me. "We might as well head outside." She waved her hand in the general direction of the sliding glass door in the dining area. "Glasses and ice are on the bar. I'll just grab my death sticks."

I carried the bag outside, leaving the door open. The backyard was designed for entertaining. Covered barbeque and bar. Large rectangular pool. Graveled paths meandered between desert trees and plants chosen for their color. It was an artist's palette of magenta, lavender, scarlet, gold, and twenty shades of green. And judging from the tools, well-used gardening gloves, and bags of fertilizer in the small ramada that served as a potting shed, Margaret did much of the work herself. Damn. She'd have been easier to dislike if she hadn't had a green thumb.

Margaret closed the sliding glass door behind her and called to me, "Don't bother with the orange juice in mine."

I set the bag on the bar and turned to find her ensconced on a padded chaise, cigarette lit. She'd lost the sundress. She was wearing a gold one-piece bathing suit cut down to her navel. The skin that showed was as smooth as her face. I wondered if she and Derek used the same plastic surgeon.

Philo came out and took the seat farthest from Margaret. He accepted orange juice without comment. A frown touched his forehead. I wondered if he had any positive memories of this house.

I handed Margaret a plastic tumbler with ice and vodka. Although we were in the shade of the patio, round sunglasses now covered half her face, screening her eyes. She tapped ash into a Lenox porcelain candy dish and then focused on Philo. "You didn't come to see me for old times' sake, so . . . ?"

"Heather's dead."

Margaret's expression didn't change. "Really. Where?"

"The mansion."

"What in Christ's name was she doing up there? They haven't lived there in a year, maybe more. Is it still for sale?"

"There wasn't a sign up, but it's on the market," Philo said. "They've been living in the guesthouse."

"No shit?"

"God's truth. What do you know about Derek's business interests?"

Margaret took a long pull on the cigarette, tapped more ash. "I'm still receiving my alimony checks on time, if that's what you mean. I'm doing okay—our settlement took into account cost-of-living increases." Her laugh was just short of a bray. "Derek was luckier with his next ex-wives. They remarried after a year or two, and the alimony stopped."

"The way I heard it," Philo said, "Derek sort of engineered those second marriages. Attractive young men, casual introductions at charity functions, whirlwind romances, the suitors' bank balances increasing by a quarter mil . . ."

"He got off cheap, when you consider how young they still are and how long they'd be collecting alimony." That laugh again. Margaret's face turned red and she started to cough. She held out her empty glass.

"Water?" I said, getting up.

"You kidding?" she gasped.

At the bar, I added a little ice and a lot of vodka to what was in the tumbler. If Philo wanted to pump her for information, I might as well help him along.

She'd caught her breath by the time I returned, and was

lighting a second cigarette from the first. "Derek tried that with me, you know—a whole string of attractive men, some young, some long in the tooth. But I'd been down that road. With Derek subsidizing me, why settle for one when I could have them all?"

"At once?" I muttered.

Philo sent me a warning glance, but laughter lurked in his eyes.

It bothered me that Margaret didn't seem at all curious about Heather. I said, "As far as you know, were Derek and Heather having problems?"

"The police think Derek killed Heather? Bullshit."

"He discovered the body."

"It's still bullshit. Derek and Heather were two sides of the same coin. Killing Heather would have been like killing himself—and Derek's not the suicidal type."

"She left him yesterday," Philo said. "Flew to her sister's in Menlo Park, then took a late flight back."

Margaret took a long swig of vodka, chased it with nicotine. "Makes sense. They had a row, probably over money or sex, and she wanted to scare him. So she took a time-out."

"A time-out that got her killed?"

Margaret's answer was a shrug and another swig.

"Derek seems to have liquidated most of his property over the last year or so," Philo said. "Except for the mansion, of course."

She sat forward, sloshing some of the vodka on her chest. She wiped it away unconsciously, scattering ash in an arc. "You're saying he and Heather were leaving town?"

"Or leaving the country. Derek and Heather moved their money offshore. Bought a house in Costa Rica. You'll have a tough time garnishing Derek's wages in a foreign country."

"The *bastard*." She slumped back, thought for a minute. Inhaled more nicotine. A frown creased the smooth forehead. "I haven't heard word one about this, and my ear's pretty close to the ground."

"Was Derek in over his head anywhere?"

"Not locally. But he backed a big development in California, Rancho something-or-other. Those damn palaces would have made his Tucson mansion look puny—if they'd ever been built. But when the market went belly-up, buyers started walking away from their earnest money. Or defaulting outright . . . You sure he didn't sell out here to keep the California thing going?"

"It's possible. I'll check."

She relaxed. "That must be it. Derek's not going to stiff me, not after all this time." But she was having trouble convincing herself. "Tell you what, Philo. I'll do a little checking on my own and get back to you, okay?"

"Thanks, Margaret. I couldn't go into it with Derek. He was pretty broken up about Heather, and I didn't want to give the detectives any ammunition."

Rather belatedly, from my point of view, Margaret said. "How'd she die?"

"Shot in the head. But she was tortured first."

Margaret's face lost color, except for the alcohol bloom on her nose. "For God's sake, why?"

"Damned if I know. Nothing was taken from the house, unless . . ." Philo paused, as if considering a new line of thought. "Do you know anything about my grand-father's coin collection?"

"Derek occasionally fiddled with it. But it wasn't worth much, according to the estate appraisal. A few thousand bucks."

Only a few thousand? Philo looked at me. I shook my head. Derek's story had more holes than a screen sieve.

Margaret was still chewing on the motive behind Heather's murder. "Do you think she was killed to send Derek a warning?"

"Maybe. That's why I was asking about his business."

Inside, the phone rang. The extension on the bar chimed in on the second ring.

"That'll be Grady," she said. "My trainer. Calling to say he'll be late." She made no move to get up. "He does Stella before he does me."

I choked on my last sip of juice. Philo slapped me on the back a couple of times. I sucked in a mouthful of dry air and set down my glass.

Margaret went on as if nothing had happened. "I don't

mind—Grady gives full body massage like nobody's business."

"Yes, well, we've a plane to catch," Philo said, setting his glass next to mine. He handed her his card. "This is my office number. They can always reach me. If you find out anything, give me a call?"

Margaret took the card. The answering machine on the bar extension clicked on. We could hear Scott Munger's voice leaving a message.

"You'll want to take that," Philo said. "It's up to you whether or not you tell him about our visit."

A less-than-sober Margaret said, "I won't—unless he asks me directly."

"Fair enough."

"You said you're catching a plane? To where?"

Philo picked up my hand, intertwined his fingers with mine, saying nothing.

"You're going to see Heather's family." Margaret's face took on a pinched look. "It's what I'd do in your shoes. And you should drop by your grandparents' place when you've finished your business. The Hendersons are still running the ranch. Robbie and Lorraine. They're in the manager's house." She stared at her empty glass as if the melting ice could tell her fortune. "I haven't been back to the ranch . . . Too foggy for me. I need sun. Plus, I heard that the other wives had their way with the decor." She set the glass down so hard it nearly cracked the little glass side table, and stood up. "Wait—I've still got a key to the kitchen door. I doubt if Derek took the trouble to change the lock."

Margaret trotted unsteadily into the house, came back a minute later with an envelope. She handed it to Philo, saying, "Directions, key, and gate code for the private road. If they've changed the code, you'll have to hoof it in." She put her arm around his waist. "It really is good to see you, Philo."

Caught off guard, Philo tucked the envelope in his pocket and gave her a quick kiss on the cheek. "I'll be in touch. Don't open your door to strangers."

"I have a gun, dear boy. And I'm not afraid to use it."

15

"Margaret stole that line," I said, climbing behind the wheel of Philo's truck. "Though I think the original mentioned bananas."

Philo thought for a moment, then laughed. "The monkey in *Babar*. Margaret adored those books . . . And she's not above stealing."

"Coins?" I reversed out of the driveway and pointed the truck toward my house. We had plenty of time before our flight, but we still had to pack and stop by Philo's office.

"It's possible." He rifled through the box of memorabilia Margaret had given him.

"But is she capable of murder?"

"If she were angry enough."

"At Derek and Heather? Could Margaret have known they were planning to leave the country?"

"Maybe. You can never tell with Margaret. She and Derek met in an acting class. She was even better than Derek, my father said. He didn't trust anything either of them said."

Yet KC and Ann's will had designated them as Philo's guardians. It didn't make sense, unless there was no one else. I let it go, saying, "I wonder if Margaret will tell Scott Munger about the gun?"

"If she doesn't, I—" Philo paused, holding a large rice-pattern porcelain ginger jar in one hand, a high school baseball trophy in the other. The jar was taped shut, the fiber tape yellowed with age. He put down the trophy, undid the tape, and lifted the top off the jar. "Jesus," he said.

"What is it?"

"Ashes. They must be my parents'. The jar used to hold cookies . . . I always thought I couldn't remember a memorial service because I was in shock. Looks like Margaret and Derek never bothered to deal with the cremains."

Back at my house, Philo watched me open the small suitcase I'd packed to take to the Grand Canyon. "We need to travel light," he said. They were the first words he'd uttered since finding his parents' ashes.

I grabbed my daypack and set it on the bed. "How light?"

His left hand held a packet of letters he'd found. The ginger jar was tucked like a football into the crook of his right arm. His backpack gaped open on the bed. "We can buy whatever we need once we're there," he said, placing the urn on the bedside table and sticking the packet of letters into a side pocket of the backpack.

I took my clothes out of the suitcase and stuffed whatever would fit into my daypack. Changes of underwear. Field pants that converted to shorts. Field shirt. Couple of T-shirts. Hoodie and jacket. Pair of sandals. Essentials only. No frills.

Finished, I looked over to see Philo removing the magazines from his Beretta 92 and Glock 27. He put the magazines, each enclosed in a zippered plastic bag, in a carrying case with the guns, and tucked the case into the backpack. I said, "You'll never make it through the metal detector."

Philo slid his left arm into the shoulder straps and smiled. "Trust me."

"I do. But I'll tell *them* I've never seen you before in my life."

"Judas."

"You mean Peter." I picked up my daypack. "Peter disavowed Jesus. Judas sold him out."

"Two faces of betrayal," he acknowledged, eyes clouding. Then he shook it off and gave me a kiss. "Ready?"

A bird whistled as we opened the door. Philo looked out at the sun-drenched courtyard where so much had happened today. He said, "And the cock crowed the first time."

"That was a curve-billed thrasher."

"Close enough."

Turning, I locked the door of my little guesthouse and followed him out to his truck.

We pulled into the parking area behind Philo's office on Tucson Boulevard. *Dain Investigations* was written in discreet gold letters on the glass entrance door. Philo's savings, coupled with Killeen's business expansion into the lucrative area of personal security, had helped them afford the new digs. Conveniently, property values had taken a nosedive just when they needed extra space.

Killeen had found this property, only a few blocks away from Philo's house in the Sam Hughes neighborhood. Plenty of off-street parking. Killeen snapped up the house next door for himself and his expanding family. Repairing and updating the two buildings had taken all of his spare time this last year.

A cinder-block wall with a wooden gate in the middle separated the office parking lot from Killeen's house. I could hear voices coming from the other side. I peered over the gate. Killeen and his wife, Sylvie, had recently uprooted the native cacti and planted herbs in small raised beds. Rosemary, basil, and chives scented the air. Chile peppers, tomatoes, eggplants, and squash grew around the borders. Sylvie and Tommy, Killeen's adopted son, were weeding the bed. The mother was as fair as her son was dark. Tommy favored his Jamaican father, the man who'd unwittingly caused our paths to cross in Nevada nearly two years ago.

As we closed the gate behind us, a golden blur erupted from a patch of shadows and launched itself at Philo. He dropped to his knees. Penelope, his golden retriever, covered his face with kisses. She might have been loyal to Killeen's family while Philo was overseas, but she let him know where her deepest attachment lay.

I helped Sylvie, eight months pregnant, struggle to her feet. She smiled as Tommy brushed off the knees of her maternity jeans, knees obscured by her protruding belly. Job done, Tommy threw his arms around my waist. He was six and a half now, tall for his age, and had just finished kindergarten. He looked up at me from velvet-brown eyes. "Mom says I can stay with you while she's at the hospital having my brother or sister."

"Your room's all ready—new bed, new paint, new rug. I thought you could help me decorate the walls. And we'll go out to the Desert Museum to check out the snakes." Tommy loved snakes.

"And scorpions and tarantulas?"

"He's widened his scope since we moved to Tucson," Sylvie said, lifting a strand of strawberry blonde hair off her forehead and tucking it behind her ear. "Now it's anything that moves in the desert."

I remembered the fascination I'd had with desert animals at his age. It hadn't faded with time. "What would life be without scorpions, tarantulas, and snakes?"

"And Gila monsters?"

"Those, too."

Something moved at the periphery of my vision. Philo and Penelope. Giving a final pat to her head, Philo said, "Back in a minute." He let himself out through the gate, crossed the parking lot, and entered the office.

"Lena's in the kitchen, messing with her newest recipe," Sylvie said, following him with her eyes. "There's plenty."

Spicy aromas drifted from the house. Something with chicken—and chiles from the garden. We were in for a treat, if we had time. I glanced toward the office.

"I heard about Heather Dain," Sylvie said softly. "Promo for the evening news. Is Philo okay?"

"I think so. They weren't close, but the way—" I caught myself before I could say more. Tommy was at my elbow, listening intently. I took the bucket of weeds from Sylvie and dumped them in a nearby trashcan. "Philo and I are heading out of town."

Sylvie didn't ask where we were going, but said, "You have to eat."

I grinned. "I'm starving. We missed lunch."

"Then go tell Philo you refuse to take a step until you're fed."

"Great," Tommy said. "I'll go set the table."

I took the same path as Philo and pressed the button by

the office door. Killeen buzzed me in and gave me a bear hug. Philo's new partner was as broad, solid, scarred, and homely as a sod smokehouse. But a grin transformed his face. "Philo's in his office."

Killeen led me through another secure door and into the heart of the building. He pointed to where a rectangle of light fell on the polished hardwood floors. I walked down the short hallway to the open door. Inside, Philo was collecting paper as it spewed from the printer. He flipped through the stack to make sure the papers were in order, then handed me an Arizona Department of Public Safety private investigator registration application. He'd filled in the employer part and most of the employee information. "Just needs your social security number and signature," he said. "Killeen will submit it for us."

I filled in the missing number, signed and dated the form. When I looked up, Killeen was there, holding a fingerprinting kit. "Is that necessary?" I asked. Philo pointed to the list of instructions. I said, "A color photo, too? What am I getting into?"

"You can still change your mind," Philo said. "I can go to California without you."

"Not on your life."

Once I was fingerprinted and photographed, Killeen left us again. "There's one more thing," Philo said. "But we'll need witnesses."

"For a temporary employment contract?"

"I've updated my will."

"Okay, what haven't you told me?"

"Nothing. But I don't trust Derek and his associates, especially after what happened to Heather this morning. I'm leaving the business to Killeen, and my share of the Sam Hughes property jointly to both of you." He cut me off as I started to protest. "It's just a precaution. I can change it back when we get home if you want."

"I want."

"Duly noted. I've added a clause about Azim and Ziba. As my father's grandchildren, they're in line for the Dain Trust."

"Azim is," I reminded him. "Not Ziba. Females aren't included."

Philo could tell it rankled. "Don't worry. I'll find a way to fix that clause, once I know it's safe to tell Derek about them. At the moment, I want to protect them. They've lost too much as it is."

"I'll hold you to that," I said, remembering the thrasher's call back at my house. The cock crowing in the garden. Betrayal. "Now, as for witnesses—Lena's in the house making dinner, and Killeen's in the next room."

"Perfect." Philo smiled. "And yes, we have time for Lena's latest concoction."

Ten minutes later the will was signed and in the safe. Killeen would take a copy to my brother Kit, the family lawyer.

Tommy had accompanied Lena to the office. He reached up and tugged on Killeen's sleeve. "Can I show Frankie?"

"Show me what?"

Killeen smiled at his son. "As long as you promise not to tell any of your friends about it. It's very, very important."

"I promise." He was almost jumping with excitement.

"Show me what?" I repeated.

Tommy took my hand and led me across the hallway to what was originally a wood-paneled den. He pulled on a section of built-in bookcases, revealing a staircase. "You have a basement?" I said to Philo.

"A bomb shelter, straight out of the fifties. Killeen showed it to me on Monday." When I looked puzzled, Philo added, "I stopped by on the way home from my debriefing. I needed my iPhone to start reconnecting with work." Reaching around me, Philo flipped a light switch.

"Come on!" Tommy pulled me down the stairs. Killeen and Philo were right behind us.

"It's buried deep under the parking lot," Killeen said. "Didn't show up on any plans. I found this entrance when I was rewiring the office. There's a second entrance in my house. That's one reason I bought that property."

"The entrances were sealed off years ago," Philo said. "The previous owners of the properties didn't seem to know it was here."

The steps led to a concrete bunker with two bedrooms,

bathroom, large kitchen/dining/living room area, store-room, and laundry. Dented appliances and used furniture. The walls and floors, still bare, were painted in neutral tones. They begged for landscape photos or paintings. But the air smelled fresh, and I said as much.

"I upgraded the plumbing, lighting, and air filtration system." Killeen looked like a child on his first trip to Disneyland. "You should have seen the storeroom—it was like a time capsule, complete with canned goods from the fifties."

"We can use it as another safe house, if we need one," Philo said.

"Another?" I said.

"There's a lot our new employee needs to learn," Killeen said. "We can cover some of it over dinner."

We dug into Lena's chicken-and-eggplant enchiladas, jicama salad, and cinnamon-laced sopapillas. Tommy wolfed his down, refused seconds, and said, "Dinner was great, Tía Lena," and to Sylvie, "May I be excused?" But he was already headed toward the sink, plate and silver-ware in hand. "Have to check on Griselda." The back door slammed shut behind him.

"Griselda's expecting kittens any day now," Killeen said, as Tommy walked by outside, carrying a large orange-striped cat. Pen stood, nose against the screen door, watching them pass. A small whine escaped her throat.

A minute later, Tommy was back, minus the cat. He went to a kitchen closet, pulled out a bucket, a squeegee, and a stepstool. At the kitchen sink, he added a squirt of detergent to the bucket and then carried everything into the side yard. This time, Pen slipped out with him. Tommy turned on the hose, filled the bucket, and dropped in the squeegee.

"He wouldn't try to wash Griselda or Pen, would he?" I asked Sylvie.

"I hope not."

Killeen grinned. "Not with a squeegee, anyway."

Tommy and Pen passed the window, heading toward the front. A soft buzzer sounded and a red light flashed on a wall panel. Under the blinking light were the words FRONT GATE.

"Just hooked that up this morning," Killeen said.

Five chairs pushed back from the table in unison. Philo, Killeen, and I sprinted out the door. For a big man, Killeen moved fast. Philo peeled off toward the side gate to the parking lot. I followed Killeen to the front gate, now slightly ajar. Tommy was standing at the top of the steps, bucket in one hand, stepladder in the other.

"Tommy?" said Killeen quietly.

Tommy looked back at the four adults, lined up behind him. Smiling, he said, "That alarm works pretty good, Dad."

"So this was a test?" Killeen said.

"Kind of. But I saw that car drive by twice when Mom and I were weeding." Tommy nodded toward a car parked across the street. "Only I can't get a good look at the driver because the car has dark windows. I figure he'll just drive off if you or Philo go over there, but he might roll down the window if I ask to wash the windshield. And then I'll see his face."

Tommy noted the glance his parents exchanged. Sylvie's freckles stood out on her pale skin. "I'm nearly seven," he said, as if this were a deciding factor. "And I waited for you to come out before I went over there." Tommy set down the bucket and took Sylvie's hand. "Please, Mom. This is my chance to be Encyclopedia Brown. I'll be safe. I'll have Pen with me. And if that man starts to open his door, I'll run away and let Pen take care of him."

"Okay," Killeen said, "but I'll be right behind you."

Tommy grinned as he picked up the bucket. With Pen leading the way and Killeen in tow, the boy stumped down the steps. The trio paused for a long time at the curb, then crossed the street, heading for a white car parked under a mulberry tree. The car had a good view of the parking lot and entrance to Dain Investigations. Coincidence? I wondered.

Tommy set down the bucket and stepladder. Pen sat and stared up at the car, while Killeen leaned against a nearby tree. The stance seemed relaxed. I knew from experience it wasn't.

Tommy knocked on the passenger-side window. The darkened window stayed shut. The outside temperature still hovered around a hundred. "He must be roasting in there," Sylvie said.

"I think his engine and air conditioner are running," I said.

Tommy, undeterred, knocked twice more. No luck. On the fourth try, the window slid down. Tommy's voice carried on the still, dry air. "Please, mister, can I wash your windows? I'll do a good job."

The driver gunned the engine and roared off up the street. Philo materialized from the Tucson Boulevard side of the office building and jogged across the street. He was wearing his Glock in a belt holster. He and Killeen had a little powwow before escorting the window washer home.

After Tommy dumped the bucket in the garden, we trooped into the house. I took the stepstool from Philo and set it in the corner.

"Well?" Sylvie said.

"It worked! I saw him," Tommy said. "He had black hair, like Frankie's. But shorter, and real curly. Brown eyes . . . skin lighter than yours, Mom. His face got red when he talked to me. And his shirt was white, with blue lines. He made me think of the flag—red, white, and blue. But no stars, of course."

She ruffled his hair. "Very good. What did he say?"

"*Get lost, kid.* His voice was kind of low and scratchy sounding, and he had a bad cough. He was smoking, but not the regular kind of cigarette. It was long and skinny and brown."

"Like thin cigars?" Philo said.

"I guess."

Killeen crouched down and put his hands on Tommy's shoulder. "Anything else about the car?"

"The seat was gray . . . Oh, I almost forgot. I saw the license plate when he drove away. I memorized the number."

Philo handed Tommy his notebook, pointing to something he'd jotted down. "Is this it?"

"Uh-huh," said Encyclopedia Brown. "Can I have dessert now?"

Killeen called a contact to run the license number, but got an answering machine. "None of our current cases would have triggered surveillance," he said to Philo. We were standing in Killeen's office.

"Then we have to assume that Frankie and I were being watched."

"A man jotted down your license number back at Derek's house," I said. "I assumed he was a reporter."

"He could have been," Philo said. "The truck's a business vehicle. If someone ran the plate, they'd come up with the office address."

"I'll let Munger know once you're well away," Killeen said. "You don't want any delays."

"I also don't want anyone but Toni and Scott knowing we've left town," Philo said.

Killeen nodded. "Plan B is ready to launch."

"What?" I said.

"Alternate transport," Philo said. "Should confuse anyone following us."

"You planned this from the beginning. That's why you told me to pack light," I said. "But you'll still have trouble with security."

Philo grinned. "We'll see. Ready to go?"

We went back to the house, hugged Lena, Sylvie, and Tommy, then drove Philo's truck to his garage, three blocks away. Killeen followed us in Sylvie's minivan. He'd been checking his rearview mirrors. "We're clear. But you might want to use a different cell while you're on the road." Killeen pulled a bag from under the seat and handed it to Philo. "This cell's from an old batch. No GPS, so you can't be tracked that way. The charger's there, too. Where to now?"

"Toward the interstate," Philo said as he turned off his iPhone. "I'll tell you where in a minute."

I handed him my cell. He removed the batteries from both phones and punched numbers on Killeen's cell. After a clipped conversation with someone named Justin, Philo tapped Killeen on the shoulder and said, "Ryan Airfield." To me, he said, "Dain Investigations owns shares in a small air charter company. They've a hanger out there."

"You have shares in an air charter company?"

He smiled. "Taxi, cargo, and courier service."

"What did you do, capture the King of the Leprechauns? Make him reveal his pot of gold?"

"Much more prosaic. A silent partner with similar interests and plenty of disposable income."

"In this economy?"

"He seems to be recession-proof."

"That's all I get?"

"I expect you'll find out eventually, when he's ready. Until then, no one knows except the three of us and Uncle Sam. And Justin, our pilot. Speaking of whom, I hope you don't mind being listed as cargo."

16

Wednesday, May 17
6:00 p.m.

Killeen drove slowly between the buildings of Ryan Airfield till he reached an anonymous, numbered hangar. The bay door was open. We decamped into the cool depths, which revealed a small Learjet.

Philo introduced me to Justin the pilot—my height, swimmer's build, wide smile. Twin cowlicks lifted the short brown hair at his temples. The two men huddled with Killeen for a moment. When they finished, Killeen came to where I waited next to the scale.

"One of our people will take care of your house and mail," he said. "Anybody you want me to notify?"

"I called Mom on the way to your place. She hadn't heard the news about Heather. I told her Philo and I needed to get away for a few days. She read between the lines. She also offered to call Derek, make sure he's okay."

"Good. Lena has the same cover story, just in case." Killeen gave me a hug. "Take care."

As Killeen and his minivan departed, a white limousine pulled in and disgorged a young woman in a sunny yellow golf skirt and matching top. Justin looked up from where he was entering the combined weight of my body, backpack, and purse onto a form. Voice carefully neutral, he said, "Ah, Cecily. On time, for once."

"She's a regular?" I said.

"Her Silicon Valley gazillionaire hires us to fly her to and from golf clinics."

Must be nice, I thought, though I had no desire to jetset to clinics. But if I were to be offered a helicopter and pilot to ferry me to remote areas for geologic mapping, well, *that* would be a different story.

A little more than two hours later, another limousine picked up Cecily at a similar hangar at San Jose International Airport. Justin filled out some paperwork, turned the jet over to his mechanic, and led us to a twin-engine Cessna tied down nearby. I climbed in first. Philo handed me our gear, saying, "One more leg. This puddle jump'll make it even harder for anyone trying to track us."

We flew to the small Palo Alto airport farther up the peninsula. The control tower there was shut for the night. Justin taxied to his tie-down spot and parked next to a Miata. We collected our backpacks and joined him on the ground. He pointed to three American-made vehicles in a small lot on the other side of the boundary fence. "New batch of loaners since you were here last," Justin said. "Take your pick. No GPS units."

"Good," Philo said. He looked at the three vehicles, two sedans and a small pickup. "I might need to switch cars."

Justin didn't bat an eye. "Thanks for the warning. Procedure hasn't changed. Just leave a phone message."

"And fill the tank, park the car where we found it, and wipe it down?"

Justin nodded, turned to me, and extended his hand. "It's been a pleasure, Frankie. Look forward to working with you again." He clapped Philo on the shoulder. "Watch your back trail," he said, and began tying down the airplane.

Philo chose a dark green Ford Escort. "Good for night work," he said, pulling the keys from under the driver's seat. He handed them to me. "I'll navigate and work the phone."

Highway 101, the Bayshore Freeway, ran beside the airport. "North or south?" I said.

"Doesn't matter. We won't be on it for long."

I turned north. A few miles down the road, Philo placed a call. When someone picked up, Philo said, "Remember that prototype metal detector you were telling me about? . . . Yeah, the indoor model—the wand . . . Gold . . . Right. Mind if I borrow it for a couple of hours? . . . Be there in ten."

I said, "Does the wand have a phoenix feather in it?"

He laughed, a real laugh, with echoes of our old lives. Before Afghanistan. Before Derek's visit and Heather's death. Philo was on the scent, in his element. This was the Philo I knew and loved, engaged in night games full of magic like those we played as children. Scavenger hunts. Sardines. Hide-and-seek. Searching for buried treasure.

I expected him to head for a rendezvous in the graffiti-marked back alleys of East Palo Alto. Noir central. Instead, Philo directed me to a neighborhood a few blocks off Jefferson Avenue in the hilly part of Redwood City. The road climbed and curved back on itself. Occasional street-lights produced spotty illumination between inky pools of darkness. Plenty of privacy for the sixties-era split-level homes cut into the steep hillside. On a clear day, the owners would have stunning views of the bay. Tonight, I could see necklaces of light defining the Bay and Dumbarton bridges, and the colored running lights of ships plying the waterway.

I rolled down my window, catching a whiff of wild mustard and freshly mown grass. The scents brought back my first year at Stanford. How naïve I'd been. Death hadn't touched me till later.

Philo directed me to pull into the driveway of a darkened house on the downhill side of the street. The headlights revealed a line of scraggly juniper trees around the perimeter. A pepper tree cast sheltering branches over the postage stamp-size lawn. I dimmed the headlights, left the parking lights on. A figure disengaged from the deeper shadows of the porch and walked briskly down the brick path, stopping under the pepper tree. A woman, by the way she moved. Another stereotype broken. I'd expected a scarred veteran of black ops, maybe with a limp. This woman moved like a Gen Xer. She carried something in a long dark case. The wand, I presumed.

"Lights off," Philo said, flipping the switch on the overhead light before slipping out. I stayed put. I couldn't speak about what I didn't see or hear. He was gone no more than thirty seconds.

"Where to, Kemo Sabe?" I said, backing out of the drive.

"There's a Starbucks at Whipple and El Camino," he said. "FedEx office next door. I can use one of their computers to hunt up Gwen Helmsley's address."

Gwen. Heather's sister.

I turned north on a tree-lined street. Alameda de las Pulgas, the Avenue of the Fleas. One of my professors had lived along here somewhere . . .

I parked behind Starbucks. The light was still on. We separated—I to rustle up some caffeine, Philo to search the Internet. When I arrived back at the car with two lattes, Philo was already there. "Took less than a minute," he said.

He directed me down the Bayshore toward Menlo Park, my old stomping grounds. I sipped my latte as I drove, remembering those early years. I'd left Tucson after high school to attend Stanford. I'd worked at the U.S. Geological Survey in Menlo Park during and after college. I'd come of age in the Bay Area. Now we were back on my turf.

Memories crowded out the events of the day. I was working here when I learned Philo was MIA in Colombia. I'd presumed him dead. A tragedy of miscommunications, no one's fault, had kept me from the truth . . . until I returned to Tucson. The intervening years had evaporated. Almost.

But then he'd left again for Afghanistan. I was still getting to know the man who'd returned. He was still getting reacquainted with the woman he'd left behind.

"Turn here," said Philo.

The street looked familiar. I remembered a Halloween party at a house rented by four other young geologists. I'd dressed as Cleopatra. It was an eon ago.

Tonight, the neighborhood seemed to have rolled up

the sidewalks during the eleven o'clock news. Gwen Helmsley's small house was set back from the sidewalk. Not even a front-porch light broke the darkness. The closest street lamp was four houses away.

I drove past the house, turned around, parked in front, in the deeper shadow of a magnolia tree. Turned off the lights. A hedge screened us from the house across the street. A huge redwood blocked the line of sight from the house on the left. The one on the right had a six-foot fence and a motion sensor light. A curious cat triggered it. It seemed to take forever for the cat to jump down, but it was only a minute or two till the light went out.

"I'll be quick as I can." Philo opened his door and started to slide out.

I grabbed his arm with both hands. "Not so fast. I'm coming with you."

He looked at me. Waited.

I said, "I won't learn anything sitting in the damn car."

"Okay, follow my lead."

I stuffed my purse under the seat, and was out of the car before he could change his mind.

Our clothing—dark pants, T-shirts, and running shoes—merged with the more solid darkness of the one-story house. We listened at the first window for noise or movement inside. Nothing. We moved to the second window. Same story. The front door had a lockbox. Philo examined the box by touch. "This'll take too long," he whispered. "Let's try the back."

We retraced our steps, creeping from shadow to shadow. The offshore wind had died. No longer held at bay, fog crept over the coast range and down into the valley, silent and stealthy as our own passage. No one was out and about, but dogs barked in several houses and backyards. The night smelled of roses and jasmine, sea salt and marshland. Springtime in California. Heady. Nothing like it in the world.

Once back at our starting point, we tiptoed the opposite direction, across the front of the garage. On the far side was a wooden gate. Reaching over, I touched the latch. No padlock. I tugged gently on a bit of knotted rope dangling from a hole in the gate. The rasping squeal pierced the night. Somewhere a dog barked, but nothing moved in the house next door.

I pushed on the gate. It stuck three inches in. Philo reached past me to grab the edge. He lifted while I pushed it open just far enough for us to ease through.

"Wait here," he breathed in my ear.

He slipped back through the gate before I could answer. Seconds later the Escort's engine started. Philo moved it up the street a couple of houses.

The house wall, on my right, was only two feet away. A faint green light glowed in Gwen's kitchen, reflecting off pale appliances and a tiny kitchen table. I started down the narrow concrete path. The redwood fence on my left was only four feet from the house next door. I could hear a television, tuned to the late-night news. I looked at my watch. Almost eleven thirty. Would the occupant stay inside once the news was over? Did he or she have a dog?

The fence was six feet high. Philo is six four. I'm six one in running shoes. To make it to the backyard undetected, we'd have to double over as we ran.

Just as Philo reached me, a door opened on the far side of the fence.

17

Philo and I crouched and made like rocks.

Sounds filled the night. A closing door. The creak of a lawn chair under stress, accompanied by a man's grunt. The strike and flare of a match. A drift of cigarette smoke. A pop top. Glugging, as a can drained. He was so close I could smell the beer. If we tried to creep away, he'd hear it.

My heartbeat slowed. My calves cramped. I wondered if we'd be here half the night. I eased down until I was sitting on the concrete.

A phone rang in the house. A string of epithets floated over the fence. Other noises followed. Shoe grinding cigarette. Chair creak. Door opening. I found Philo's hand. As soon as the smoker closed the door behind him, I was on my feet and hightailing it to the backyard.

Light from next door fell over the fence, showing Gwen's tiny lawn fringed by rose bushes. Philo tried the windows. No bars, thank heavens. I stepped onto a patch of concrete at the corner of the house. A lemon tree dominated the little courtyard. I spotted a door, took a step. The tree rustled. A lemon glanced off my head and hit the concrete. It sounded like a bomb.

Philo touched my shoulder, pointed to the French door I'd been aiming for. He tucked the wand case under his arm and pulled a small black rectangle from his back pocket, unzipping it to reveal a set of fine tools. I could just imagine what my family would say if they knew I'd added breaking and entering to my résumé. I knew what Toni would say.

Philo handed me a penlight. I pointed the beam at the lock. Twenty seconds later, I heard a click. Philo opened the door. Like the gate, these hinges needed oil. I clicked off the flashlight. Once inside, I began breathing again.

We were in a small combination living/dining room. I drew the front and side curtains before turning on the penlight. Honey-colored carpet. Recycled-brick fireplace. Built-in bookcase, mostly empty. No furniture to speak of, except for a couple of side tables with dusty silk plants. The house was as devoid of personal touches as Derek's mansion had been. Not a photo or treasured knickknack in sight. And damn few hiding places.

Philo already had the magic wand out of its bag. It resembled a long microphone attached by an umbilical cord to a small box. I handed back the penlight. While he swept the room, I went through the house closing curtains so our stealthy light wouldn't leak out. I didn't trip over furniture. The bedrooms were bare. Not even a sleeping bag and air mattress. Gwen didn't live here anymore, and there was no sign Heather had camped here.

In the kitchen, I used the dim light from the appliances to investigate the cupboards. Gwen had cleaned the place well. No sticky surfaces. No dust. But I checked every drawer and nook and cranny for treasure. Came up empty, except for an Earl Grey teabag, lodged at the back of a cupboard shelf.

There was, however, a flashlight above the sink. I took it. Covering the glass with my hand I opened the door to the garage. Half the space had been turned into a den. An empty wall unit hugged the far end. A fire door led into the one-car garage. It didn't hold a car. It was stuffed to the rafters with furniture and boxes.

I squeezed past the washer and dryer, around the stacked loveseats and rocking chairs, the on-end mattresses and disassembled beds, to reach the door to the side yard we'd just traversed. Philo arrived as I was confirming that the black curtain over the window in the door would prevent smoker-man from seeing our dim light.

I poked around while Philo directed his magic wand toward the faded cupboards lining the far wall. He was wearing earbuds so the hum wouldn't be heard outside. Occasionally he'd stop and examine a spot more closely.

As far as I could see the shelves held jars of canned tomatoes and berries, china and crystal, paint, rollers, and brushes. The lower cabinets revealed worn tools nestled among odds and ends.

"Done," Philo whispered, removing the earphones.

"Find anything?"

"Gold detail on porcelain china, gold leaf on some wooden trays and figurines."

"No gold coins."

"Nope."

"So that's it?"

"Not exactly. I found a locked safe in the master bedroom. The wand didn't get excited, but I'm not confident enough of the technology to wager that it'll pick up a signal from inside a steel safe."

"Why lock an empty safe?"

"It might not be empty. We'll have to come back in the morning to check. I didn't have the right tools."

"Won't it be risky to come back in daylight?"

"We'll think of something."

"I presume your sorceress has the tools?"

"Yup. But not tonight. She's . . . working."

We returned the curtains to their pre-visit state and retraced our steps down the path, pausing just outside the gate to listen. We were lucky. The neighborhood dogs must be in for the night.

"Okay," I whispered, and led the way to the car. Just as we closed the doors headlights turned onto the street.

"Duck," Philo said.

"What?"

He pulled my head down. We were both below window level. The lights swept over us as the car drove slowly past. Philo waited until it was farther down the block before raising his eyes high enough to peer into the side mirror. "Police," he said, sitting up straight. "They've gone around a curve. Let's get out of here."

I started the engine and pulled slowly away from the curb. "Routine cruising?"

"I think so. If they'd been alerted to a suspicious vehicle, they'd have stopped and checked us out."

"And we'd have had some explaining to do."

Philo's smile was very white in the darkness. "I'd already thought of an excuse."

"I'll just bet you had. Where to now?"

"To ditch this car. When we come back tomorrow, I don't want nosy neighbors making the connection."

Back at the Palo Alto airport we switched our gear to a Malibu. Philo took the wheel and pointed the car toward Redwood City, saying, "Got to return the wand."

Ten minutes later he dropped the wand through the oversized mail slot in his contact's front door, then drove to a little inn on El Camino Real.

Philo was asleep by the time I'd showered off the gritty layers of the day. In the room next door, someone was listening to a soft, droning voice. I found it soothing. It reminded me of dorm life, late at night, and of my first roommate, Alana Calloway.

I drifted off, wondering, *Whatever happened to Alana?*

18

The Afghan boy stopped fifty yards away and shouted a greeting to alert Philo's camp. His voice was changing, shifting registers. He was twelve and small for his age. He carried a book in his right hand. Philo recognized his own battered copy of Louis L'Amour's The Lonesome Gods.

When Philo answered his greeting, the boy began walking again, slowly, as if he were counting steps. He raised the book, and called in English, "I liked this one very much, especially the big man, the monster."

The movement lifted the boy's woven vest. Philo glimpsed the edge of another vest underneath—black and gray webbing, bulky. His heart stopped, then started again with a thud he felt down to his toes. He had to say something to let the boy know he understood.

"The man who didn't fit in?" Philo called.

"Yes, that one. It says that he loved to read. And I like that it had maps. I like maps." The vest dropped back in place as he lowered his arm. Another two steps and he paused for a moment, crouched, set the book on the ground, and tightened his sandal strap. Straightening, he called softly, "They have the detonator, Philo. I am sorry."

The slow steps continued. The book lay where the boy had left it.

Philo raised his hand. "Don't—"

"You must do what you must do." The boy's smile lit the dusk. "Insha' Allah, they will have books in Paradise . . . and no war."

"And no war," Philo said.

The boy was still smiling when Philo shot him.

19

Thursday, May 18
Menlo Park, California
2:15 a.m.

Awakened by his nightmare, Philo lay in the dark motel room, deciding whether to go for a walk or work on his computer. Sleep wasn't an option. He didn't feel like getting dressed again, so he got up, turned on the desk light, and pulled out his computer.

Thirty minutes later, he looked up. The mirror over the desk showed Frankie, black hair draped over the white pillow. She was breathing so softly he could barely hear it. She gave a soft snore and rolled over. Philo smiled and touched a string of worry beads he'd draped over one corner of the laptop. He'd found them among his half brother's effects after the bombing. They were Nasrullah's everyday beads—a deep blue mineral, with filaments of rusty red, brown, and gold that shimmered with the changing light. Nasrullah's children had said Philo could keep them. They had other, more expensive beads of amber and lapis lazuli—beads with memories attached.

After Nasrullah's death, Philo'd thrown himself into work and used the demands of the job to keep himself focused on what he *could* do, not what he couldn't. Until today—yesterday, now—when Derek swept back into his life, resurrecting old ghosts. But this time Frankie was there, standing with him.

Philo fingered the beads. When the nightmares came, the beads helped him find that still, tranquil place deep within. Nasrullah had taught him breathing meditation during their months in Afghanistan. His brother had lost many members of his family during the Soviet invasion.

Nasrullah knew how memories, horrors, and regrets could consume you if you let them.

Long breath, Philo thought. *Short breath. One per bead . . . Repeat . . . Be aware of each breath, of the body, of the mind—*

The cell phone rang. Frankie jolted awake, gray eyes wide. It was the phone Killeen had given them on the way to the airport. Only Killeen knew the number.

Philo grabbed the phone, pressed TALK, said, "Yes?" Just the one syllable. Don't give anything away.

"Philo?" Aunt Margaret sounded pissed. "I called the number on the card you gave me. Got someone named Killeen. He wouldn't say whether or not you'd already left town. Are you in the Bay Area?"

Voices in the background, male and female. Philo swore under his breath. *Tell the whole world, why don't you?* But Killeen wouldn't have forwarded her call if it weren't important. So Philo gritted his teeth and said, "It's nearly three in the morning, Margaret. What's wrong?"

"Someone was in my den. The fucker had a gun. I shot at him. Missed, unfortunately. He got away."

Philo stood and began to pace. "You're okay? You called 911?"

"I'm not stupid. The police are here now. And Killeen sent me a little one-armed girl named Cinna to stay with me. She looks like a bloody Arab. How the fuck can *she* help?"

Cinna Hightower was a black belt in everything from jujitsu to tae kwon do, an expert in communications, and fluent in Farsi, Pashto, and Arabic. She'd served with Philo in Afghanistan—until she lost her left arm at the elbow. Philo had offered her a job as soon as she finished rehab. Six months later, she'd shown up in Tucson with a letter of introduction from Philo. Killeen had hired her on the spot.

"Cinna's half-Iranian," Philo said, dealing with the least of Margaret's comments. "What kind of handgun do you have?

"What? Oh, a little revolver, why?"

"Ask Cinna to empty the cylinder. When she gives it back to you, point the gun at her."

There was a rustling at the other end as Margaret put

down the phone and followed directions. "Jesus!" she yelled, then came back on the line. Voices laughed in the background. "She damned near broke my wrist."

"Yes, well, you know you're in good hands."

"Hand, dear boy. She's only got one, remember? I'd still rather have you."

"Tough. Now, I want you to call Scott Munger, that police detective you talked with this afternoon."

"I already did. He'll be here any minute."

"Good. The man in the den—did he get in with a key?"

"No. He jimmied the sliding glass door. At least I think he did. Can't remember locking it after Grady left. I had a drink or two . . ."

"Did you get a good look at the intruder?"

"Yes. I flipped the light switch so I could get a better shot at him. He was Hispanic, I think. Short, quick, young. I'd know him if I saw him again."

"You said he had a gun. Did he shoot back?"

"He tried, but his gun got stuck in his pocket. So he ran for it."

"Okay. Tell Detective Munger everything you've told me, Margaret."

"I wasn't born yesterday, dear boy."

No matter how Philo responded to that he'd get into trouble, so he settled for, "Would you put Cinna on, please?"

Again, Philo heard rustling as the phone was passed, heard Margaret say, "He wants you."

"Hey, Philo." Cinna's voice was a clear alto. "Welcome home."

"Thanks for coming over in the middle of the night."

"No problem. Wasn't sleeping anyway. You know how it is."

Philo did. "Margaret's a pain in the ass, and you'll want to shoot her yourself before long."

"I'll practice patience and tolerance."

"You'll need both. I want you to move her to the safe house tonight. Make sure she leaves her cell phone behind. Use your car. Have Killeen follow you. Switch cars midway."

"I take it this was more than a break-and-enter?"

"Could be. I don't want to take any chances. My uncle's latest wife—number four—was murdered yesterday morning. And we caught a guy watching the office a few hours later. Killeen will give you his description."

"And now someone's broken into the house of wife number, what, one? Two?"

"One. And he was carrying."

"We'll assume it wasn't a coincidence." Cinna hesitated, then said, "Since this is a twenty-four-hour detail, I'll need a partner. Shifts of four on, four off, would be best."

"How about Griff, if he's not on another case?" Griffin Blessing was an old army buddy Killeen had hired while Philo was overseas.

"Griff's available, I already checked," Cinna said. "And we work well together."

"Good. Have Killeen call him. Three cars will be better than two for the drive to the safe house."

"Got it. Soon as the police are done, we'll spirit Maggie away."

"Just treat her as a regular client," Philo said. "Call her Ms. Dain."

"Yes, well, Maggie reminds me of a cat in heat. At the moment she's hitting on a detective who just arrived."

"That'll be Scott Munger. He's immune, I think. Would you put her on for me?"

"Sure thing. And don't worry about her, Philo. Griff and I can handle her—as long as it doesn't last too long."

"Never fear. I'll be home Monday."

Margaret was purring when she came on line. "If I'd known Detective Munger was that attractive, I wouldn't have been so short with him on the phone this afternoon."

Munger was on the gray side of forty and had a face like a pit bull. Philo wondered if Margaret was losing her sight. He sighed. "There will be two people looking after you—Cinna and a man named Griffin Blessing. Please, do what they tell you. No arguments."

"I'll be the soul of cooperation, dear boy, as long as they let me carry my gun."

Philo weighed the pros and cons. "Sorry, Margaret, there's too much chance of you shooting them in the middle of the night. But they'll both have weapons. You'll have to be content with that."

It was Margaret's turn to sigh. "Content, no. Resigned, yes. Can I at least bring the Grey Goose?"

"What happened to the Absolut?"

"It was a long day."

Philo sighed. "Bring your whole damn bar, if you want."

"And a deck of cards. Can't play strip poker without one."

Philo shook his head as he ended the call. "Problem at Margaret's?" asked Frankie from the bed.

"Yes. She's okay. Killeen's on it."

"Good. The night's half gone." She smiled and tossed back the sheet. She wasn't wearing nightclothes. "Come to bed."

The First Threshold

Beyond the threshold, then, the hero journeys through a
world of unfamiliar yet strangely intimate forces, some
of which severely threaten him (tests), some of which
give magical aid (helpers).

—Joseph Campbell, *The Hero with a Thousand Faces* (1949)

20

I looked at Philo as he stowed his laptop away in its case. Though he'd had only a few hours sleep, he looked refreshed. Getting away for the weekend was serving its purpose. The driven, haunted look was gone from his face, at least for the moment. I wanted that moment to last.

Setting my daypack on the bed, I stepped behind him and slid my arms around his waist, resting my chin on his shoulder.

"How hungry are you?" I said, hooking my index finger into the V of his knit shirt.

He smiled at me in the mirror, then glanced at his watch. "Sorry, but we're due at my contact's house."

"Ah, yes, your sorceress."

Philo smiled. "I call her Galadriel. She's a Tolkien fan. Earns me a few points."

"She keeps track?"

"Everyone keeps track."

The fog had lifted but still obscured the sky by the time we'd collected the tools and made our way back across town to Gwen Helmsley's neighborhood. In the pale morning light the houses seemed scrunched together, shoulders touching. Philo pointed to a for-sale sign lying in the grass behind the magnolia. It had fallen out of the hooks that suspended it from a wooden post.

"Explains the lockbox on the front door," I said.

Climbing out, I reattached the sign and snagged a flier from the plastic tube on the post.

"Let me guess," Philo said, when I was back in the car. "Nine hundred thousand?"

"Close enough." I studied the flier. "This is almost too easy. Gwen's the realtor. We can meet her and check out the house, all without raising an eyebrow." I plucked the cell phone from his breast pocket. "I'll call. She won't recognize my name."

"Even so, it would be better to use an alias. Let's keep it simple. Fran and Phil."

I punched in the number listed on the sign. "Mindy Brunewald," said a strong, rich, Germanic voice.

"Oh," I said. "I was calling Gwen Helmsley. I'm interested in looking at the house on Hedge Road." I gave my name and the house number. We spoke for another thirty seconds. Pressing END, I said to Philo, "Gwen's taking some personal time. Another agent's covering for her. Mindy Brunewald."

"Sounds Wagnerian."

I smiled. "We'll see. She'll be here in ten minutes. What's our backstory?"

Philo thought for a moment. "I'm expanding my security company, opening up a local office."

"I should be able to remember that. And I'll say I've snagged a postdoc at the Survey. How much time do you need to get into the safe?"

"Five minutes or less."

I rolled down the car window. The morning scents were different from last night's. The wind had switched direction. I thought I smelled the ocean, geraniums . . . and frying bacon. We'd made do with the motel's continental breakfast. I was hungry again.

My side mirror reflected a woman in jogging shorts and tank top pushing a baby stroller down the street. I climbed out of the car as she approached. "Excuse me," I said, gesturing at the sale sign. "We're thinking of buying in this neighborhood. Could I ask you a few questions?"

"Sure." She paused and moved the stroller forward and back, forward and back. "If I stop, he'll wake up," she said. "He's teething. I just got him to sleep." Her bloodshot hazel eyes had circles underneath. She hadn't slept in a while.

"Why don't I walk with you?" I leaned into the car window and said to Philo, "Be back in a minute, honey." He gave me a thumbs-up.

"When I worked at the Survey," I said to the mother, "one of my coworkers lived in the neighborhood. He loved the convenience."

"My husband's an anesthesiologist at Kaiser," she said. "We bought here because he could hop on the freeway and get to work quickly. It's been a godsend." She maneuvered the buggy over a broken patch in the sidewalk. "Will you be working at the Survey again?"

I nodded. "A postdoc. My fiancé will be working at home a lot. He owns his own business."

"Gwen—that's the woman who owns the house, Gwen Helmsley—she works at home a lot, too. She's a realtor. Her hours are terrible."

"So this hasn't been a rental unit. We're a bit leery of rentals. They tend to need a lot of work at the outset, and we won't have time."

"No, Gwen's lived here as long as I have. Eight years. We moved in the same month. She loves this neighborhood—comes to all the block parties and yard sales. She threw me a baby shower before Jesse was born."

"Why's she selling, then?"

"Her dad died. Her mother's in poor health, Parkinson's or something. She needs a full-time caregiver. Gwen has a sister somewhere—Arizona, I think, or New Mexico. But she's married and can't, or won't, help out much." She shook her head in disgust. "So Gwen moved back in with her mom a few months ago. Her mom's house in Daly City is worth twice this one, and houses sell pretty quickly here—or they used to, anyway, so . . ." Her voice trailed off.

"I'm surprised she didn't just rent it out," I said. "That way, she could return."

"I suggested the same thing. She said you can't go back, and this phase of her life is over. When she no longer has to care for her mother, Gwen plans to liquidate everything and see what the world has to offer."

"The world outside the Bay Area," I said.

"That's how I took it. I gather Gwen's been the daughter-on-call for all her adult life. Her father battled cancer for years. It was draining for Gwen and her mother, but Gwen never complained."

We'd reached the corner. A sixties-model mint-condition Mercedes sedan slowed as it approached Hedge Road and turned left toward Gwen's house. The realtor was right on time. She parked across the street and opened the car door. I said good-bye to the neighbor and walked briskly back to where Philo stood on the sidewalk.

Though Philo'd expected a blonde Amazon in breast-plates, Mindy Brunewald turned out to be a petite brunette fifty-something in a black skirt and blouse, red blazer, and three-inch black-patent heels. Her highlighted hair was pulled sternly back from her face into a ponytail, held with a red silk scarf. Not a wisp escaped.

Red's a power color. Mindy meant business. Her heels clicked as she crossed the road to greet us. She held her pen like a sword.

I introduced Phil, leaving off the last name. I didn't know how well Mindy knew Gwen's family. In a pinch, I would use his middle name, Graevling.

"Was there a particular reason you were interested in this neighborhood?" Mindy said, leading us to the front porch and opening the lockbox.

I gave Mindy the cover story we'd cooked up, ending with, "I'd like to be close enough to bike to work. I hate commuting."

"Especially on these roads at rush hour."

"I remember them all too well," I said, as she opened the heavy front door with its tiny security window. I smiled, remembering how easily we'd gained entrance the night before, and said, "The house has been on the market for some time?"

Mindy hesitated, then opted for the truth. "Five months."

Philo, on his knees, pushed aside a cascade of silk philodendron leaves obscuring an electrical outlet. At least that's what I hoped he was looking at. He might have gone round the bend.

Mindy Brunewald gave him an arched eyebrow. "Can I help you find something?"

"You'll have to forgive Phil," I said. "While I check out the aesthetics and flow of a house, he focuses on the electrical and plumbing. He needs state-of-the-art hookups, and plenty of outlets in each room."

She nodded, satisfied. "That may be a problem. This house was built in 1948. As you can see it's been remodeled, but that was twenty-five years ago."

"Before the personal computer revolution."

She nodded. "The present owner retrofitted where she could, but she didn't need much beyond a computer, printer, and wireless service provider."

"You know the owner, then?"

Mindy hesitated, as if I'd caught her out in a lie. "Gwen Helmsley owns the house."

"I see."

Philo rose and crossed to a grate set into the floor. "Central heating?"

"Yes. Gas. Just the two openings, here and on the other side of the wall, in the hall. No openings in the bedrooms. But the house is only eleven hundred square feet. And the converted room in the garage has a separate heating system—electrical."

With a noncommittal grunt, Philo headed down the hall toward the bedrooms and baths.

I wandered into the small kitchen, hoping Mindy would follow. She did.

Wanting to give Philo as much time with the safe as possible, I opened every cupboard and drawer, explored the refrigerator, tested the taps and garbage disposal. Ditto the garage, though it was hard to move between the piles of furniture and boxes. Mindy began tapping her toe on the oil-stained concrete floor. "Let's look at the bedrooms and bathrooms," I said, praying Philo had had time to check out the safe.

But when we retraced our steps to the hall, I saw him outside the first bedroom window, checking the junction box. I made a quick circuit of the rooms. I was hoping to find a family picture of Heather and Gwen, something I'd overlooked last night.

Philo met us in the living room. He nodded. Mission accomplished.

"If you like the area but don't want to commit right away," Mindy said, "Gwen's willing to offer a lease with an option to buy."

"The electrical's not up to my needs," Philo said. "Would she be willing to rewire?"

Mindy frowned. "I doubt if she'd do that for a lease/option, but she might come down on the price to offset those costs. I can ask."

"It's a deal breaker," Philo said, then turned to me. "Seen enough?"

"I think so."

"Are there any other properties I can show you?" Mindy said when we reached the sidewalk.

"Not today," I said. "But you'll let us know what the owner says about the electrical upgrade?"

"As soon as I can."

Feeling like a fraud, I wrote down a fictitious phone number and we said our formal good-byes.

"Was the safe empty?" I said, watching Mindy's Mercedes turn around and drive away.

"Not exactly." Philo was looking over my head. "Shit," he said under his breath. He put his hand under my elbow. "Hop in the car, Frankie. I'll drive."

I heard an engine start up as I slid into the passenger seat. I twisted around. A dented Saturn was parked across the street. It hadn't been there when we arrived.

Was the driver alone? I couldn't tell. The windows were tinted. Would he follow us?

Philo drove slowly up Hedge Road. The Saturn fell in behind.

"We've picked up a tail?" I said.

Philo pressed a finger over his lips. I got the message. Turning on the radio, I found a rock station loud enough to cover our voices.

"We'll know in a few minutes," Philo said, heading toward the Bayshore Freeway. "But I've been tailed often enough to spot the signs."

"But how did he find us?"

"He was probably watching Gwen's house, waiting for

anyone backtracking Heather. And he had plenty of time, while we were inside, to stick a tracking device or bug on this car."

Silently, I considered the implications. First off, we couldn't risk returning Galadriel's tools.

Philo must have been thinking along the same lines. "Don't worry, we'll lose him. But not before I get a good look at him—and maybe talk to him."

"I'm game. But he's already told us one thing." Philo glanced at me, eyebrow raised. I said, "Whoever killed Heather is still after the coins. Why else would we be followed?" Philo merged onto 101, heading north. I watched the car speed up to merge behind us. "And so blatantly, too. But how did he know to tail *us*, specifically? We could be any couple out looking for new home."

"There were photographers outside Derek's house yesterday. Our pictures might have been on the news, or in the papers."

"Or the man watching your office yesterday afternoon could have taken photos."

"True enough. So, let's assume he recognized us when we left Gwen's place. He's after the coins. They might be in your bag, or still hidden in the house. Or," Philo paused for a moment as he changed lanes, "if he knows they weren't in the house, he might be hoping we'll do the work of tracking them down for him."

"And once we find the coins—"

"*If* we find them."

"Right. *If* we find the coins," I said, "he'll try and take them from us."

"I would." Philo moved into the slow lane and signaled a right turn.

"Where now?"

"Somewhere I can remove any extraneous devices before we switch cars again. I don't want to expose Justin's setup by returning a compromised vehicle."

He took the Whipple Avenue exit and headed back to the center with the Starbucks and copy shop. The L-shaped parking lot had entrances on two cross streets. The only way our tail could watch both exits was to shadow us in the lot.

Philo parked at the angle of the L. The Saturn followed us in, circled the lot, and took up a position close to the Whipple Avenue exit as Philo began a search of the underside of our vehicle.

"I'll grab us some coffee," I said, getting out. "And then see if I can locate the Helmsley address in Daly City."

"Use this." Philo's voice was muffled by the rear fender. He fished his iPhone from his pants pocket and held it up to me. "I put the battery and SIM card back in. They know where we are at the moment anyway."

When I came out ten minutes later, Philo was leaning against the corner of the building, watching the man in the car. I set the coffees in the cup holders and handed back his phone. "Success?" I said.

"Didn't find a tracking device or a bug, so I think we're good to go," Philo said. "But I'll double-check with Galadriel's equipment." He took a photo of the Saturn's license plate. "There's just one man in the car. I'm betting he's flying solo," he said. "Otherwise, another car would have taken over the tail. And he hasn't talked to anyone while I've been watching. I'm going to try to draw him out, see if I can photograph his face."

"Are you kidding me?"

"We're safe, as long as we don't have the coins."

"But he can't know that—not for sure."

"Point taken. I'll be careful."

"Slip me the car key," I said. "I'll pick you up on the next block north in five minutes. If you cut between the buildings he can't follow you."

Philo gave me a kiss and tucked the key in my hand. I climbed behind the wheel and turned on the engine. Just as Philo reached the Saturn, I backed out. The man, distracted by Philo at his window, missed my exit onto El Camino. I drove south a couple of blocks, then followed a zigzag route back north. When I reached the designated street, Philo was standing midway down the block, half-hidden by an oak tree.

"Nobody followed me," I said, as he folded his long legs into the car. "How'd he react?"

"Turned on the engine, stalled the car, then backed up so fast he nearly ran over my foot."

"Amateur hour. Did you get his picture?"

"Yes. I've sent it and the license number to Killeen. And I've decommissioned my phone again." Philo was still watching the road behind me. "Did you get Gwen's mother's address?"

I pointed to the scrap of paper on the dash. "You want to switch cars first or drop off the tools?"

"Tools, first."

I turned toward the hills, let Philo out near his contact's house, and watched from a distance as he once again fed the tools through the oversize mail slot in the door. The door opened a crack, then closed. Philo waited. Pretty soon the door opened again and a woman's arm handed something black to Philo. He brought it to the car, ran it over and under the body, nodded, and returned it through the slot.

"Well?" I said when he got back into the car.

"We're clean. I don't think we need to switch cars after all."

I put the car into reverse and waited for a school bus to trundle by. "Isn't her mail slot a security risk?"

"She has a couple of Dobermans."

"Would she loan us one?"

He turned, smiling as he ran a hand down my cheek. "Scared?"

"Not exactly," I said. "Which reminds me—what *did* you find in the safe?"

"Photos."

I took the car out of reverse and turned off the ignition.

21

"Photos of what?" I asked.

Philo reached over the seat, plucked a gallon-size clear plastic bag from the floor, and handed it to me, saying, "I'm betting we won't find any prints, even on the bag—other than yours and mine, of course."

He said something else, but I missed it, my attention caught by a black-and-white, eight-by-ten photo of a den or family library. Built-in shelves crammed with books flanked arched windows, standing open. Beyond, a lawn stretched out and down until it was lost in rolling hills. In the far distance light glinted off the sea. Which sea, I couldn't tell. But it looked like the Pacific, Coast Ranges in the foreground.

Philo tapped the center of the photo, the focal point, occupied by a pedestal game table. On it stood a chess set. A game was in progress, though no players were in view. He said, "I recognize the chess set. It belonged to my grandparents. This was their den."

"The house Margaret gave you the key to—Foggy Gulch Ranch?"

He stared out the front window at the bare strip of land between two houses. A pair of robins poked for worms in the tall grass. On the bay, far below, ships moved like toy boats in a bathtub. "There's a note with a date on the back," he said, as if I hadn't spoken. "It's in my father's handwriting. He must have taken this picture on our last visit with them."

"Then Heather must have put these in the safe. Gwen wouldn't have had access to your family photos."

Philo pulled his gaze back to the photo. "I shouldn't think so—unless Heather gave them to her. But check this out." He took the bag from me and turned it over, revealing two smaller photos, this time in color. The same chess set. In one photo, the gold- and silver-toned pieces lay in an ebony case lined with red velvet. In the second photo, the kings faced off at the center of a marble game board, the one in the black-and-white photo. The pieces had been intricately crafted and cast by a master. The opposing profile views showed identical shoulder-length flowing locks, long bearded faces, heavy-lidded eyes. They wore Roman armor, including a crown and lion's head atop their Roman helmets. Around their bases were parts of words, —ERICI— (or —EVICI—), and —REGI—. The remainder of each inscription was obscured by the curves of the bases.

"Looks like Latin," I said.

"I agree. And these color photos are recent," he said. "Taken with a digital camera. No stamp of a commercial printer, so they likely were reproduced on a home or office printer."

Philo took a clean handkerchief from his back pocket and used it to pull out the photo of the kings. A white label with a typed quotation had been stuck on the back: *Reinfeld said: Chess is a game played by two opponents who are always referred to as "White" and "Black." White always makes the first move. Thereafter the players take turns in making their moves.*

Philo turned the photo over and put it back into the bag. I studied the somber-faced kings. Did the message have literal as well as metaphorical meaning? If so, was the writer playing White or Black? Had he set the ball rolling by murdering Heather, or was she killed in retaliation for something she or Derek had done? I said, "Does Derek play chess?"

"He thinks board games are a waste of time. But my father—" Philo smiled. "KC took after my grandmother. She was a ranked player. Grandpa was almost as good. And Dad could give them a run for their money. They all loved the game."

"How about Heather?"

He grimaced. "I only met her the one time, and she wasn't interested in chess."

"Well, someone's thrown down the gauntlet, either to

Derek, or to you. Could Heather have planned something this elaborate just to get back at Derek—something that backfired?"

"It's possible." He tapped the photo of the twin kings. "It's also possible her death had something to do with this specific chess set."

"Instead of the missing coin collection?"

"What if Margaret was right about the value of the coins? What if there *is* no Double Eagle?"

I reached over and smoothed the frown lines from his forehead, saying softly, "But why would Derek send you on a wild goose chase?"

Philo captured my hand and kissed the palm. "Haven't a clue. But it's the first question I'll ask him." He took out his cell, punched in a number, and waited. "Lena, would you route me through to my uncle? Right." Long pause. "Hey, Lena. He's not answering. Would you keep trying, please? If you reach him, tell him I have some news, and set up a time for the call. But don't give him this number. It's for you and Killeen only."

I picked up the plastic bag. "Tell me about the day your dad took the photo."

"We'd moved to Bishop from the Oregon commune the summer before. My parents wanted to get settled before I started kindergarten. I was five, nearly six, that Christmas."

Philo stared out at the bay again. I doubt he even saw the boats.

"We arrived at my grandparents' house on Christmas Eve," he said. "It was late afternoon. They were in the middle of a chess game. They let me watch. But afterwards, when I picked up the king to examine it, Grandma Claudine told me to set it down—that I wasn't to touch the set, at least till I grew up. It was her dowry, she said, all that she'd been able to bring from Europe . . . all that was left of her family." He picked up my hand and absently stroked the back. "I asked her what a dowry was." He laughed. "I learned a lot about the history of bride price, medieval marriage customs, and even how they were represented in Flemish art. She kept pulling art books off the shelves. I remember how big and heavy they were . . . Dad told me later that she'd gotten a degree in art history at the Sorbonne. She stayed on in Paris to study art conservation—at the Louvre, I think. She was there when the Germans invaded France and Belgium in 1940."

"Did she try to go home?"

Philo shook his head. "Her family lived in Tournai, a small Belgian city that was nearly destroyed during the fighting. But somehow her parents managed to send the chess set to her before the Germans arrived."

"Did they survive—her family, I mean?"

"None that she could ever find. She stayed in France during the war years, met my grandfather when the Allies liberated Paris. After the war they corresponded for a while, then he sent her a ticket to America."

He took his hand from mine and traced the outlines of the gold king with his forefinger. "I'd forgotten about the chess set till now. Wish I could remember what the inscription said."

"It looks old. And if it's made of gold and silver, then . . . could this be the treasure Derek wants you to find?"

"Could he have been lying, you mean?"

I shrugged. "We keep going in circles. Derek's the starting point . . . When you and he were talking at my house, I sensed tension about how Derek handled your grandparents' estate. What was that about?"

"My grandparents died in a car crash a couple of months after that Christmas visit. My father blamed Derek for their deaths. I'm not sure why. All I know is that I miss them."

"If they'd lived, your life would have been very different. They'd have taken you in after your parents died. Chances are, we'd never have met."

A smile touched his lips. "We'd have met. I'm sure of it. Maybe on a granite outcrop in the Sierras, or at a Stanford game. I'd probably have gone to Stanford, like my father did."

Philo's comment jiggled my little grey cells. I suddenly saw my Stanford roommate, Alana Calloway, head bent over a chess game. "Wait—" I kissed the corner of his mouth and snagged the phone from his pocket. "I have an idea where we can get some help on the chess set. Alana Calloway, my college roommate. She worked at a London auction house."

But the cell rang as I flipped it open. "It's Killeen."

"Why don't you drive while I talk?"

I started the engine again and pulled away from the curb, curving through the hilly streets toward Highway 280 as I thought about Alana. She'd majored in art history and been a chess junior master. After graduating from Stanford she had married Chet, the man she'd dated all through high school and college, the man her parents had picked out for her. Their families were part of the same Hillsborough social set. Alana and Chet had known each other since childhood.

When the marriage broke up, Alana found a job with a London auction house. But I'd heard through the grapevine that she was back home, living and working somewhere on the Peninsula. Her mother could tell me. She'd always liked me because I was a "sensible girl."

Did I have any other contacts in the art world? Michael Zorya, who lived next door to my parents in Tucson, dealt in art and antiquities. He was also a flamenco guitarist. World-class. When I'd seen him at Easter, he'd said he was heading for San Francisco—something about giving workshops and a few concerts. Was he still in the area?

I merged with the stream of traffic heading north on 280, a road that parallels the San Andreas fault zone. Below us, a little farther south, was the U.S. Geological Survey, where I'd worked for three years—until I lost my position in one of the reductions-in-force that have plagued the Survey for the last quarter century. I'd planned to stay here in the Bay Area, a place I'd come to know and love. Instead, I packed my things and went back to graduate school, this time in Southern California.

I hadn't visited the Bay Area in years. After the slow pace of the Southwest, the congestion here, the mass of humanity jockeying for space on the freeway, triggered culture shock. My thoughts must have been reflected on my face, because Philo put his hand over the phone and said, "Staggering, isn't it?"

"Thank heavens it's dead quiet on the ocean side of the hills."

Philo turned his attention back to Killeen. Judging by Philo's side of the conversation, they seemed to be covering more than the Heather Dain case. I knew little about the nuts and bolts of their work. Private investigation doesn't lend itself to small talk. Or shouldn't. I knew that Killeen had worked in military intelligence and that Philo was an expert in communications. And in patterns. In the twenty-first century, everyone leaves traces of where they dine, what movies they rent, what food they purchase, where they buy gas, what music they download. I knew there had been other work of a more clandestine nature, and I knew better than to ask for details Philo couldn't share.

We were driving on the rim of the world. In terms of population density, the two sides of the peninsula were yin and yang. Heavily forested hills, their bases wreathed in fog, dropped away toward the ocean on the left. On the right, houses crowded the slopes between 280 and the bay. All in all, I preferred the foggy side.

Philo said good-bye to Killeen and tucked the phone in his pocket. His face looked tight. I said, "What's up?"

"An anonymous caller reported finding a car, with a body inside, parked behind a Circle K on Valencia early this morning. Hadn't been dead long. His name was Arnulfo Sánchez—a small-time hood with a record. He matched the description Margaret gave the police, so they showed her a photo this morning."

"Munger went to the safe house?"

"No, he asked her to come to the station. Killeen stood in for me. Margaret ID'd a photo of Sánchez—who was also the registered owner of the car parked outside the office yesterday. Tommy described him exactly."

I considered the ramifications of a second body in Tucson. "How was he killed?"

"Throat slit. His wallet was gone, but he still had a weapon—a pistol, recently fired. His prints were on it, and he tested positive for gunshot residue."

"They think Sánchez looks good for Heather's murder."

"They're waiting on ballistics, but they're cautiously optimistic."

This was the break we'd been looking for. "If Sánchez's gun killed Heather, then he provides a link between her death, the break-in at Margaret's, and, presumably, the coins. And *his* death confirms there's another person involved—one who isn't worried about being connected with the murders. Otherwise, he wouldn't have left the body where it would be found so quickly."

"A pro," Philo agreed. "Ex-military maybe. He used a knife. Quick, quiet, efficient. No torture. He wasn't after information. He was eliminating a weak link."

It made sense. Sánchez was seen by both Tommy and Margaret. He was a liability. "Sánchez's killer—could he be the man who followed us from Gwen's house?"

"As you pointed out, he was an amateur," Philo said. "Besides, I doubt he'd have had time to find and kill Sánchez in Tucson last night and make it up here in time to catch us in Menlo Park this morning. No, I think our tail was local." He scratched his head and stared out the window. "Someone's giving orders, someone with the wherewithal and contacts to hire the work done."

"The person who put that chess quote on the back of the photo?"

"Why not? We know that Heather wanted to leave Derek. But if she wanted to maximize her gains, she had to void the prenup. She stole Derek's coins for leverage. But she also covered her bases. She found a buyer in case Derek didn't come through. Maybe he was her lover—who knows? But he's unscrupulous enough to traffic in stolen goods. That was her mistake."

"You think he double-crossed her, hired Sánchez to steal the coins. Only Sánchez fucked up. Twice. He didn't get the loot, and he killed the golden goose."

Philo nodded. "So, Sánchez and his boss went into crisis mode, scrambling to come up with their own Plan B."

"Sánchez watched Derek's house to see who showed up. And we entered, stage left."

"He probably followed us to Margaret's and then to my office."

"Sánchez must have been fairly competent. We never noticed him behind us."

"Ten to one he put a tracker on the truck while we were in the house. It would've been easy with that crowd milling around. Then he could have hung back, no problem. We'd never have seen him." Philo pulled out his computer and made a note to have Killeen check the truck for tracking devices.

"That would explain why he showed up last night at Margaret's," I said. "It was our first stop."

Philo made another note. "But once Sánchez was seen at both her place and my office, his boss sent a cleanup crew."

"Can you call one man a *crew?*"

"Cut me some slack, I'm on a roll. Where was I?"

"Somehow the boss learned that we'd left town for the Bay Area. He hired the man in the Saturn to find and tail us. The logical place for him to start was Gwen's house, where Heather had been staying—"

"And where they'd left the photos."

"Which is where our entire scenario breaks down," I said. "Problem number one—"

"There's no sign Heather *had* been staying there. Problem number two, the photos are of a Dain family residence and chess set, not the coin collection both Heather and Derek claimed she'd taken."

I nodded. "And problem number three: that quote on the back of the photo. Whoever wrote it *expected* Derek, or someone he hired, to backtrack Heather to Gwen's house. And Heather must have been aware of that *before* she left the Bay Area for Tucson."

"So her death can't be the first move in a chess game between Heather's team and Derek."

"If Heather never planned to return the coins, if all she was trying to do was give herself enough time for a clean getaway, then I can see her leaving a taunting note for Derek. Or asking Gwen to do it."

"You're right," Philo said. "And there'd be an added bennie—the photos of the chess pieces would have Derek obsessing over what other family treasures she might have taken. He'd have to do an inventory, which would buy her even more time . . . Maybe things started to go wrong when Heather flew back to Tucson. Maybe that wasn't part of the plan, and the buyer got spooked."

"But why did Heather return—especially to the empty house she and Derek were trying to sell? What made her interrupt her carefully laid plans?"

"And lie to me on the phone about where she was," Philo said. He had his cell out again. "Lena? Were you able to reach Derek? . . . OK. Please keep trying." He gave her a couple of messages for Killeen, then signed off.

"What now?" I said.

"We stick with our original plan while we wait to hear from Derek. But we watch for falling rocks."

I left 280 and circled onto Highway 1. California poppies carpeted the verge. Shreds of blue-gray fog crept between the Monopoly houses of Daly City.

"We kind of got sidetracked after we left Gwen's place," Philo said. "Did you find anything?"

"A used condom in the master bathroom. I doubt if it was left over from Gwen's tenancy—the house had been cleaned."

"How did the realtor react?"

"Mindy just shrugged and shook her head. No sign of guilt or embarrassment. I don't think she had a quickie with a client."

Philo laughed. "No, that's more Heather's style. But if so, who was her partner—the person who put the note on the back of the photo?"

"Or a stranger she met on the flight from Tucson, who offered to carry her bag—"

"Bags," Philo said. "Derek once complained that she always traveled with at least two."

"A clothes horse."

"More like a stable full. And her clothes were custom-made. That way, she'd never be caught wearing the same outfit as any other woman at the party."

I thought back to the body on the tile floor . . . Off-the-rack or catalogue clothes. Inexpensive shoes and watch. Lack of jewelry. Fingernails clean and shaped, but not manicured. Fair skin pale, not tanned. Fair hair showing darker roots. Things a woman was more likely than a man to notice.

Philo interrupted my musings. "Heather's only luggage was an overnight bag—exactly what you'd expect if she'd made a spur-of-the-moment decision to fly to Tucson. But when she left Derek, she would have had at least her usual two bags, if not more. So, where are they?"

"Not in Gwen's house," I said. "I checked every closet twice. I was trying to give you as much safe-cracking time as I could."

"The garage?"

"Nope." I realized I didn't know anything about Heather Dain. Wasn't *know your enemy* the first rule of war? "Was there anything else Heather brought with her when she traveled? Something we should be looking for at her mother's house?"

"I asked Derek that. Heather traveled with her favorite teas—Yogi, and her own special blend of South African rooibos. There was some in the cupboard in the mansion kitchen—"

"But none at Gwen's house. The cupboards were bare . . . Did you find tea in Heather's purse or overnight bag?"

"Shit," Philo said. "That body in Tucson—"

"Definitely wasn't the Heather you just described."

22

If the victim wasn't Heather, who was she? And why had Derek ID'd her as his wife?

I reviewed the mental tape of yesterday's events. Derek's pleading phone call to Philo. The white-faced man who'd answered the mansion door. The way he'd disassociated from the body on the floor and focused on the coin collection, as if clinging to that external problem so that he wouldn't have to deal with the emotional havoc triggered by the horror in front of him. Had he been in shock?

If so, he might not have forced himself to look closely at the body. He said he'd checked to make sure she was dead. He must have touched her neck or her wrist, because the body wasn't disturbed. She lay on his kitchen floor with a bullet hole behind her ear and blonde hair covering her face. Maybe he'd just assumed, *Who else could it be?*

I could make a case for Derek's misidentification. But what about Philo's? He didn't have the same emotional connection with Heather. There was nothing to do but ask him point blank.

"I've been thinking about that," he said, "wondering how I could have accepted Derek's ID without question. I guess the answer is that it's been years since I've seen Heather, and the body size and hair color match the woman I remember. She was found in their kitchen. Heather's driver's license and plane ticket clinched the deal. But you can bet I won't make that mistake again."

"I have three little questions," I said. "Who's the mystery woman? Where is Heather? And does she still have the coin collection?"

"Those're just the tip of the iceberg. For instance, how did Sánchez and the victim gain access to Derek's home? There was no sign of forced entry, so either Derek or Heather had to have given them a key."

"Unless the lockbox was on the door," I said. "Then, any realtor could have entered the house."

"Suggesting that the victim might be a realtor who brought Sánchez with her."

"Un-huh. Derek could have stowed the lockbox behind the bar just before we got there."

"One more question to put to my uncle when Lena finds him."

Our previous "facts" were falling like trees in a clearcut. I said, "I'd like to toss something radical into the mix."

"Go for it."

"We assumed that the purse belonged to the victim, and that she'd been alone with her killer. But Heather could have been *with* the victim—"

"In which case they'd have had a key, and we wouldn't need the lockbox on the door."

"Right. Or Heather could have come home and interrupted Sánchez. If he forced her to go with him, she might have left the purse behind to let us know she was in trouble."

The miles slid by under the tires as Philo mulled over the different scenarios. "If Sánchez took Heather with him, then she didn't give up the coins. Otherwise, he wouldn't have shown up at the office and visited Margaret's at one thirty in the morning."

"And been killed a short time later, presumably for failing." I sighed. "Speculating further's a waste of time. We've got to find Heather."

"She used her cell to call Derek." Philo pulled his phone out again, jabbing numbers as he spoke. "It'll have GPS."

"She said she was getting rid of it."

"Maybe she was lying. And maybe the phone's dead.

But if it isn't, Killeen might be able to pinpoint her location."

While Philo brought Killeen up to speed and discussed options, I pondered the niggling issue of the physical similarity between Heather and the victim. They could have been sisters. Mindy Brunewald, the realtor, said that Gwen was taking personal time . . .

When Philo ended the call, I said, "Have you ever met Gwen or seen a picture of her?"

He was silent for half a mile. "She might have been in one of Derek and Heather's wedding photos—there were some on the wall in the living room the day they brought me home from the hospital. But I was in no shape to notice such details."

"Any photos in the dead woman's wallet—other than the one on Heather's license?"

"None."

"Strange."

"Very. But Killeen said that Toni and Scott are tracking the victim's movements. They have people reviewing airport security photos at SFO and Phoenix–Sky Harbor and footage from the motel cameras. With luck, they'll find something that will shed light on whoever used Heather's ticket."

"Well, we'll have an answer in a few minutes," I said. "If Gwen's at her mother's house, then the victim's a stranger. And if Gwen's not there, her mother will have some idea where she went."

"And Gabrielle will have photos."

I took my hand off the wheel and touched his knee. "Have you considered that Heather might be in Daly City, too? Derek might not know that Gwen moved back home."

"We couldn't be that lucky." Philo pointed to a freeway sign. "Here's our exit."

I looked at my watch. Twenty-six minutes. Not bad.

We drove a few blocks to a neighborhood perched on eroding cliffs. The spaces between houses offered glimpses of the Pacific under a drifting marine layer. On this side of the peninsula the sun struggled to break through the amorphous mix of fog and clouds. Mist collected on the windshield. I turned on the wipers.

Three left turns took us to a two-story home, painted sage green with white shutters and a brick-red door. An unassuming house, simple and welcoming. Baskets of fuchsias hung on either side of the door. A concrete walk, bordered with daisies, bisected a recently mowed patch of grass.

The woman who answered our knock had fair skin, strong cheekbones, white-streaked blonde hair caught back in a clip, and pearl studs in delicate ears. She wore a silky, off-white top, brown pants, and a camel cardigan. Light makeup, carefully applied, enhanced brown-flecked hazel eyes. Her right hand held the doorknob. Her left, a slim cane.

I wasn't sure how Philo wanted to play this. But before he could open his mouth, she said, "Did you feel that?" She tapped the foyer floor with her white cane. Her voice was low and musical, with traces of a French accent.

"Feel what?" I said.

"The earthquake. A minute ago." Excitement colored her words. "It had to be at least a 4.5."

"Sorry," I said. "We've been in a car. Didn't feel a thing."

"Oh. Well, then . . ."

Philo stared at her, looking puzzled. I stepped into the breach. "Mrs. Helmsley? Gabrielle Helmsley?"

"Yes." Gabrielle turned her head a bit to the side, as if she were trying to see me with her peripheral vision. "You're the couple who called about the dining room set?"

"Ummm, no." I paused to give Philo a chance to jump in.

"I'm Philo Dain, Derek's nephew," he said. "And this is my fiancée, Frankie MacFarlane."

It was the first I'd heard of an engagement, but I limited my reaction to a choking sound. Philo tightened his grip on my hand.

"Philo?" Gabrielle's head swiveled so she could see

Philo from an angle. Reaching out with her left hand, she touched his face. "Ah, *c'est vrai*. You're very like your father." A smile touched her lips. "It's been a long time."

Philo drew back, looking confused. "I'm sorry, have we met?"

"Of course, you wouldn't remember. You were very young when your grandparents died." A shadow of old sorrow darkened her eyes. "Your Grandmama Claudine was my godmother. And I knew your parents well."

I think it was the first time I'd ever seen Philo at a loss for words.

"Come in, my dears." Gabrielle Helmsley stepped to the side and pushed wide the door. "We have so much to catch up on."

And, easy as that, we were in the Helmsley home.

23

Transferring the cane to her right hand, Gabrielle Helmsley closed the door and led us into the living room. She moved easily between the chairs and tables, touching them with the tip of the cane but not using it for support. Whatever afflicted her, it wasn't Parkinson's.

The house was small enough that I'd have known if Gwen or Heather were there. But I heard only Jacques Brel's "Ne Me Quitte Pas" coming softly from speakers in the corners of the room. Gabrielle seated herself on the end of an ivory-silk loveseat. She patted the cushion next to her. Philo sat without a word.

I remained standing. I wanted to check out the photos on the walls, the upright piano, and the slender-legged occasional tables. I drifted from one photo to another, comparing Gabrielle's two daughters. They were perhaps two years apart in age, near-clones in coloring and build— both blonde and fine-boned, like their mother. There the similarity ended. Gwen's face revealed a sweetness, an inner reserve. Her eyes held a wistful innocence. But if Heather had ever been innocent, the lens hadn't captured it. Even in the earliest photos, her eyes and poses suggested intimacy and self-awareness. She courted the camera.

I hadn't seen the victim's face in Tucson, but the general build and hair color fit either woman.

"We actually stopped by to see if Heather was here," Philo said. "She and Derek had a, well, a falling out, and she left Tucson. Derek's worried about her."

"I'm so sorry," said Gabrielle. "Heather left, oh, an hour ago. Maybe two."

Philo sat back and looked at me. This was progress. To Gabrielle, he said, "Did Heather mention where she was going—or how you could reach her?"

"No, dear. She left rather quickly."

"That's too bad." Philo paused. "Is Gwen home by any chance?"

"I'm afraid not. Heather gave Gwen a little vacation." A smile touched Gabrielle's lips for a moment, then disappeared. "It was only supposed to be for one day, but when Gwen didn't return last night . . ." She put her hand on Philo's arm. "You said Heather and Derek had a falling out?"

"She didn't tell you?"

"Heather said she was in San Francisco on business."

Philo covered her hand with his. "Heather left him. She's asking for a divorce."

"That can't be. She seemed quite happy." Gabrielle paused, then proceeded more slowly. "Until she got a phone call this morning."

"Who was it?"

"A man—Derek, I assumed. But maybe not." Worry deepened the lines of Gabrielle's face. "A minute later I heard Heather throwing things into a suitcase. She said she needed to get home."

"To Tucson, you mean."

"That's what I supposed."

"Do you mind if I use your phone to call Derek?"

She gestured toward the phone on a side table, saying, "I've been trying to reach him. He doesn't answer. Gwen's not picking up, either. Their numbers are on the speed dial." She massaged her right hand with her left, as if pain had settled in the joints. "Gwen bought me that special phone when my sight started to go," Gabrielle added. "She programmed the numbers in. I'm hopeless at that sort of thing."

Philo crossed to the phone, sending me a glance that said, *Your turn.* I stopped my circuit of the room and sat gingerly on the edge of a formal silk-covered armchair. The chair was surprisingly comfortable.

"Does Gwen often stay away for a couple of days?" I said, as Philo lifted the receiver and pressed one of the buttons.

"Not since my eyesight deteriorated. It's macular degeneration. There's nothing they can do." She was quiet a moment, then gave herself a little shake. "I was going to hire live-in help, but Gwen didn't want a stranger in the house. And this way, there's someone here with me at night. Or there was." She looked at Philo. He was leaving a message, simple and short. He touched another number on the speed dial.

"When did you see Gwen last?" I said, recapturing Gabrielle's attention.

"Late Tuesday afternoon. Heather called. She was in town for only a few hours, she said, and she asked Gwen to meet her for dinner at Benihana's."

"The one near the airport?"

Gabrielle nodded. "Gwen fixed a light dinner for me and then drove off. Around seven, I believe. She said she'd be home late, and not to wait up."

"But in the morning, Heather was here."

"Yes." A smile lit her face. "It was lovely to see her. Her life with Derek keeps her so busy that she can't visit very often."

Philo resumed his place on the sofa, saying, "Neither of them answered."

Gabrielle's smile drained away. "When I couldn't reach Gwen on her cell this morning, I started to worry. She always calls me to let me know she'll be late . . . But Heather said Gwen was probably just enjoying her time away, and to give her a few more hours."

"Let me see what I can find out," Philo said. "Is there another phone line? I'd like to leave this one free in case anyone calls back."

"Gwen has a business line in her office. Upstairs, second door on the right."

Philo dropped a kiss on my head as he left the room. We both knew how that phone conversation would go. My job was to distract Gabrielle while he linked the local police with Pima County detectives.

I leaned toward Gabrielle and said gently, "Do you have any recent pictures of Gwen?"

"There's the photo Gwen uses for her real estate ads. I have a copy in my bedroom. Would you mind getting it for me while I put the kettle on? You do drink tea, don't you— Frankie, is it?"

I nodded, then remembered she couldn't see well. "Yes. Short for Francisca. And yes, I love tea."

"Good. My bedroom is just down the hall." Gabrielle got to her feet. Her shoulders slumped. Her slender body seemed to have aged years in the past quarter hour. "The photo's on my bureau."

Gabrielle's bedroom must have once been her husband's office, converted now so she wouldn't have to deal with the stairs. A sturdy black file cabinet stood in one corner. Simple shelves attached above it held books on real estate, long outdated. Large windows in the east wall let in muted gray light. The small backyard, fenced in redwood, held a glass-topped table and metal chairs, forms only half-grasped through dimensions flattened by fog.

I turned on the overhead light. The bed was made, the antique, white-painted furniture uncluttered. The impression was of neatness, order, every object in its place. A blind person's room. Three large photos stood on the bureau—head-and-shoulder shots of a middle-aged man and a thirty-something Gwen, and a snapshot of Derek and Heather wearing swimsuits and Santa hats, hoisting glasses on a beach. *Mele Kalikimaka,* it said along the bottom. Christmas in Hawaii.

I carried Gwen's photo to the kitchen and set it on the counter. "Oh, good, you found it," Gabrielle said. "She received a realtor's award last year. It included a formal portrait."

I studied the photo Gabrielle could no longer see clearly—an adult Gwen, in a sleeveless black top, diamond and pearl earrings, matching pendant. Blonde hair, no roots showing, brushed her shoulders. Gentian-blue eyes shone. Life was good that day.

Heather and Gwen had become even more alike as they aged, I noted. Perhaps Derek shouldn't be faulted for not recognizing his sister-in-law. Clearing my throat, I said, "She's lovely."

"Inside and out." Gabrielle put a hand on my wrist. "She's dead, isn't she? She's dead, and you don't know how to tell me."

"Gabrielle, I—"

She turned away to stare sightlessly out the kitchen

window at the gray mist now shrouding the house. "I think I knew. Yesterday morning I felt my heart stutter. It went on for a long time. Heather wanted to take me to the hospital, but I wouldn't let her . . . couldn't let her. And then it stopped."

I turned the photo facedown on the counter and wrapped my arms around Gabrielle. Her husband and one daughter were dead, her other daughter on the run. Who was left to comfort her?

"How did it happen?" Her voice didn't tremble. There was steel in Gabrielle Helmsley.

"There's a chance it might not be Gwen."

"How did it happen?"

Telling her was Philo's job, once Gwen was positively ID'd. I stalled. "Why don't I fix you some lunch to go with our tea?"

She stepped away from me, straightening her shoulders. "I could use something warm. Can you do lentil soup? My mother used to make it on cold days. I think I have all the ingredients. I was going to make some with Heather today."

"My mother makes it, too," I said. "It's one of my favorites."

She waved her hands. "Go then, explore. The pots are in the cupboard next to the oven."

I rustled out the soup pot, opened the large pantry door, found a package of lentils and a couple of cans of stewed tomatoes. The fridge yielded carrots, celery, onion, and garlic.

Gabrielle took a basket of assorted teas from a cupboard, set them on the counter next to a rose-splashed china pot, and sat silently at the kitchen table. When the water finally came to a boil she made a pot of jasmine tea and left it to steep, then resumed listening to the rhythmic rise and fall of the cleaver. The music in the living room had stopped. She didn't move to put in a new CD. Chopping vegetables makes a comforting music all its own.

I tossed all the ingredients into the pot with the rinsed lentils and water, set it on the stove, and joined her at the table. I'd made a decision as my hands worked. Why prolong her agony? In her shoes, I'd want to know the worst.

I poured a cup of tea for each of us, and told her the story of the past two days, leaving out our illegal entry into Gwen's house last night and the details of how we'd reached the Bay Area. Philo was still in Gwen's office when I finished. He must have had to work his way through the chain of command to find a local detective who could interface with Scott Munger.

My hands smelled like onion. Maybe that's why I was crying. Gabrielle handed me a box of tissues from the sideboard. Somehow she remained dry-eyed. She wasn't screaming or yelling or pounding the table, none of the things I'd be doing if I'd just found out my daughter had died.

I tossed my little pile of tissues in the wastebasket, turned down the soup to simmer, and poured myself another cup of tea. Gabrielle took my hand in both of hers and said, "What can I do to help you find whoever did this?"

"Philo will have questions. I have questions."

"Anything."

"Thank you. But first, I'd feel better if I knew you'd be with relatives once we leave. Is there someone I can call?"

"I have no other relatives, not even in France. My father died in the war—in the Résistance." She gave it the French pronunciation. "My mother passed in 1962, just as I finished my schooling. That's when I came to visit Claudine . . . and never left."

I had such a large family I couldn't imagine what it felt like to be that alone. "I hate to leave you, especially tonight."

"Don't worry about me, Frankie. I'll be fine here. There will be leftover soup, and the grocery store delivers. So do several local restaurants. I won't starve."

Philo stood in the hallway, just outside the kitchen, as if unwilling to commit to stepping into the room. I wondered how long he'd been there.

Gabrielle must have sensed his presence. She stood up and walked over to him. He dwarfed her. Taking his face between her hands, she said, "Have they confirmed it? My Gwenneth's dead?"

"Not yet," Philo said, a confirmation in all but words.

"The police are on their way to talk to you."

"Promise me you'll find who did this thing. And promise me you'll find Heather. She's all I have left."

Philo wrapped his arms around her slender form. She dropped her hands and put her forehead against his chest. I saw tears darken his navy shirt.

"Promise me." Her muffled voice broke on the second word. Philo stood, eyes closed, lashes wet.

There was nothing I could do. I went to the stove, stirred the soup, reduced the heat a hair further, and replaced the lid. All the meal needed was some warm sourdough bread and maybe a bottle of wine. *I* could use a glass or two right then—wine and wilderness. I needed a break from the suffering that infused this house, from the emotions that threatened to swamp me again.

Philo led Gabrielle back to the living room. I heard their voices murmuring softly. Philo was saying something about letters. I heard the front door open and close, then open and close again a minute later. When I entered the room, I found them sitting, heads together, Philo rifling through the bundle of old letters Margaret had given him. "Claudine sent KC letters while he was in the Peace Corps," he said. "Would you like me to read them to you?"

When the present robs you of family, sometimes the past must suffice. I found my bag on the armchair where I'd dropped it. They wouldn't even notice I was gone. I said, "I'm going to the store for bread."

Philo's eyes lifted from the old blue airmail stationery covered with cramped script. He handed me the car keys and Killeen's cell phone, saying, "Be careful out there."

24

I passed a police cruiser turning onto Gabrielle's block, two officers inside, coming to question the grieving mother, fill in the blank lines on their forms, and turn a tentative ID into a definitive one.

I had no desire to be present for the formalities. I wanted to remain autonomous and anonymous as long as possible. The soup could simmer for an hour or so, giving me time alone—time to think, to piece together the things Philo and I knew, things we couldn't give to the police without pointing the finger of blame directly at his uncle. Even if Derek had lied to us, even if he was hungry to recover the coins or chess set, it didn't mean he was guilty of having Gwen killed.

At a nearby market, I grabbed bread and a bottle of BV Coastal Cabernet, then stopped for a large coffee at McD's. Mussel Rock Beach was only a few blocks away. I knew it well from geology field trips, long ago. Pastel cliffs and sharp winds, the sounds of gulls and crashing surf. Wildflowers and solitude a mile from bustling, chaotic civilization.

I parked in the lot at the end of Westline Road, beyond the entrance to the mass transfer station. The post–World War II houses of Daly City perched on the edge of the cliffs above, ready to tumble down when the Big Quake hit. The cliffs slouched seaward, the Tertiary sedimentary rocks so fractured and weakened by one tectonic plate moving against the other that all sense of bedding had been lost. The lone exception was a landslide block of white strata with clean sharp bedding planes. The eroded face resembled teeth, bared in defiance of the forces tearing at them.

Locking the car, I set off down the dirt path. I'd arrived at low tide. The empty beach, flanked by more pale cliffs, stretched northward to San Francisco. Gulls soared and skimmed the water. Two men flew model airplanes, and a helicopter and single-engine plane droned overhead. Perspective played games. I had difficulty distinguishing the models from the real thing. They all looked like toys, though the models sounded as loud as a swarm of killer bees.

The wind whipped my hair. I tucked it under the hood of my sweatshirt. Poppies, daisies, and buttercups, penstemon, lupine, and lavender ice plant covered the slopes, with, here and there, a twisted cypress. The saturated color seemed to catch and hold errant beams of sunlight that seeped through the lowering mixture of cloud and fog.

The mass wasting of the cliffs reminded me of change, that universal constant. I stood at the juncture of two vast blocks of the Earth's crust—the Pacific Plate, moving north, pressing against the southwestward-moving margin of the North American Plate. This narrow strip of crust wedged between the San Andreas fault and the coastline, what geologists call the Salinian block, is a hodgepodge of Tertiary and Cretaceous marine rocks—a mélange of deepwater ribbon chert, isolated granitic plutons, and shallowwater sandstone, siltstone, and fossil-rich mudstone. Mussel Rock, standing just offshore, was a remnant of a once-continuous sandstone unit, now truncated by the fault zone. I picked up a chunk of ochre-colored sandstone. Weathered, friable, easily shattered. Only the ice plant and bracken and blooming wildflowers kept the rocks from eroding quickly to join the beach sand.

I threw the rock as far as I could out to sea, watched it land with a satisfying splash, followed it with more missiles until my arm was tired and I'd cleared a large circle around me. And then I ran—down the zigzag asphalt path to the sandy beach, and up the damp sand until the sheer cliff on my right met the limitless ocean on my left and there was no more room to run. I collapsed in a heap, breathless.

I'd left people and noisy model airplanes behind. I sat in a cone of wind and mist and emptiness, looking back at that foreign block of crust. We both had traveled here from points far to the south. My air journey from Tucson had been quick and smooth. But the Salinian rocks, deposited in the deep ocean and sutured onto the continent somewhere in Mexico, had crept northward at a rate of two centimeters per year. They'd ridden the plastic upper mantle like a bird on a hippo's back. And they were still moving, though the San Andreas fault zone was locked here, pressures building, as the world waited. The small quakes, like the one Gabrielle felt today, didn't relieve enough stress on the system. The "Big One," when it hit, would jolt the block from its stasis—jolt it as surely as Philo, Gabrielle, and I had been rocked by recent events.

What then? The ticky-tacky houses on the cliffs above, the North American Plate's western edge, would slide down to this beach. Mud, dredged from the bay on the other side of the Peninsula to make the foundations for cities, would liquefy, the water molecules coalescing until foundations cracked, houses fell, and roads split. Bridges would collapse. The Marina District in San Francisco, built on unconsolidated sandfill, would face a similar threat.

When would the Big One happen? Soon. Time and change are the inevitabilities, the certainties. In terms of endless, unfathomable geologic time, origins and endings and major ruptures are as transient as fog.

I felt raindrops, cold as stone, on my face. Time to turn back.

25

I was halfway to the car when I remembered that I'd never tracked down Alana Calloway or Michael Zorya to discuss the chess set. I checked for a cell phone signal. It was weak, but doable. I started punching in numbers . . .

The police were gone when I reached the house, but a Ram pickup was in the driveway. Gwen's dining room table and upended chairs were in the bed. A young couple was spreading a tarp over the furniture and lashing it down. Gabrielle stood in the garage, looking forlorn. "I didn't know what else to do," she said, watching them drive away. "Gwen put the ad in the paper. They wanted the set . . ." She gave a helpless little shrug and pressed the garage door opener, shutting out the world.

I carried the wine and bread into the kitchen, tasted the soup, added some sea salt and cayenne pepper. Philo's voice murmured overhead in Gwen's office. He didn't sound happy. By the time I'd sliced the bread and put it in the oven to heat, Gabrielle had set the table for three. The placemats were pink Belgian linen with appliquéd flowers. Philo came in as I uncorked the wine.

"That looks wonderful. Thank you both," he said.

"Claudine gave these placemats to my mother, back when they were schoolmates," Gabrielle said, carefully positioning matching napkins and silverware. "I'd planned to give them to Gwen when she married. They don't suit Heather. She's not . . . *douce.*"

Philo and I exchanged a glance. Gabrielle was right—Heather was anything *but* sweet.

Gabrielle took china plates and soup bowls from the sideboard and handed them to me. "I'll just go wash my hands," she said, and left us alone.

"I reached Alana Calloway's mother," I said. Philo looked blank. "Alana, my college roommate. I called her mother while I was gone."

Light dawned. "Oh, right. The roommate who works at a London auction house."

"Not any more. She's expecting us for supper. Sixish. And we can spend the night there, as well. She can't wait to meet you."

"And if I don't pass muster?"

"I'll have to toss you out and start looking again."

"Fat chance." Philo opened a fresh stick of butter and plopped it on a saucer. "Where does she live, exactly?"

"Moss Beach. Convenient for whenever we decide to head down to Woodside. I told her we need some advice on old chess sets. Turns out they were a significant part of her work in London. Now she's gone out on her own—deals on the Internet."

"She'll save us a hell of a lot of time. Did you describe the photos to her?"

"I thought it would be better to show her." I found the salt and pepper shakers and set them on the table. "Oh, and I called home while I was gone. Mom says Michael's in San Francisco, teaching at the Conservatory. I made the mistake of asking for Michael Zorya the first time I called the school. Drew a blank of course. I could have kicked myself. He doesn't exactly spread his real name around. Anyway, I called back and asked for Alessandro. He was in the middle of a flamenco class, but the receptionist said she'd get my message to him. I gave her this cell number and asked her to have him call at three."

"Seems like ten years since I've seen Michael." Philo took the bread from the oven, placed it in a basket, covered it with a napkin.

Michael Zorya, his father, and aunt lived next door to my parents in Tucson. The disappearance of Michael's sister had united our two families. It had also brought Philo back into my life.

"Mother said he's doing well." I dished up the soup, adding softly, "Did you reach Derek?"

"No, and Lena said his message machine's full." Philo stepped to the doorway and checked to see if Gabrielle was within earshot. The coast was clear. "I called Scott Munger. Got kicked over to Toni. Derek's disappeared."

I nearly dropped the soup bowl I was filling. "I thought Scott had someone watching the place."

"He put a deputy at the bottom of the driveway."

"Not much of a view from there."

"So he discovered late last night when a fire started at the back of the house."

"The kitchen?"

"You guessed it. The fire had spread to the garage and guesthouse by the time the deputy noticed it, around two in the morning. Once it was out, they checked to see if Derek was caught in the blaze. Took them a while. No body. So they broadened their search. Turns out Derek hiked up the ridge behind the house—to that new development."

"A Derek Dain project?"

"Um-hmm. One of several that he pulled out of in the last year. But he still had a key to the development office. He called a cab from there. Munger found the cabbie. He dropped Derek off at Margaret's house. Her car's missing."

"I bet she's spitting tacks right now." I smiled, picturing Margaret's face when she learned the news. Something pinged in my brain. "Wait a minute—didn't you say Killeen escorted Margaret to see Scott Munger this morning? So she could ID photos of the guy who broke into her house last night?"

"I know where you're going—"

"Why didn't Scott or Toni mention the fire to Killeen? And why didn't Killeen mention the fire to you during one of your conversations on the drive up here?"

"The fire was reported on the morning news. Killeen saw it. That's why he went with Margaret to the station— for a private conversation with Scott and Toni while Margaret was viewing the photo lineup. They weren't sure whether Derek had died in the fire or not, and they weren't sure how I figured into everything. Killeen gave them my alibi. They asked him not to say anything to me about the fire until they knew whether Derek was alive or dead."

"And until they checked your alibi."

"I expect so. Killeen said they grilled him—and talked to Justin. And once they knew for sure that Derek wasn't in that house, they started tracing his movements."

"A path which led to Margaret's missing car. Did Derek know you hid Margaret away?"

"Not from my end. And Toni says not from their end, either. Margaret claims she can't remember calling him. Killeen checked. She talked to him once, right after we left."

"To ask him if he were planning to pay alimony from Costa Rica?"

"That sounds like Margaret. But she doesn't remember details too well when she's been drinking."

"I assume Toni and Scott think the fire was a diversion, to give Derek a head start."

"What else could they think?" Frustration colored Philo's words. "His alibi for Heather's murder was a hardware store receipt for lighter fluid and a lighter."

"When they find Derek, there'll be no question about him facing charges—arson, destruction of a crime scene, interfering with a criminal investigation . . ." My voice trailed off.

"And first-degree murder," Philo said, finishing the list. "Alibi or no alibi, Toni was pissed. She and Scott put out a multistate BOLO on the car, and they've got officers checking Derek's vacation homes. No hits."

"I thought he'd sold all his homes."

"Didn't put the Cabo San Lucas condo on the market, and the others are in escrow. He's still got access."

"Where are they?"

"Coronado, Sanibel, Vancouver Island."

Coronado Island was the closest to Tucson—a six- or seven-hour drive. I looked at my watch. He could be on the coast by now—a good jumping off place for points south. I said, "Did he usually drive to Cabo?"

"No. Toni called one of his business associates. He said Derek sailed a Switch 51 catamaran, berthed in San Diego. Heather usually crewed for him, but he wouldn't have a problem finding someone to take her place."

"From Cabo he could easily fly to Costa Rica."

"Or sail," Philo said. "Rename the boat somewhere in Mexico, take on a local crew. They'd be hard to track."

"Who'd be hard to track?" Gabrielle said from the doorway.

Philo turned, put his hands on her shoulders, and said, "Derek. He's gone missing."

She sighed. "Things just keep getting worse, don't they." It wasn't a question.

We talked about simple things over lunch—what Philo had been doing since Gabrielle last saw him, how he'd come into my family's sphere, and how he and I had found each other again. "It sounds like you both lead very exciting lives," she said. Then, "Philo, did Derek or Margaret ever tell you that Russell and I wanted to raise you after your parents were killed?"

Philo paused in the middle of buttering a piece of bread. Pain darkened his eyes, but he didn't say anything.

"Apparently not," Gabrielle said. "I'm so sorry. We had the space, here, and the girls liked the idea of having a brother. It's what Ann and KC would have wanted, and you would have known you were loved . . . But Derek and Margaret wouldn't hear of it. I suppose it was the inheritance."

"I didn't know," he said, running a hand over his eyes. He leaned over and kissed her cheek. "It would have been—wonderful."

"But you wouldn't have met your Frankie," she said. "So all things happen for a reason." She pushed back her chair and stood. "And now, if you don't mind, I'd like to lie down for a few minutes."

"Of course. We'll just tidy up."

Philo cleared the table in silence, dealing with the newest black mark on Derek's slate. "I'm glad we came," he said. "It changes everything."

I wrapped my arms around his waist and held him for a long moment. "I hope she lives forever."

"So do I." He kissed me swiftly, then let me go. "But Heather sure as hell doesn't deserve her."

"Speaking of Heather," I said, handing Philo a plate to dry, "that fire solved the problem of selling the mansion.

But Derek's not the only one with a motive. Heather's partner could have set it to kill two birds with one stone—destroy the crime scene and scare Derek into running. With the police chasing *him,* the pressure would be off everyone else."

"And give Heather enough breathing space to find a new partner or buyer." Philo dried the last plate and set it on the table. "I can't imagine she still trusts the old one."

"Not after what he did to Gwen," I said. "Unless Heather thinks he's the only game in town."

"Or he's got some hold over her."

The phone rang in Gwen's office. I followed Philo up the stairs. It was Cinna. Philo put her on speakerphone. "There was a natural gas leak at the safe house," she said. "We had to move Maggie—er, Ms. Dain."

"Did someone find you?"

"Don't know. The leak might have been a routine maintenance problem. It's an older line. The repairman said he'd get back to us on that. But Killeen went ahead and did some digging—contacted city records. Three days ago, a man searched for Derek Dain properties. The clerk pulled all the Dain records. Yours were in there. Maggie's house, too."

"Which may explain how Arnulfo Sánchez came to be parked outside my office, and how he found Margaret later that night."

"Looks like it," she said. "Killeen checked your truck. Didn't find a tracking device."

"So Derek was targeted *before* Gwen was killed," I said. "And whoever ordered the search—Heather's partner, presumably—didn't just rely on what he could find on the Internet, he looked for Derek's relationships."

Philo took a string of midnight blue worry beads from his pocket and slid them between his thumb and forefinger. Cinna's voice came over the line. "What's up, Philo?"

"We have to assume Heather's partner knows about Gabrielle. He might not yet know that Sánchez killed Gwen by mistake, but he will as soon as it hits the evening news."

I put a hand on his arm. "We'll have to find Gabrielle a place to stay until we can figure things out."

Philo nodded and stowed the beads back in his pocket. "Margaret's secure?" he asked Cinna. "No one followed you?"

"An atom bomb couldn't touch her."

Philo smiled. "Perfect. Keep an eye on her. We don't know if she's got a role in this."

Back in the kitchen, Gabrielle was just finishing the cleaning up. She must not have been able to sleep. Or she wanted to prove she wasn't helpless. Or both. Philo explained the situation in Tucson. "I'm sorry, Gabrielle, but it might not be safe for you to stay here after all."

"You told us you didn't have relatives," I said, "but what about friends?"

"Well, there's Bea. She drives me to church when Gwen's . . ." Her voice tapered off. Her face was tight with exhaustion.

Philo put his arms around her and said to me, "That connection would be difficult to pick up, unless whoever's looking had a lot of time to poke around—or a lot of people working for him. He hasn't shown that he has either. So Gabrielle should be safe at Bea's."

"May I call her for you?" I said.

"Would you? Please. She's on autodial there. Just press 4."

I touched the keypad and felt the four raised dots under my fingertips. Closing my eyes as the phone rang, I ran my fingertips over the keypad, feeling the dots and lines that signified the numbers, trying to imagine Gabrielle's life as my own.

A woman's voice answered. "Gabrielle?" she said. Texas twang. Or maybe Oklahoma. "We all missed you at Bible study last night. Hope everything's okay?"

I introduced myself and explained about Gwen without going into the details. I said that Philo and I were having trouble locating Heather and Derek, and didn't want Gabrielle to be alone while we worked. Would it be possible for Gabrielle to stay with Bea for a short time? Of course, Bea said, promising to come over as soon as her husband returned with the car. Twenty minutes or so. And she'd let their pastor know he might be needed.

When the call ended, Philo deleted all the numbers

from the speed-dial file. He also placed a call to Gwen's office line, to replace the last-called number in the phone. "Just precautions," he said to Gabrielle. "I'll reprogram your phone later, when this is over."

Gabrielle nodded and said, "I'll go pack a few things, then."

When she was gone, I said, "Would it be better to drop everything and take her back to Tucson?"

Philo weighed that for a moment. "I don't think she'll go—not until we find Heather, anyway. This is where she was last seen."

I smiled. "And the Bay Area holds the clues to Derek's treasure."

"Yup. We're getting closer."

I wondered again at Derek's involvement in the events of the last two days. He was the strongest link between Margaret, Heather, Gwen, and the coin collection. Did he start that house fire and disappear from Tucson because he thought someone was hunting him, or because *he* was the hunter?

I said, "Does the U.S. have an extradition agreement with Costa Rica?"

Philo must have been tracking my thoughts. His mouth tightened to a grim line. "Not for death penalty cases."

26

I carried Gabrielle's overnight bag to the front hall. "Is there anything else you need, anything you want us to do?"

"I don't think so. And if I've forgotten anything, well, Bea only lives a few blocks away." Gabrielle hesitated, then said, "Should I leave a note for Heather, in case she stops by for the rest of her things?"

Gabrielle's bag slipped from my hand, landing on the floor with a thump. "The *rest* of her things?"

"She told me she was taking her laptop computer and her small suitcase, and that she'd be back for the large one."

"Philo!" I called up the stairs. He was on the phone. His long legs came down the stairs five at a time.

"What's wrong?"

"Heather left a bag behind."

"Gabrielle—" he began.

"Look wherever you like, my dears. Take anything you think will help find her. But are you looking for something specific? Perhaps I can help."

Philo raised an eyebrow in my direction. I shrugged. In for a penny . . .

He led Gabrielle to the sofa. Once she was seated he explained about the mission Derek had given us, and about the photos we'd found at Gwen's house.

"A chess set?" She seemed surprised.

"That rings a bell?"

"Of course. On her deathbed, my mother asked me to bring Claudine a chessboard. Claudine had brought the chess pieces with her when she married Kenneth Dain, but she'd had to leave the board behind in Paris. It was so heavy and bulky, you see."

"Excuse me a sec," I said, and ran out to the car. The

photos were where Philo had left them, on the floor of the back seat. I showed them to Gabrielle.

"Ah," she said, holding the plastic bag of photos close to her nose. She sighed in frustration and reached for a magnifying glass on the nearest end table. "Yes, that's the chess set—on the table Kenneth made to hold the board. I remember the set well. My mother and Claudine would play, during the war, when I was small. But I was never allowed to touch the pieces."

"I wasn't either," Philo said, smiling.

Gabrielle tilted her head, squinted into the magnifying glass, and ran a finger over the black-and-white photo. "Claudine and Kenneth decorated the library like that every Christmas." She pointed to an evergreen garland, suspended by big bows and draped over the lintel of the open window. "Did your father take this? It looks like his work."

"It is," Philo said. "Dad took it that last Christmas. His name and the date are on the back."

"I can't imagine where Gwen would have gotten these, or why she'd leave them in her safe."

"She wouldn't. Only Heather or Derek had access to our family photos."

"You think Heather put them there?"

"Yes. But she wasn't alone. They seemed to have left the photos for whoever followed her to the Bay Area. That means Derek, from whom the coins—and perhaps this chess set—were taken. I'm just his surrogate." Philo used a clean tissue from the box on the end table to lift one of the small color photos from the plastic bag, turning it over so he could read the note to Gabrielle. "Whoever put that on the back of the photo either had the chess set or knew of its existence," he said. "It might be the price they're demanding to settle a debt. It might be the secret red flag Heather waved at Derek, saying, 'I mean business about voiding the prenup.' But we won't know till we find her."

Gabrielle looked as if someone had struck her across the face. "But that quote you read, that means . . . Gwen's death is part of someone's game?"

"Not intentionally. But it's linked somehow. We think Gwen was in the right place at the wrong time. Unfortunately we can't ask the man who killed her. Arnulfo Sánchez was found murdered last night."

"Good," she said, revealing a very different Gabrielle, fierce, intense. "I'm glad I'll never have to see him, never have to forgive him." She was silent for a time. Her mind must have been leaping from one dark thought to another, because the lines on her face deepened as she said, "If Gwen went to Tucson in Heather's place, and Gwen was killed, was someone after Heather?"

"It would explain why she bolted from here when she heard about her sister."

"Ah, Derek's call . . . And neither of them told me about Gwen. They left it up to you—and the police. Oh, Philo, it all seems so random, so pointless." The tears she'd been holding back spilled over.

I grabbed the box of tissues and handed it to Philo, who'd put his arm around her. "I promise you," I said, "we'll find out who's behind it."

"Gabrielle," Philo said, "this is important. Someone wants whatever Heather took from Derek. Maybe the chess set, maybe Grandpa's coin collection. Did you ever see the collection?"

She mopped at her eyes, took a deep breath. "Often. I lived with Kenneth and Claudine for a year, you know. They introduced me to Russell, my husband. He was a realtor, just starting out. He'd found the old ranch property for them."

"Really? I didn't know that," Philo said. "Did Grandpa ever show you a gold Double Eagle, one his father had bought for his mother?"

"He said they'd had one once, but they'd had to turn it in."

"Then Derek lied to us. Again," I said.

Philo's smile was a bitter twist of the lips. "He has a fluid relationship with the truth."

"He always did," Gabrielle said. "That's why Russ and I hated it when Derek and Heather eloped."

We heard a car pull into the driveway. Gabrielle took a key off her key ring and handed it to Philo. "Just lock the back door when you're finished, *cherí*. You can leave the key under the geranium."

"If you need us, call the number I gave you," he said. "You'll get Killeen, my associate. He'll reach us. You can trust him with your life."

"It's Heather's I'm worried about. And yours." Gabrielle stood and kissed first his cheek, then mine as the doorbell rang. When I was halfway across the room, Gabrielle said, in a low voice, "If you don't mind, my dears, I'd rather not tell Bea any more than you have already. She's a lovely woman, very helpful, but the worst gossip in town."

PART IV

A Tale of Two Treasures

The chess board is the world, the pieces are the phenomena of the universe, the rules of the game are what we call the laws of Nature. The player on the other side is hidden from us. We know, . . . to our cost, that he never overlooks a mistake, or makes the smallest allowance for ignorance.

—Thomas Henry Huxley, "A Liberal Education" (1868)

27

Philo and I searched the guest bedroom first. This had apparently been Heather's childhood room. Photos stuck into the edges of the dressing table mirror showed a young Heather with a sequence of best friends— in junior high cheerleading costumes, tennis whites, and swimsuits, holding up trophies. Several slumber-party photos showed the princess bed in the corner, then draped with white eyelet and lace. The present palette was green and peach.

Though she'd left in a hurry, Heather had made the bed and put out fresh towels in the adjoining bath. While Philo made a thorough search of the room's nooks and crannies, I headed for the narrow walk-in closet. Hangers held a few out-of-date wool suits, a couple of robes, and a black velvet floor-length coat. I found her suitcase under a pile of blankets at the back and towed it out into the room. Though small, the suitcase was heavy. But unlocked. Heather couldn't have prized whatever it contained.

"Looks like she was planning to head for warmer climes," Philo said, peering over my shoulder as I sifted through bright cotton sundresses, swimsuits, and assorted cover-ups. Lots of sandals. And one rectangular nylon travel case, the size of a thick school binder. Inside were heavy plastic sleeves, twelve pockets to a sheet, like the kind I used to use for slides. The pockets were empty except for little printed slips of paper. Each one held the name of a coin—ancient Roman, Greek, Byzantine, and European; Spanish reales, English doubloons, and a host of others. But no slip of paper with the words "1933 Saint-Gaudens Gold Double Eagle."

"This is the collection Derek told us to look for," Philo

said turning the empty sheets. "Heather must have taken them with her."

"If so, then why's the case so damned heavy?"

"Excellent question, my dear Sherlock." Philo took over, poking and prodding the suitcase. No obvious secret compartments.

"The handle and frame?" I said.

Philo turned the handle, unscrewing it from the frame. It was roughly a foot long, with end-pieces that also screwed in.

"Customized," Philo said. Unscrewing one of the end pieces, he pulled out some cotton stuffing from the tube and upended it. A plastic tube of coins slid into his hand. Gold coins. Silver coins. History stamped on precious metals, each separated from the next by a circle of glassine paper. The center and bottom crosspieces of the frame were likewise filled.

"Derek's treasure," I said.

"Or part of it. An X-ray machine wouldn't pick them up because they're encased in metal."

"But why the hell would Heather go off and leave them?"

"Damned if I know. Maybe she decided to take the Double Eagle, if it exists, and leave the coins of lesser value."

"What good would the Double Eagle be to her if she can't sell it?"

"She can't sell it in *this* country. Costa Rica and Mexico might be a different story."

"We have the coins," I said. "What next? Find a courier?"

"This is the first evidence we've found that says that Derek told the truth about something. But he's not in Tucson. There's no reason to send them home. Problem is, we can't leave them here, and we can't keep them in the car."

"Why don't we take them with us to Alana's house, then find some way of getting them to Michael? If anyone knows how to transport artifacts around without raising suspicion, it's Michael." I looked at the bedside clock. "He should be calling any time now."

Gwen's office phone rang just then. Philo went next door to answer it while I slid the coins, one by one, into their protective pockets. I tried to match the coins with their paper labels, but I didn't obsess about it. When I finished, there was one empty slot. The faint impression the coin had left on the plastic was about the size of a fifty-cent piece. How long ago it had been removed, I couldn't tell, but it hadn't been in the 1930s. The coin case had a Velcro closure. Velcro was invented in the fifties.

"All here but one," I told Philo when he came back.

He flipped through the sheets. "No gold coins of recent vintage. Grandpa Dain died before owning gold coins became legal again."

"Who was on the phone?"

"Gabrielle. She asked if we'd find Gwen's car at the airport and bring it home. Every day it's there, it's costing her money, and she can't drive it herself."

"It's a big airport."

"Gabrielle said that Gwen always parked in the same section—Garage B, near the Southwest concourse. The license number's on the fridge, and she had a spare key in her desk drawer." He held up a car key with a remote-entry bud. "We'll just keep squeezing this till we find the car."

I had a brilliant idea. "I don't suppose you asked—"

"Yes, we can borrow the car." He grinned. "No one will be looking for us in Gwen's Honda."

"We just have to make sure no one follows us from the airport to Alana's."

"Trust me. No one will follow us." Philo looked at his watch. "We have time to pick up the Honda and still arrive in Moss Beach on schedule."

"As long as rush-hour traffic doesn't slow us down."

"It'll work. We'll make it work."

Finding the coins had energized us both. We had part of the treasure, use of a new vehicle, and a sense of our next step—getting Alana's and Michael's help with the chess set. It was a start.

My cell phone rang. The bedside clock with the over-sized numerals showed 3:00 exactly.

"Francisca, I have missed you." Michael Zorya's voice

was like butter melting on a hot croissant. "Is this business, or pleasure?"

"It's always a pleasure, Michael."

Philo snorted, and had to rethread the crosspiece he was attaching to Heather's luggage. The men knew and liked each other—mutual respect tinted with a healthy dose of competition. The snort was for me.

"Was that Philo I heard in the background making animal sounds?"

"Yes. We're in the Bay Area on business. We could use some advice and, er, expertise, if you can spare the time."

"I finished my last class today. My final concert isn't till Wednesday night. I'm yours till the dress rehearsal Tuesday afternoon. I do hope it's something difficult and dangerous. I need a change of pace. I'm going stale from all these hours indoors."

"Murder, missing persons, and treasure. I can't say more on the phone."

"Enough. You had me at 'treasure.'"

Michael had a car and welcomed a drive down the coast, so I invited him to dinner at Alana's. I'd already cleared it with Alana, on the off chance he'd be able to join us. He asked if there was anything I needed him to bring. "A good bottle of wine," I said.

"I'll bring two. See you at six." He rang off.

I smiled as I shut down my cell and removed the battery. We had a team of experts assembling down the coast in a few hours, and a second team working in Tucson. I felt the adrenaline pumping.

"Quick, Watson," I said to Philo, who was parking the suitcase at the back of the closet. "The game's afoot."

28

Alana Calloway's bungalow stood on a terrace above a marine reserve. Riprap, broken boulders brought in from elsewhere and piled at the base of the cliff, formed a bulwark against wave erosion. So far, the plan was working, though I thought the cliff might have given up some of the property since my last visit.

I had stayed here many times with Alana during our years as roommates at Stanford, weekends stolen from science, volleyball practice, and the narrow confines of dorm life. The Calloway family was richer than Croesus, their wealth going back to the gold rush era—mining and railroads and supplies for the miners. Alana's mother had tried to pressure her only child into joining a sorority, but Alana wasn't a joiner by nature, except for honor societies, chess club, and a group that planned regular junkets to art museums. She didn't anticipate needing to network for employment. Her future, once her undergraduate work was complete, centered around marriage to the young man she'd dated since seventh grade.

Everything began according to plan. She married Chet right after graduation, as expected. Six months later, she discovered her husband preferred men.

Alana had somehow put together a career that satisfied her. She didn't need the money. Her trust fund had kicked in when she turned twenty-five. By then she'd been single again for four years, her marriage annulled. She had come back to the States two years ago. Her mother told me she would prefer to have Alana living on their Hillsborough estate, but Alana had opted for their seaside house.

She had made changes to the place. Added a second floor and two rock towers where the rear corners used to be. Bougainvillea and clematis climbed a white-painted perimeter wall, while a twisted cypress leaned landward like a large bonsai tree. Digger pines dropped cones and needles onto the newly paved courtyard. The bungalow had become a tidy little castle.

I'd called from SFO to tell Alana we'd be bringing an extra car. The wrought-iron gate stood open. Moving lightly as a dancer, she was out the front door and down the steps before I'd even shut off the engine of Gwen's Honda.

Alana hugged me tightly. We hadn't seen each other since her wedding. Interim correspondence had been hit-and-miss. But it was reassuring to see she hadn't changed. She was of medium height, slender as a reed, and beautiful in a fragile, red-haired, ivory-skinned, waiflike way. Body and build of a model. She was dressed in black cotton pants and brightly colored Guatemalan jacket. No shoes. The hall lights turned her cascade of curls the color of flames.

"I'm *so* glad to see you, Frankie," she said. "And this must be Philo. Love the name." She held out her hands to Philo. A hug would come later, if she approved. "Come in, come in."

She led us through a wide hall lined with art—small sculptures in niches; oils, etchings, and watercolors on off-white walls. Original art works. Nothing abstract. Eclectic. She wasn't obsessed with one artist or school, but preferred Impressionist and earlier periods. I saw Seurat and Monet, and landscapes and seascapes by Turner and Constable. Mostly small paintings in well-spaced groups, pleasingly arranged and illuminated by inset lights in the high arched ceiling.

"You're looking for a theme," she said, smiling at us from the end of the hall.

I thought for a moment. Philo was mum.

"Water," I said. "Each one offers a glimpse of an ocean, lake, or stream."

"Appropriate for a beach house, don't you think?"

"But did you know, when you began collecting, that you'd be living here?" said Philo.

"I think so . . . subconsciously, anyway. I was always happiest in this place. Did Frankie tell you we used to escape here to study for midterms and finals?"

"She hasn't had a chance to tell me anything much. We've been . . . preoccupied."

"And you have to tell me all about that. But first let me show you your room."

Alana took the long circuit, starting with the eat-in kitchen, which had a cauldron of clam chowder simmering on the stove and well-used cookware dangling from hooks over a large butcher-block island. She moved quickly through the living room, with its view of the patio garden and ocean, and stopped at an imposing door to the south tower. "A fireproof walk-in safe," she said. "I put the art-work in here when I travel. Above this is my closet."

"You always wanted a round closet," I said.

"Because my father made me a dollhouse when I was five. It had tiny closets in the turrets—good for storing secret treasures."

"What's in the other tower?" Philo said.

"Something much more prosaic—baths, above and below." She led us down the hall to the round bathroom. Sky-blue tiles from Mexico. Walls of redwood. The window faced the sea. "And the pièce de résistance," she said, throwing open the door on the right. An ornately carved four-poster bed, massive enough to have held Henry VIII and all of his wives, dominated the room. The four posts nearly touched the high ceiling. They supported a damask canopy held back with gold cord. "I found this monster in Cambridge," she said. "Shipped it home. Mother hated it, so it stayed in storage until the remodeling was finished."

"It deserves a museum room all its own," I said.

Philo smiled. "Imagine the stories it could tell."

"The conceptions, births, and deaths of a long line of British nobility," said Alana. "A few churchmen among them. It goes back to the Normans."

"Being of Norman descent myself, I shall treat it with due respect," Philo said.

The second bedroom held simple, Mission-style furniture, not nearly as old as the bed in the adjoining room. Alana's childhood furniture. It fit better here, somehow, than on the grand estate on the other side of the Coast Range.

"I thought your friend Michael could have this room." Alana smiled. "Philo looks too long for the queen-size bed. But I leave the room choice in your hands. Now, you have to see what I've done upstairs."

She led us up a wide staircase at the end of the hall. "We had to rig up a pulley system to hoist the larger pieces over the deck, but it was worth it, don't you think?"

The curtains were pulled back from the windows, showing an expanse of ocean and headland and beach. It was like being in the Swiss Family Robinson treehouse, untouchable by dangers from below. The room covered the entire top of the house, except for the tower rooms. A balcony jutted out over part of the backyard, providing cover for the patio and a private area for sunning, reading, or painting.

An easel stood just inside the sliding glass door. On it was a watercolor showing the northern part of the nature reserve below. The Seal Cove fault ran just offshore. Her detail was such that I could pick out the dark sedimentary rocks of the Purisima Formation, folded into a plunging syncline on the landward side, and the pale ochre rocks of the cliff wall. She'd captured the scene at low tide, when the arching black rock ribs of the syncline, planed off by the ceaseless to-and-fro action of the waves, stood out in sharpest relief. I'd visited the rich tide pools there, first as her roommate, then as a geology and oceanography student. The memories swirled up.

"I think that if this room were here back when we were in school, I might have refused to budge the first time you brought me to visit. It's heaven."

"I knew you'd like it. The painting's almost finished. I'll send it to you."

I dragged my eyes from the sunset view to take in the rest of the room. The east wall was shaped like the top half of a trapezoid, a long flat part in the middle, against which the bed stood, and two shorter, curved tower wings. A triangular fireplace of local stone fit neatly where tower and wall met. Above the mantelpiece was the only wall decoration in the room, aside from a Flemish tapestry hanging behind the bed. The large photo was of flamenco guitarist Alessandro. He'd just finished a concert, and was about to take a bow. His left arm, outflung to the side, held his guitar. The other, folded across his waist, held a white rose.

"I took that in Spain," she said, "the third or fourth time I heard him play."

I looked at Philo. He grinned back. Tonight should be fun. I said, "I've heard he's playing in San Francisco next week."

Alana's eyes seemed to lose focus for a moment before returning to the room. "I've had tickets for ages. I go to his concerts all over the world." She smiled like a child with a new toy. "What good is having all that family money if I can't use it?"

"Have you ever met him?"

"Oh, no. I'm not very good with people—you know that, Frankie. What would I say? That I love his music? He must hear that all the time. I'd have nothing to talk to him about. I can't play a note. Never could."

Maybe I'd better give her a bit of warning. "Alana—" The doorbell cut me off. I started for the stairs, saying, "That'll be Michael. Let me—"

"Don't be silly." Alana scooted around me, danced down the stairs, and opened the door on the second chime. I was right behind her.

Michael Zorya stared from a startled and silent Alana to me, standing behind her left shoulder, and back. "Well, well," he said softly, "if it isn't the lady of the rose."

Alana's welcoming smile dissolved as her face turned from white to brick red. She ran down the steps and disappeared around the corner of the house. Michael stared after her.

"I didn't know," I said. "I couldn't warn her." That made no sense. "She's terminally shy," I started to say, then turned to Philo. "You tell him, then bring him to the beach. But for God's sake, take down that photo first. And close the courtyard gate. There's a king's ransom in art here."

"Got it." Philo gave me a gentle push in the direction of the courtyard. "Go."

I kissed Michael's cheek on the way past. He hadn't uttered a word after that first sentence. Smart man.

Alana had followed the house wall around to the cliff side, where a smaller iron gate gave onto a flight of steps. I stopped at the top, searching the curving strip of sand and rock for Alana's slim form. Finally saw her halfway down the beach, huddled on a riprap boulder, facing out to sea. Her hair streamed and fluttered in the wind like a bright, fluffy scarf. I ran down the steps and across the sand, slowing as I approached. I didn't want to startle her again. Her every muscle seemed tensed for flight. I sat next to her on the boulder, using my hip to shove her over so my butt had a bit of purchase.

"I swear on your red hair, Alana, I didn't know till you showed us that photograph. I was starting to tell you when the doorbell rang."

"This wasn't some stupid joke, then?"

"When did I ever? Okay, there was the time that I didn't bother to warn you that my brothers were showing up at our dorm room—"

"En masse! And I was still in bed."

"I remember. I honestly didn't think it was a big deal—"

"But you grew up with four brothers and enough male cousins to staff a football team. I was an only child."

"I thought you handled it with great aplomb."

"I escaped into the shower and stayed there an hour."

"You grew to like them soon enough."

"Yes. They were the brothers I would have wanted . . ."

She was calmer. I gave her a moment, then made the leap. "I feel the same about Michael. Alessandro is his stage name. His real name, which he keeps private, is Michael Zorya. He lives next door to my family." When she gave me a skeptical glance, I said, "No, not when you visited Tucson. They moved in two years ago. His sister was engaged to my brother Jamie before she . . . died."

She put her hand on my arm. "Oh, Frankie, I'm so sorry."

"Jamie's doing fine. He's marrying a lovely woman who's like a sister to me. But Michael took it pretty hard."

"I meant it before, you know, when I said I couldn't talk to him. I freeze up at the very thought."

"Michael Zorya deals in art. I don't ask too many questions about that side of his business, but I know he worked for Sotheby's Paris when he finished school. He owns a store in Tucson, which his aunt manages. He's got a photographic memory and knows as much as you do about the art world. Perhaps more. And, damn it, Alana, I need both of your expertise in order to figure out what Philo and I are dealing with."

"Still, you must have heard his music—"

"Many times. The guitar is his art, Alana. Chess is yours. You're both masters. I doubt he can hold a candle to you on the chessboard."

I looked at the two men walking slowly up the beach, tall Philo with his short hair and subtle limp, Michael wearing his trademark black pants and white shirt, his chin-length hair tousled by the breeze. Alana was updating the picture she had of him with the new data I'd just given her. "Michael," she said, trying the name out to see how it felt, sounded. She gave a little nod and stood up. "Michael I can deal with. Will you introduce me? I'd like to start over."

We met them at the strand line. "Alana Calloway, I'd like you to meet my friend and neighbor, Michael Zorya. Michael, this is Alana."

The Spanish Gypsy took her outstretched hand, bowed, and kissed the back. As he straightened, she said, "Forgive my lapse. I'm not usually prone to . . . drama."

"I understand. I was not who you expected to find on your doorstep. I know nothing of you except that you are Francisca's friend. I look forward to learning more."

The setting sun dropped below the clouds and struck her hair. His left hand lifted, catching a strand that had blown across her face. She didn't pull away. He rolled the strand between his fingers. They both seemed to have forgotten they weren't alone. I slid my arm around Philo's waist and leaned into the curve of his body, wondering what would happen next.

"Do you play chess, Michael?" she said.

He smiled, tucked the strand behind her ear, and said,

"I'm better on the guitar, but I didn't bring one."

"Then it'll have to be chess. But I warn you, I always win."

His smile widened. "I promise to lose gracefully." And taking her by the hand, he started up the beach toward the stairs.

"Did I hear what I think I heard?" Philo said.

"Yup. The white queen just captured the black knight."

29

"I'm starved," Alana said. "Food first, business with dessert."

We put the chowder, crab legs, and sourdough bread in the middle of the round table, a hand-carved slab of redwood. The tree rings seemed to echo the rock arcs in the bay. Alana uncorked the wine and sat across from me, but she and Michael were focused on each other.

I reached for Philo's hand under the table. Michael took his eyes away from Alana's face and said, "How's the charter business going, Philo?"

"Making you money, despite rising fuel prices. Killeen's savvy that way."

The penny dropped. I said, "*You're* Philo and Killeen's silent partner, the money man behind their air cargo company?"

"I had to find some legitimate vehicle to absorb my earnings. Alessandro's been quite lucrative the past few years." When Michael said the name, Alana didn't even flinch. "And I still track down the occasional art object for those who have neither the time nor the knowledge to do it themselves." Michael laughed. "The rich will always be with us."

Alana cracked a crab leg and sucked out the meat. "Do you have a problem with wealth, Michael?"

"I have more money than I will ever need."

I could see Alana's shoulders relax. Her wealth had been an issue ever since she and her husband broke up.

"It doesn't hurt either business to have a private mode of transport," I said, wrestling Philo for the last crab leg. I won.

Philo smiled and said to Michael, "Killeen's been sending you the reports?"

"All in order, according to my accountant. But I do have a few suggestions. How about we set up a meeting for Friday? I'll be back in Tucson by then," he looked at Alana, "unless something delays me."

"You could always bring a date to Jamie's wedding," I said.

Michael smiled. "I just might do that."

Rain began to patter against the windows as we cleared the table. Michael and I did the dishes while Alana and Philo found dry wood for a fire. Though it was May, the northern coast was chilly at night, especially during a storm.

Michael emptied a bowl of crab remains into the trashcan. His face was striking, rather than handsome—bronze skin, wavy black hair turning silver at the sides, a beak of a nose. He met my gaze with a level one of his own. Where Alana's eyes were the pure blue-violet of tanzanite, his were the dark gray-blue of hawk's-eye, with bands of light that shifted as he moved. Watchful eyes, revealing nothing he didn't want revealed. He said, "You really did not plan this?"

"How could I? Alana and I haven't seen each other in years."

"I rather think she is a witch."

"Then she'll get on well with your aunt." Tía Miranda was a *curandera,* a healing woman—though her actions weren't always benign.

Michael laughed, the most carefree sound I'd ever heard from him. "Alana may have to borrow the knife Tía gave you."

"Alana wouldn't know what to do with it. Her intellect has always been her blade. Between her mind and her money, she's put off almost every man she's ever met."

"Ah, but she and I have a bridge. Music."

I put the last plate in the dishwasher, straightened, and put my hands on his shoulders. "Don't trifle with her, Michael. I'm not sure she could stand it."

"It is far more likely to be the other way around. Your Alana may be much stronger than you think."

Alana came in just then. "Am I interrupting?"

"Never," Michael said.

"Good. Then help me with dessert."

We took our coffee and vanilla ice cream, both dosed with Frangelico, into the living room. The fire was going strongly in the glass-fronted fireplace. It was stormy outside, but who cared? We were snug for the night.

I let Philo tell the story of our adventure. It had begun, after all, with his uncle and wicked stepmother, and with a murder at his family's doorstep. While he filled Alana and Michael in on the details, I brought in our backpacks and laid our bits and pieces of evidence on the coffee table. I didn't open the case containing the coins. I left it there, in the center, to tantalize Michael. He sent me a glance. His lips twitched. He was willing to play along.

When Philo told them about being followed from Gwen's house this morning, I saw the concern on Alana's face. "We weren't followed to Gabrielle Helmsley's," I said, "and we haven't been followed here. But we'd like to keep it that way by not using our cells. Which reminds me—I need to call Tucson. May I use your landline?"

She directed me to the guest bedroom. As I left, Philo was launching into the Gabrielle saga and Derek and Heather's disappearances. I called Teresa, my almost-sister-in-law, to make sure the wedding plans were going smoothly. She had things under control. I then checked in with Killeen, to update him on the case. No word on Derek, he said. Margaret was asleep in the bomb shelter, after eating a light dinner and finishing a bottle of Grey Goose. Cinna and Griffin were having a terrible time with her. She'd decided she was claustrophobic. How much longer, Killeen asked, did I think this was going to take?

I told him about finding the coin collection—minus the Double Eagle—and that we had Michael and Alana helping with the "treasure" end of things. I wasn't sure how long it would take to find Heather, but at the moment, there was only one more place in the Bay Area where she was likely to be staying—the Dain property in Woodside. We were headed down there sometime tomorrow, once we knew more about the chess set. I said, "Did you get any hits on the photos Philo sent you?"

"The license plate of the guy who followed you is registered to a Lenny Wilson. His passport shows frequent trips to Mexico, but he's not in the system. I'm still waiting on info on the chess set, but the gas company got back to me about the safe house. Rust had eaten through the line—it wasn't tampered with."

"That's a relief," I said. "How's Sylvie doing? Not in labor yet, I hope."

"Nope. Still on schedule for next month."

"Well, give her my love."

"Of course. Frankie?"

"Hmmm?"

"Whoever you're chasing wants something badly enough to kill for it. Remember that."

"I'll ask Alana to keep the coins in her safe. It's built to withstand a magnitude 8 quake, she says."

"I can't wait to meet your Alana."

"I think she's Michael's Alana, as of tonight—and vice versa."

"Well, well. Didn't think I'd live to see the day."

"Nor did we."

I was smiling when I rejoined the others. Pheromones were thick in the air. Michael and Alana were now sitting hip to hip on the sofa in front of the fire. Michael was saying that he doubted Derek's story about the Double Eagle.

"Yes, a few escaped the recall," he said. "Besides the Farouk coin, the Smithsonian has a couple. And Treasury has stashed nine others in Fort Knox, trying to figure out what to do with them. So, the odds are slim that Derek had one."

I opened the coin case and flipped the plastic pages till I found the empty pocket. Michael picked up the case and took it close to a light. Alana got up and rustled in the drawer of a little inlaid table, coming up with a magnifying glass.

"The impression in the plastic is the right size for a Saint-Gaudens Double Eagle," Michael said. "But whether it is the 1933—" he shrugged. "Who can tell?" After flipping casually through the rest of the pages, he closed the coin case and set it back on the table. "The other coins are real enough. I could sell them for you for perhaps two hundred thousand."

"But Derek knows that I wouldn't have gone to this effort for that small an amount," Philo said.

Michael nodded. "Makes you wonder what his real objective is."

"The chess set?" I said.

"They can run to the thousands of dollars these days, but nothing like the money Derek described," said Alana. "Unless the chess set has a history that makes it unique." She picked up the plastic bag with the photos. "This one looks French, or maybe Belgian. I'd say nineteenth century."

Michael pulled his computer from a case at his feet. "You have wireless?"

Alana nodded. "It's password protected." She typed in a long sequence of letters and numbers, and Michael was up and surfing. He said, "The chess pieces are probably stamped with the artist's signature on the bottom."

"That would help," she said, "but I think the clue to the story is in the face of the king. For some reason his visage was rendered in a much older style. It doesn't really match the style and simplicity of the rest of the pieces."

"What about the Latin inscription?" I said. "Philo's partner hasn't gotten a hit on the partial. Does it ring a bell with you?"

"Perhaps it was tied to the piece these were copied from. Because I'm sure they're copies." Alana picked up the magnifying glass and held the photos close, just as Gabrielle had done. Alana said to Michael, "I swear I've seen the original somewhere before. But it wasn't on a chess piece. I seem to see it as a drawing—part of a larger work."

"The headpiece, armor, spear, and cloak are Roman," Michael said, "but statues from that period show soldiers with short hair. And that face does not look Roman—though it could be one of the Holy Roman Emperors. I am a little rusty on those."

"Yes." Alana was on her feet, pacing in front of the fire. Philo and I moved aside to give her room to think. She stopped abruptly, in front of me. "The early Frankish kings. They worked with the Romans, then laid claim to northern Gaul as the Roman Empire disintegrated. To the

Franks, long hair signified virility and royalty. But this isn't a conventional depiction of Clovis or Pepin or Charlemagne. I'd have recognized them."

"Childerici Regis," Michael intoned.

We all looked at him as if he'd gone round the bend. Then I got it. "The Latin inscription on the base."

"It was also on a gold signet ring engraved with the likeness of Childeric the First," he said, "the same figure we see on the chess king." Michael turned his computer around so we could view the Web site. "The ring—or a copy of it—is in the Paris Mint."

"That's it!" Alana said, comparing the partial inscription shown in the photos to the digital image on the screen. "Clovis's father. He died in 481, or thereabouts. The only reason we know what Childeric looks like is that they found his grave goods by accident in, in . . ."

"1653," Michael prompted.

"No fair. You're reading from a Web site."

"So why does some fifth-century footnote wind up on a nineteenth-century chess set?" I said.

"Haven't a clue," Alana said. "But we're a step closer to knowing than we were ten minutes ago."

Philo got a funny look on his face. "Where was this burial site?"

"In a little Belgian town called Tournai," Michael said.

Philo and I exchanged glances. Tournai, where Philo's grandmother was born. And the chess set was her dowry. But the set couldn't be worth more than a few thousand.

"What?" Michael said.

"Another piece of the puzzle," Philo said. While he related what Gabrielle had told us about the chess set, and her part in getting the board to America, I studied the chess pieces in the photos. One king looked like gold. The other was silver-toned. But was it silver, or a gold-silver alloy such as electrum? Platinum hadn't been discovered until the late nineteenth century. Commercial white gold wasn't produced until the twentieth century, though "white gold" had been described by Pliny, and the Egyptians had used electrum. Silver plate over gold was a possibility, but why go to all that trouble? It was cheaper just to use silver. I picked up the magnifying glass and looked closely at the silver-toned king. I thought I saw an area of tarnish. Gold and platinum didn't tarnish. Silver did.

I turned the magnifying glass on the chessboard. The squares looked like veined marble, black and white. Nothing out of the ordinary. I'd love to get a closer look. But I'd have to find it first.

Alana stood up and gave Philo and me each a hug, saying, "I'll send out some e-mails about the chess set, see if I get a nibble. I should have answers by morning. These guys live on their computers in the wee hours."

"Can you do it anonymously?" Philo said. "We don't want to put you in danger."

"Don't worry, I'll be discreet."

I handed her the coin case. "Will you keep this in your safe until Michael or Philo can take it south to Tucson? With Derek missing, there's no point rushing them home."

"My safe is your safe," Alana said, and carried the case to the tower door.

Michael slid his arm around me. "You would trust me with them?"

"You saved my life once."

"Twice."

"Now you're making things up."

He watched Alana close the safe door, turn, and disappear down the hall. No backward glance, no coy gestures. She knew he'd follow. "Once, twice, what does it matter? Tonight we are even." He stood and stretched. "I think I will retire also."

Philo grinned. "Don't you have a chess game scheduled?"

"I do. And I never make a lady wait."

Michael kissed my cheeks and walked leisurely toward the stairs at the end of the hall. I said to Philo, "Did you lay a fire upstairs?"

"Alana did. Should be going nicely by now."

"Ready to turn in?"

"Not yet."

"That bed a bit daunting?"

"I think whoever commissioned those posts had just come from a battle that tested his manhood."

"Luckily, you have no such problems." It was my turn

to stretch. "Well, while you sit and ponder, I'll shower. Then I can dry my hair by the fire."

Ten minutes later I padded back wearing a white toweling robe Alana had left for me on the bathroom door. Philo took the brush from my hand and pointed to two large cushions in front of the fire. I turned my back and sat. My hair had grown a foot since I'd cut it in Nevada nearly two years ago. I could now weave a respectable braid. But the long, thick, black mass took forever to dry.

Philo was silent. Hairbrushing didn't require that much concentration. I said, "You know, there's nothing you can't tell me, Philo." The brush stilled. I turned around to face him. "Share. Don't share. I'll love you either way."

"I'll hold you to that." He put down the brush and took my face in his hands, then drew a deep breath. "I killed a boy in Afghanistan."

Sweet Jesus. "What had he done?"

"Nothing. He was my friend. He loved books, so I taught him to read English. He just wanted peace and a chance to study. But they turned him into a walking bomb."

Tears blurred my vision and spilled over. Philo wiped them away with his thumbs, then dropped his hands and looked into the fire.

"He warned me," Philo said. "He didn't have to, but he did, knowing I'd have to stop him before he reached my camp. And he left me a map to where I could find his killer—the man who'd killed my brother." I gripped his hands, searching for words of comfort. When I found none, Philo added, "Now the boy's ghost comes to me in dreams."

I touched my head to his. Philo said, "You're not running."

"No."

He leaned back to look at my face, my eyes. He wanted more.

I kissed him, then said, "We can't change the past, Philo. All we can do is learn from our mistakes—and make amends, if possible."

"How do you make amends to a mother who's lost her only son?"

"When that path is closed, you can only pay it forward. I'll help. We can do it together."

"Together," he repeated softly. "A perfect segue." He put his hand in his breast pocket and took something out. A gold ring with an oval wine-red garnet, surrounded by smaller stones. "I found this today, among the letters in the box Margaret gave me. Gabrielle told me that it once belonged to Grandma Claudine. My father gave it to my mother after Claudine died." He ran a fingertip over the red stones. "I remember Mom wearing it on special occasions."

I saw a shadow cross his face. Some losses hurt forever. "Philo, are you asking me to marry you?"

He smiled ruefully. "I was heading in that direction."

"I married you before you went off to Afghanistan, and again when you came home."

"You might have mentioned it to me—"

"I didn't want to scare you off."

"—and I'm not sure it would hold up in court."

"You should have thought of that before you introduced me to Gabrielle as your fiancée."

He turned the ring until it caught the firelight. "Oddly enough, that was just before I found this." He slipped the ring on my finger. "A perfect fit," he said, surprised.

The ring was warm on my finger. I'd never been partial to diamonds, preferring colored stones. This one suited me. Garnets and gold.

"Ready to face that bed?" I said.

30

**Thursday, May 18
San Jose, California**
10:15 p.m.

The man who killed easily and swiftly unlocked
the door to a second-floor apartment. Not his. He owned
nothing except the clothes on his back, enough spares to
half fill an overnight bag, a shaving kit, a laptop computer,
and a traveler's chess set. Anything he needed for a job he
bought and then discarded, like the no-contract cell phone
in his pocket. Neither property nor pets tied him down—
only his bond with the woman in the bedroom. Soon,
nothing on earth would own him.

"Hey, Ma, I'm home," he called softly. If she were
sleeping, he wouldn't disturb her. If she were awake, the
call would reassure her.

He heard a murmur of soft voices as he crossed the
living room carpet to the bedroom door. Barbara, the
woman from next door who checked in on his mother
when he worked late, had her feet up on a small divan in
the corner. The floor lamp beside her shed a glow on the
Bible open in her lap. Barbara was a woman of faith and
compassion. And hope. Hope that once this man's mother
had passed, he'd turn to Barbara for consolation. In the
meantime, she read Psalms to his mother, who loved the
music of the words, if not the content.

His mother's face had wasted away until there
remained only the thinnest layer of flesh and sinew molded
over her bones. Her hair was gone. She'd been so lovely
once. Now, all that separated her from whatever happened
next was her refusal to depart. But he could see that

tonight she was already halfway to that other plane. It wouldn't be long.

"You're home late, Rico," she said. It was little more than a whisper.

Rico was not his name. It was the name he and she had chosen long ago, when they'd run away from his father. Rico was Spanish for *rich*. They'd hoped saying it often and aloud would bring good fortune to their little family.

"Meeting took longer than expected." He sat on the edge of the bed and gently took her hand, the one his father had purposely slammed in the car door. It had never healed quite right.

His mother didn't ask questions. She no longer cared for details, even the little fictions he made up to explain the money that paid for this apartment, for the chemotherapy that hadn't worked, for the experimental treatments that hadn't worked for his sister last year, either.

"Your mother didn't eat today," Barbara said. "But I got her to drink some water and a little ginger ale."

Rico looked into Barbara's kind brown eyes. "She's made a decision, then."

"I guess. I asked if she wanted to go to the hospital, but she said no, she'd wait for you. I helped her shower. She wanted to look her best for . . ." She gave a little shrug. There were tears in her eyes as she looked at the figure on the bed.

"Thank you, Barbara." He handed her an envelope with more than enough cash to cover the hours she'd spent with his mother.

"That's too much," she said, and tried to give it back. "I was just—that's what neighbors do."

"No, keep it, please. I don't know what we'd have done without you these past few weeks. If you don't want it, you can donate it to your fellowship." The money was his way of paying his debts and tidying up loose ends—of allowing a clean break from this time, this place, this identity.

"I might do that," she said. "You'll call if you need anything, even just to talk? This will be a hard transition for you."

"Yes," he said, meaning, *Yes, it will be hard for me,* not

Yes, I'll call. But she seemed satisfied, because she closed her Bible and stood up on short, sturdy, Levi-clad legs. "Would you like me to stay and pray with you now?"

"No, thank you. I think we need a few moments alone before I call the ambulance." He escorted her to the door.

"Oh, I left some dinner in the refrigerator, in case you're hungry," she said as she stepped out. "I'll pick up the dish tomorrow."

"That'll be great."

His mother's eyes were closed, her breathing even and regular. They'd agreed to wait as long as possible before calling an ambulance. That way, she would die in a hospital, making everything easier. He would have her cremated, and would spread her ashes in a place they'd discovered when he was a child, a forest glade in the eastern Sierras. He, his mother, and his sister, Esperanza, had camped there for a month when they'd first run away. The owners of the private campground had hired his mother to help clean the restrooms and cabins. They'd paid cash, and been glad to do it. It was the happiest time of his life.

Rico and his mother had spread Esperanza's ashes there last summer. Soon the two women would be together again.

His mother's eyes opened. "Barbara's gone?"

He smiled. "Finally."

She smiled back. "Goodness is wearing, isn't it?"

"Not yours. Never yours."

"We have so little time. There are things I need to say." When he nodded, her words came out in a rush. "I wish our lives had been different. I wish I could have done more for you."

"It wasn't your fault that my father was who he was. At least you got Esperanza and me away from him."

"But you were smart, Rico. It wasn't right that you had to leave school so young. It wasn't right that your only choice was to go and fight on the other side of the world."

"But I returned safely, didn't I?"

"Safe . . . yes," she said. "When you came to see us, your sister and me, before you went to Iraq—that was the first time we'd felt safe in years. I never thanked you for that. I didn't know how."

He remembered that day, the day his other life began. He'd found his father in Las Vegas, shit-faced drunk at nine in the morning. They'd sat on his patio, drinking margaritas. The sun beat down on a pool the color of aquamarine, his mother's birthstone. Rico suggested a swim to cool off. No, his father said, he'd never learned to swim. The pool was just for parties. Of course Rico was free to use it . . .

Rico had tripped him into the deep end of his fancy pool and held him under. Then Rico had walked away and taken the first plane home to San Jose.

"It was a better death than he deserved," Rico said. But his mother had drifted off again.

The army had strengthened Rico's self-defense skills. They'd taught him the art of killing easily and quickly. He learned that he didn't mind killing, that the brotherhood mystique was a bunch of crap, that he didn't care one way or the other about anyone outside his family.

Life was okay for a while after he mustered out. He looked for a job. But there was nothing that paid very well. He enrolled at a community college. And then his mother and sister became ill. Breast cancer. Ovarian cancer. No health care. They both worked part-time, earning too much to be covered by health care for the poor, not enough to pay for individual health care. He quit school, took jobs teaching martial arts at several dojos. The bills mounted. He got certified as a personal trainer and took on clients at a couple of fitness centers. Helped one silent and frightened woman, bruises hidden under makeup, work off her anger in the weight room. Her fear gave him the idea. He waited a couple of days and then called her anonymously. Said he'd heard she was having problems. Offered to help her, for a onetime fee. He arranged an accident on the road to Santa Cruz . . .

He was choosy about his clients. Found them all the same way—through conversations overheard at the gym or the Race for the Cure or while teaching martial arts self-defense classes to women who'd been raped. He knew the signs. He kept it anonymous, always via the grapevine. He initiated. They responded, yea or nay. Always a choice . . . A pedophile in Sacramento . . . A rapist in Sunnyvale.

Some people were willing to pay for "justice," or maybe just to sleep soundly at night.

He'd only asked one question of his clients: What had the target done? It had to be an act so contrary to his moral code that removing the perpetrator cleansed society and kept him from hurting others down the road. And Rico made sure each client knew what would happen if they lied to him. They never did. He checked the facts he was given.

For cover, Rico kept his day jobs. He heard Theo Aristides was looking for a personal trainer, someone to work with him at home. Strictly cash. Rico was good at motivating. He got results. And knew when to be silent. He was hired three days a week at Aristides' new clubhouse not far from Monterey Bay. It was the only building in the development—ten thousand square feet, with an indoor swimming pool, fitness room, and sauna. The clubhouse complex was half of the big draw for prospective property owners. The other half was a planned golf course. Now, the pool was empty, but the Jacuzzi worked. And Rico discovered that Aristides had converted the clubhouse office to sleeping quarters. So much for selling the California dream.

Their workout sessions were frequently interrupted by phone calls. Rico overheard the mounting anger as Theo's bottom line shifted from black to red, listened as he was threatened by a money man in Reno. Rico watched Theo move the pieces on his chessboard as he argued, watched his anger turn to fear. When he got off the phone Theo attacked the punching bag until his hands were bloody.

For the first and only time, Rico changed his method of doing business. He had friends in Nevada, he said to Aristides, friends who did jobs for people. Friends who'd been in the military and were having trouble settling in to civilian life. Did Theo want one of them to call him?

Theo did. Rico himself called thirty minutes after leaving, adopting the Mexican accent he'd heard all around him in the barrio as he was growing up, the accent and way of speaking English that his mother never let him use. She wanted him to be a man with no background, no ethnicity, able to move easily into whatever field suited him. *Yes,* Rico had said to Aristides, *he could help him with the Reno problem. He was in Las Vegas at the moment, finishing a job. Could it wait till the weekend?* It could.

Rico drove to Reno that Friday night. The target was dead by sunrise. It was when he called in to report the success that the chess games began. Rico triggered it by using a chess term, something he never did in Theo's presence. The games with an unknown opponent—at least, unknown to Aristides—were something they both enjoyed.

Rico hired someone to check into his employer's background. A discreet search, done anonymously. The report held no surprises, but revealed a lot. Birth name, Theron Aristides. Nickname Theo. Mother, no father. Age forty-seven . . . At age six, Theo immigrated from Greece to Chicago with his mother. Lived with mother's unmarried uncle, Plato Aristides, a builder, until the mother's marriage. The new husband, Robert Herrod, was later arrested for spousal abuse and assault and battery on a child. Charges dropped, but Theo moved back with his uncle, who taught him the construction business. Uncle Plato died of cancer, and Theo inherited his company and home. Sold them and used the proceeds to buy a parcel of land near old Fort Ord, California. Had trouble with the permitting process. Environmental groups challenged the development. Theo looked around for a partner who could both grease the skids and help with the backing. Met Derek and Heather Dain at a conference in Las Vegas. Formed a partnership. When the housing bubble burst, Derek Dain pulled out.

The background check ended there, but Rico knew what happened next. Aristides found a substitute backer in Reno. The Reno connection called in the debt. Aristides hired Rico to take him out.

The sporadic jobs continued. They were lucrative. None were rush jobs—till Arnulfo Sánchez screwed up in Tucson. Rico had had to call in sick to work in order to make it down there in time. Rico hadn't liked being rushed . . .

He wondered now if he'd made the right decision to help Aristides in the first place. Theo and the Reno target weren't much different. If Rico's sister hadn't died that month, if his mother hadn't needed his help with the medical bills, if . . . But those were just excuses. Rico could have found another way if he'd tried hard enough. And then maybe Aristides would have been stopped earlier, and the Tucson woman would still be alive . . .

Someone yelled in the parking area below the bedroom window, waking his mother. "You have enough to pay the final bills?" she whispered.

"And enough for a fresh start. Don't worry." He picked up her water glass and guided the straw to her lips.

"Then promise me that you'll stop whatever it is you do, maybe go back to school."

"I promise—except I have to finish something. I have to make sure someone doesn't hurt anyone, ever again."

"But you're not doing it for money?"

"Not for money, no. For . . . justice."

"Don't—"

"I won't get caught." *Or, if I do,* he thought, *I'll just see you and Esperanza a little bit sooner.*

Rico's cell phone rang. It would be Theo. He put a finger to his lips. His mother gave the faintest nod.

"*Buenas noches,*" Rico said.

"Your opening, Grob's Attack, gave Black the center," said Aristides. "You crazy?"

Rico smiled. The unexpected move had put Aristides off stride. Good. "In the army they taught us that the best attacks are not always frontal assaults," Rico said softly. "A flanking move can be more effective."

"Your funeral."

"And there was a certain symmetry with the work I did for you, no?"

"Ah, the 'Spike.'" Aristides laughed. "Touché."

"You were satisfied with the job? The second payment has been sent?"

"Yes, hours ago. But I have more work for you—four jobs."

Rico looked at his mother, the lines of pain around her eyes. "I'm sorry."

"What?"

"I am unavailable."

"You want more money, is that it?"

"I have been recalled to active duty. I leave in the morning."

"But what will I do?"

"Do it yourself. Barring that, there's always chess."

"Fine," Aristides spit out. "I move pawn to d5."

"Bishop to g2." Rico closed his cell phone. He wouldn't need it any more. The unfinished game would drive Aristides nuts. But not for long.

Rico removed the SIM card, took a hammer and a Philips screwdriver from the kitchen drawer, and tapped holes in the card until it was useless. He tossed it in the trash.

"It's time," his mother said.

He used the landline to call the ambulance, then sat with her on the bed. She was smiling faintly. "All is in order. The dying will be easy—it won't take long. And then, you can go and finish your business. We'll both be free." Her breathing was more labored now, and she was even paler. "Make me a paper bird while we wait."

"I already did. On the plane." He pulled a tiny white origami owl from the pocket of his shirt and pressed it into her palm. An owl to carry her spirit into the afterlife.

She closed her fingers around it fiercely. "Tell them it goes with me—" Her breath caught on a spasm of pain.

"Can I get you a painkiller?"

She shook her head. "I hear the siren. You have the papers? The DNR? Nothing must go wrong."

He crossed into the kitchen and took the envelope from the refrigerator door where it had been waiting for this moment.

"Remember," she said, "to act cleanly. Leave no lingering—" Another spasm cut off her words.

They heard the siren burp to a stop in the driveway, followed by heavy treads on the stairs.

"No lingering consequences," he finished for her. "I'll remember, Ma."

He was folding another bird—not an owl this time, but a heron, made from a square of pale blue paper. He tucked it in his pocket as he crossed to the door.

31

Friday, May 19, San Jose, California
12:05 a.m.

Rico's mother died forty-five minutes after arriving at the hospital. Her body would be picked up in the morning. He could collect the ashes from the mortuary in three days.

Rico felt flat as he drove to Theo's development in the hills south of Monterey Bay. He parked his sister's nondescript Nissan pickup down the street from the entrance, wrote OUT OF GAS on a piece of paper, clipped it under the windshield wiper, and locked the truck. He didn't think the police patrolled this stretch of road, but better to be safe.

He'd filled his thermos with coffee at the hospital, and bought a couple of sandwiches. He picked up his backpack and walked quickly through the maze of small streets and culs-de-sac toward the clubhouse near the top of the hill. The empty, bladed lots, lit only by moonglow and starlight, matched his mood. Eventually, when the market recovered, people would come here to build new lives. He might even be one of them, he thought, watching the phosphorescent glow of waves breaking on the beach two miles away.

Aristides' car was parked in its usual place in the clubhouse lot. Rico planted a tracking device under the Caddy and made a circuit of the building. All was quiet. He climbed the hillside behind the clubhouse until he found a place he could look down into the rear of the property. He ate one sandwich, then another, washing them down with coffee. Then he settled in to wait.

On several occasions, out of curiosity, Rico had studied

his employer from a distance. Aristides was a man of habits. At 6:00 a.m. he'd stroll out to the pool area with his morning coffee. At 6:30, whether Rico was there to train him or not, Theo would begin his workout in the glass-enclosed gym. Later, he'd grab a large breakfast at one of three local cafés. Then he'd work the phones or meet with a client. In the evenings, he'd play chess and sit in the Jacuzzi.

Rico knew that Theo had begun running guns to Mexico, supplies for the constantly warring cartels. Rico hadn't bothered to check out Theo's clients. They were unimportant.

The man who killed easily and quickly knew he could take Aristides out here, at the clubhouse, but that might not stop whatever he had set in motion. Theo might have found someone else when Rico turned him down. Lenny, perhaps. It would be better to wait and see what developed. Time was on Rico's side. So was the element of surprise.

Rico looked out to sea. A fog bank, touched by moonlight, hung there like a curtain. He thought about the final moments with his mother. He'd tried to warm her hands with his, but her body was shutting down. He'd kissed her smooth forehead one last time, told her he loved her and would see her again soon.

"Not too soon," she'd whispered, before the light faded from her eyes and the breaths stopped coming.

Not too soon, the offshore breeze seemed to echo now.

"I'll be careful," he said softly.

32

A sound woke me in the night. I was alone in the bed. Needing to make sure Philo was okay, I padded quietly from room to room. The second bedroom door was open. Michael wasn't there, but the spare quilt was gone from the foot of the bed. I found Philo, rolled up in the quilt, sleeping on the patio floor. His breathing was deep and regular. His lips curved in a smile.

The rain had stopped and the moon was setting. I crawled in beside him and curled my body into his. His arms came around me automatically. "I love you," I whispered.

I woke again at dawn to stiff muscles and the aroma of coffee. Philo had turned on the coffeemaker, and it was still going through the motions. So was he. His shirtless form moved gracefully through his qigong routine on the patch of grass a few feet away. The sight took me back to Wednesday morning, on my patio in Tucson. Before there was a body in Derek's kitchen . . . Poor Gwen. The innocent victim of Heather's scheme.

I needed the cleansing feel of waves lapping at my ankles. I pulled on jeans and a sweatshirt, poured a large cup of coffee into a plastic mug, and headed down the stairs to the beach.

The fog was so thick I could barely see the folded rocks of the syncline. I clambered up on an outcrop, noting that the tide was coming in. Under the still waters of the tide pools, life bustled and bristled. *Starfish, and sea squirts, and crabs, oh my . . .*

Philo found me there, hunkered down, watching a bright orange turban shell trundle across a small pool. The hermit crab inside was hunting breakfast. Nearby, a green sea anemone waved its shell-encrusted tentacles with the swish of the waves. The fog had receded. A watery sun warmed my back.

"You look like you did when I first met you. Barefoot. Long black braid dipping in the water. Dark as an Apache, but with those great gray eyes laughing as you turned over rocks in Sabino Creek."

"Looking for sand rubies." I smiled at the memory. I'd been eight, and already entranced by garnets.

He touched the back of my hand. "My grandmother's ring suits you, but if you'd prefer something else, just say the word."

"Not on your life," I said. I lifted my right hand out of the water. Philo had sent me a ring from Afghanistan, a man's signet ring in worked silver, set with an engraved oval of bloodred carnelian. The intaglio design reminded me of a pair of water birds rising from a pond. I took off the ring, kissed it, and slid it onto Philo's left ring finger. It fit. Of course. "Consider it a placeholder till we tie the knot."

Philo gave me a hand up. I stretched and said, "You know, I'd be perfectly happy to spend the day here."

He grinned. "Ah, but we've miles to go, Sherlock. I heard rustling from upstairs. I've put quiche in to bake."

"Well, aren't you the handy man."

"I try. Alana stocked the larder with enough to feed Childeric's army."

A wave washed over my feet, rising till it reached my knees. Luckily, I'd rolled my pant legs. I picked up my coffee cup, which was floating toward Japan, and leapt onto the sand, saying, "Race you back."

He beat me by ten feet. Coming through the garden gate, I smelled croissants along with the quiche and realized I was starving.

Alana and Michael were setting the patio table. They looked . . . comfortable with each other. And as if they had secrets to tell.

"The ring's new," Michael said. He didn't miss much. "And weren't you wearing Philo's Afghan ring last night?"

Alana dropped the last placemat, and reached for my hand. "Lovely. Is it official then?"

Philo nodded. "Your castle must be enchanted."

"It is, isn't it?" Alana gave Michael a slow, lazy smile, then turned and led us into the kitchen to finish breakfast preparations. "We struck gold with our research, by the way. You tell them, Michael."

While Philo and I cut up fruit and Alana made more coffee, Michael settled into a chair, saying, "We turned up various stories about the grave goods of Childeric I, the first undisputed king of the Merovingian line."

"If this has anything to do with the *Da Vinci Code,* I'm leaving," I said.

Michael laughed. "This has nothing to do with pseudo-history or conjectured lineages of the offspring of Jesus and Mary Magdalene."

"Or Grail lore, much as we love it," said Alana. "Go on, Michael."

He smiled. "The short version is this—Childeric became king of the Salian Franks around 457 AD. He was a warrior who fought beside the Romans against the Goths and Visigoths. He also warred against the Saxons and Alamanni. For his service, Rome awarded him lands around Tournai, where he established his capital. His wife, Basine—or Basina—of Thuringia, was the mother of his son and successor, Chlodovech."

"Clovis," I said.

"Right. There may have been a second wife, unnamed. Clovis was the first Frankish king to turn Catholic."

"Which didn't stop him from murdering most of his relatives and many of his neighbors," Alana added.

Philo smiled. "Yes, well, the rules were different back then."

"The good old days," said Michael.

"Childeric's grave goods?" I prompted.

"His tomb was discovered by a mason doing repairs to

a church in Tournai. It was an incredibly rich find by anyone's standards."

"Gold and jeweled brooches, buckles, pins, and swords," Alana said, taking the croissants from the oven.

"And a pile of gold and silver coins." Michael offloaded the rolls into a basket.

"Don't forget the bees," Alana said. "Gold and garnet bees. Three hundred of them."

"Bees." Philo's tone was skeptical.

Michael handed him a photograph he'd downloaded and printed from Alana's computer. It showed the upper and lower views of two insects with gold bodies and garnet wings. "Bees," I agreed.

Michael smiled. "They might be flies or locusts—there's some dispute. You can see the faint crosshatched lines on the garnets. Those are characteristic of Merovingian work. But here's the interesting part: along with the bees and horse bones, probably Childeric's royal stable, they found *two* human skulls. One was smaller than the other."

"Basine?" I said.

"Possibly. Or his nameless second wife, if she existed."

We carried the food and coffee out to the table on the patio. The wind had calmed, and the morning was warming up nicely.

"A Belgian physician named Chifflet was commissioned to draw the collection," Alana said. "He published the drawings and descriptions, in Latin, in 1655. You can find some of his drawings on the Internet, if you're interested. That's what I remembered seeing."

"The treasure was given to the King of Austria, who soon passed it on to Louis XIV," Michael said. "He put the treasure in his royal library. A century and a half later, Napoleon, looking for a fresh emblem for his new empire—something to replace the fleur-de-lis of the old monarchy—adopted the bees. They harked back to the birth of the Frankish state, of France itself. Napoleon had them sewn onto his coronation robe."

I took a helping of fruit salad and passed it to Alana. "So what happened to Childeric's treasure?"

"This is where it gets interesting," Alana said. "The night of November 5–6, 1831, thieves broke into the Bibliothèque Nationale and took Childeric's treasure and other golden objects stored there. Roughly eighty kilograms, says one report. There seems to be some argument as to what happened next. One report says that the thieves melted down the gold, and the police later recovered most of it. Whether or not that included Childeric's hoard isn't clear . . . Another report says the thieves tossed the loot in the Seine. The police did recover a couple of bees and a few other objects that one thief had hidden in the Seine. But the bulk of Childeric's treasure was lost."

"The thieves didn't talk?" I said.

"They may have, during the trial. But forty years later, when the Paris Commune took over the city, the records were destroyed in a fire."

"Let's see if I've got this right," I said. "Judging by all those conflicting reports, anything could have happened to the treasure. The thieves, with the police hot on their heels, might have loaded the loot onto a boat waiting in the Seine, melted down the treasure, or hidden it away somewhere it'll never be found."

"Or a bit from columns A, B, and C," Philo said. "It seems we're no closer to figuring out the connection between Grandma Claudine's chess set and Childeric the First." He looked at Alana. "Any chance it might have been made for the twentieth-century tourist trade? No doubt Childeric was Tournai's most famous resident."

Alana shook her head. "I stand by my original opinion—nineteenth century. French or Belgian."

"Oddly enough," said Michael, who'd been staring out at the ocean, "the director of the French National Library at the time of the theft was a Belgian."

"You think they wanted their treasure back?" Philo said.

"I think we will never know the whole story. We will be lucky if we can divine a small part of it."

"Did any of your chess cohorts respond to your e-mails?" I asked Alana.

"Only one. An old man, and an old friend, from Antwerp. He said he'd heard a rumor years ago, when the Nazis blitzed through Belgium, that the 'treasure of Tournai' had been spirited away. He didn't hear of it again. Tournai was all but destroyed during the war, along with many of its people. There was no one to remember."

The sadness of that thought pierced the beauty of the morning. And silenced us. By unspoken consent, we focused on our food.

I pushed away my empty plate and picked up the thread. "We know the chess set exists, and we know that it's linked in some way with Philo's grandmother's line. But we haven't a clue why those pictures were in Gwen's safe."

"Though we presume Heather put them there," Philo said. "The message on the back suggests that someone, not Heather or Derek, is playing a game of chess. We also presume that game is with whoever followed Heather to the Bay Area—Frankie and me, as luck would have it. But the note and photos could also have been intended for Derek."

"How did that someone get photos of the chess pieces?" Michael asked.

"I'll bet they were taken for insurance purposes," Alana said. "To document the chess set's existence, in case of theft or fire. They're recent, digital. Once the images were in a computer, they could be sent anywhere, downloaded and printed. Then all anyone had to do was type and print out a label and stick it on. I've done it thousands of times for art objects I've appraised or sold."

"I have also," Michael said. "It occurs to me that this man may live in the Bay Area. That's where Heather rendezvoused with him. Quite possibly a longstanding affair. She might even have left Derek for him. If so, your chess player would have had access to her computer. I presume she traveled with a laptop?"

I nodded. "So her mother says."

"When Chet and I broke up," Alana said, "I had to catalogue everything we owned. California's a community property state."

"So's Arizona," I said.

Alana nodded. "I had to have an outside appraiser evaluate the assets so they could be divided equally. Luckily we'd only been married a few months. We hadn't had time to accumulate anything but wedding gifts. I sent those back."

"Heather's organized," Philo said. "This wouldn't have been a spur-of-the-moment decision. She'd have been documenting assets for weeks, months."

"We've been thinking of Gwen's murder as a Tucson-based crime," I said. "The entire picture changes if we move the brain—or brains—behind it to the Bay Area." I looked at Philo. "Does Derek have any developments this far north?"

"I'll find out," he said. He went into the second bedroom to call Killeen. "Request delivered," Philo said when he returned. "He'll get back to us."

"I could work that angle for you today," Alana said to me, "while you and Philo see if Heather's in residence in Woodside. I can keep in touch with your Killeen, if you like."

I hugged her. "I like. Divide and conquer."

Michael looked at Philo. "You take Frankie to Woodside, but not me?"

"Well—"

"Have you thought that Heather might be setting a trap for you there?"

"He's counting on it," I said.

"There's only one narrow road in and out, blocked by an electric gate," said Philo. "Frankie can cover that while I check out the house."

"I have a better plan. I will follow you in the Malibu." Michael made a wry face. He drove a silver BMW convertible. "Once we get to the property, Frankie can cover the gate, as planned, while I drive partway in with you in the Honda. You can drop me off to circle around on foot and serve as backup."

"No," Alana, Philo, and I said together.

"You promised me adventure, Frankie. Did you draw me here under false pretenses?" Michael turned to Alana. "Though I would have come anyway, of course, just to meet you."

I could hear his father's voice saying, *That boy has golden hands and a devil in his smile. He got them from his mother.* I said, "No, Michael—"

He ignored me. "Besides, not to put too fine a point on it, Philo, but I am as much a partner in this firm as you are."

He had Philo there.

Alana started to say something, then changed her mind. Michael put his arm around her. "I promise *you* to return unscathed—if at all possible." He let her go and pulled a map from his pocket. "Now, tell me where exactly we are going."

Philo pointed out the road, gave them both the Dain address, the number of the ranch manager, and the gate code. He said, "With Killeen and his group, that means we'll have three teams working, here and in Tucson—four, counting the police. I talked to Toni last night. They have a lead on Arnulfo Sánchez's killer. Sánchez was the man who killed Gwen and broke into Margaret's house that night," he reminded Alana and Michael.

"Who's Toni?" said Alana.

Philo explained his relationship with the sheriff's detective. "Toni examined the convenience store videotapes. Found a guy buying gum an hour before the murder. There was an origami bird and a bit of a gum wrapper lying not far from the body. Same brand of gum. No prints on either, but Toni put the origami description in the system and got a couple of hits."

"What kind of bird?" I said.

"A heron or stork, Toni thinks. Something with a long neck. Not a swan."

"Toni thinks this Origami Man was brought in to kill Arnulfo Sánchez?"

"Right. He's probably from out of town. The system hits she got were from Sunnyvale, Sacramento, and Reno."

"Origami is about symbolism, not just paper folding," Alana said. "A heron stands motionless in still water, waiting for the fish to swim by . . . waiting for the time to strike."

"Sánchez was killed in the early morning hours," I said. "If the Bay Area is the killer's home turf, he could be nearby right now, looking for us."

"Or for the coin collection." Philo turned to Alana. "Want to change your mind about holding onto the coins for us?"

"I'm not worried," Alana said. "Origami Man, or whoever hired him, won't be able to track you here—as long as he didn't follow you yesterday."

"He didn't," Philo said. "One operative couldn't have. We doubled back more than once on the way."

"Then he'll be working on Heather's relationships,

Philo, not Frankie's college ties. His employer has to be aware by now that Heather's on the run. The coins are safe here."

"And all roads lead to Heather," said Michael. "I look forward to meeting her." He turned to Philo. "You have weapons?"

"We're good."

"And I have Tía Miranda's blade," I said. "I hope the charm holds."

"She is not given to weak magic," Michael said.

"If you aren't back by dark, or haven't called," Alana said, "I'll alert Killeen and the authorities. And then I'll drive down there myself."

Michael studied her set face. "I maneuver better alone in situations like these."

"Then I'll wait in the car with a phone, a first-aid kit, and a pistol."

"Have you ever handled a firearm?" he said.

I laughed as she got up and walked to the safe, punched in a code on the panel, and pulled open the heavy door. Michael grinned at me and then followed her. On a rack at the back were handguns, shotguns, and rifles. I knew what Michael was thinking as he sized up the cache—yes, there was room for his knife collection. Or part of it, at least.

"My father was an Olympic marksman," she said. "He didn't have a son."

Michael ran a hand lightly over her hair. "Have I told you that you are perfect?"

She smiled. "Yes. Last night. In several languages. But I think you were most eloquent in Spanish."

"That's because you don't speak Arabic."

33

Friday, May 19
Bay Heights Development
Monterey County, California

7:00 a.m.

Theo Aristides punched the STOP button on the elliptical trainer, stepped off, and pulled on his boxing gloves. He was pissed. Not one fucking thing was going right. His trainer hadn't shown up for their scheduled workout, and he wasn't answering his phone. Worse, Theo's hit man had refused the job last night, and the backup, Lenny, was en route to the border with a shipment of arms. There was no way Theo could find a replacement for Rico on such short notice. He'd have to handle Derek and Philo Dain himself. And the girlfriend. Pick them off one at a time.

But Theo had lost track of Heather, just as Lenny had lost Philo Dain yesterday. And to top everything off, Derek Dain was missing. Was he with Heather?

Theo began beating a rhythm on the speed bag, making believe it was Derek Dain's head. Theo had mortgaged everything he owned to get the development off the ground. Dain had said they couldn't miss. Shit.

The speed bag danced on its hook as Theo poured out his fury. Dain insisted he'd been cleaned out, too. Theo didn't believe him—or Heather, for that matter. But what could he do?

Smuggling guns kept the lights on, water in the Jacuzzi, and ouzo in the bar. It paid for his trainer and the settling of scores. Smuggling would be harder now that Sánchez was dead. Lenny would have to work solo for a while. He couldn't follow people worth a damn, but he'd proved he was good at finding ways to transport merchandise into Mexico . . .

The wall phone rang. Cursing, Aristides removed his right glove. He didn't care who it was, he'd tear a strip off anyone.

"Theo?" Heather's voice.

She sounded tentative, or maybe scared. Good. "Where the fuck you been?" he said. "You playing games with me?"

The line went dead. Aristides checked back for her phone number and pressed SEND.

Without preamble, Heather said, "Why did you kill Gwen?"

"I didn't."

"Had her killed, then. Don't split hairs."

"My guy fucked up. I sent him to ask you nicely for the coins—half up front, like we agreed. Wasn't his fault your sister flew down to Tucson."

"We agreed you'd be paid today."

"I needed money yesterday. I have a buyer."

Silence on Heather's end. Aristides said, "You still there?"

"How'd you—*shit*. You had someone watching Gwen and me at the restaurant." Her voice was dead calm.

"Yeah. Then Lenny followed you both back to the airport. Saw her get a ticket to Phoenix in your name. Assumed it was you. He said you looked like twins."

"We're nothing alike."

"Yeah, well, I thought you were crossing me, going back to Derek."

"Don't be stupid."

"What the fuck was your sister doing in Tucson?"

"Picking up my passport. I had to renew it. The trip was supposed to be a, a, *lark* for Gwen—a little break . . ."

"Passport?" The edge was back in Aristides' voice. "You planning a trip?"

"Once I've scattered Derek's and Philo's ashes, I'm going to go play the grieving widow for a few weeks. Someplace cool. Vancouver, maybe."

"Travel takes money."

"Mother loaned me some. Enough to get me out of Tucson."

He didn't believe her. But it didn't matter. Once Heather paid him for taking care of Derek and Philo, he'd take care of her, too. But first he had to find his prey.

"The nephew's got a woman with him—or he did yesterday. Lenny lost 'em."

"I know. I spoke to my mother last night. She wanted to know why I'd left without telling her about Gwen. I told her I was scared. That Derek must have sent someone to kill me, and got Gwen instead."

Blaming Derek was a nice touch. "Did she mention the nephew? Say where he is?"

"He followed the clues straight to Daly City, just like we planned. Mother didn't know where they were going to spend the night, but they planned to show up here today."

Aristides noted the word *here*. "You're at the house, then?"

"Yes. I checked into a motel yesterday. Needed an alibi. Moved to the house last night. Nobody but you and Derek knows where I am. The car's hidden and I haven't used the house lights."

"You're sure Derek'll come?"

"He called last night from Santa Barbara," Heather said. "He should arrive by eleven."

"This morning?"

"Yeah. He's anxious to finish with Philo once and for all."

"Don't forget the girl."

"She won't be a problem. It may even work in our favor—Philo'll be distracted."

"What about the chess set?"

"It's here at the house. It's always been here. Derek doesn't play chess, so there was no reason to cart it around."

"You could have told me."

"Then you might just have decided to break in and steal it. This way, I get something in trade."

"At the price of your sister."

"Go fuck yourself, Theo."

"See you at ten."

Thirty minutes later, showered and dressed, Theo Aristides stood at the door of the small side room off his office. It had only the one entrance, a steel door with a biorecognition lock. The room had been furnished with display cases. Each held at least one of Uncle Plato's chess sets in ivory, jade, gold, silver, pewter, and wood. One case was empty except for two color photographs of a chess set—an unusual set. The king wore Roman garb. Around his base was a Latin inscription. Aristides knew it by heart: *CHILDERICI REGIS.*

Theo's Uncle Plato had told him about the chess set long ago. Plato had played a game against Claudine Dain when Theo was still a boy. She'd beaten the pants off Plato, but had agreed to play him again, via mail. And once, when Plato was at a tournament in San Francisco, Claudine had invited him to drive down to Woodside for a game. They'd played on the most beautiful chess set Plato had ever touched. But she wouldn't sell it, no matter how much money he offered.

Theo wanted that chess set as much as he wanted revenge on Derek for pulling out of the development deal.

Aristides closed the heavy door and set the lock. When next he opened it, he'd have the chess set in hand, or his name wasn't Theo. *Theron,* actually. Greek for "hunter." And he was hunting now.

Carrying an unopened bottle of ouzo, he left the clubhouse by a side door, setting the alarm behind him. As he exited the development, he didn't notice the tan pickup leave the curb and follow him west.

PART V

Into the Maze

To the wilderness I wander.
By a knight of ghosts and shadows
I summoned am to tourney
Ten leagues beyond the wide world's end.

—Anonymous, "Tom o' Bedlam" (17th century)

34

Friday, May 19
Marina, California

8:00 a.m.

Rico could see Theo Aristides' black Caddy in the parking lot of a mom-and-pop breakfast place on the highway. They had a drive-through window, so Rico ordered a breakfast burrito and coffee to go and then parked a little way up the road. He figured there was a 50-50 chance Theo had just ventured out for breakfast and would return to the clubhouse. But if not, then Theo was headed north on Highway 1. Rico could follow at a distance, using the tracking device.

Rico finished his burrito and fished a cordless razor from the catchall behind the seat. Might as well make himself presentable. He shaved, carefully cleaned under his fingernails, and brushed his hair. Toiletries stowed away, he settled in to wait.

Not far away, pleasure craft and fishing boats crisscrossed the deep green water of Monterey Bay. Rico would like to live on a boat and learn how to sail. There was time now. He'd go back to school, maybe work in the library, meet a nice girl. He was free and solvent. He could be anyone he chose to be. His mother's death had left him rudderless, but he would carve a new rudder, make himself a new life—as soon as he finished this one little detail. The world would be better off without Theo Aristides.

Rico looked in the mirror. Theo's SUV hadn't moved.

Anytime, Theo. Let's get a move on.

35

Philo, Michael, and I left Moss Beach in our two-car convoy. Behind us, the fog drifted in like the mists of Avalon to hide Alana's castle.

Philo drove in silence past the Half Moon Bay airfield, its western edge marked by a scarp where the Seal Cove fault disrupted the old marine terrace. In the center of Half Moon Bay we joined Highway 92, the lifeline connecting the Pacific side of the Peninsula with the San Francisco Bay side. It was the same highway we'd taken in rush-hour traffic from SFO yesterday. Now, morning commuters charged the eastbound lanes.

It was a relief to peel off onto the relative quiet of Skyline Boulevard. The road suited drivers who loved maneuvering small sleek cars on hairpin turns and narrow, winding highways. Gwen's Honda handled the curves well. Not much oomph, but a smooth ride. Michael, following in the Malibu, must be pining for his BMW.

We climbed through softly rippled hills cloaked in grass, mustard, and chaparral. Last night's drenching made them sparkle in the sunlight. The road curved back on itself, revealing the College of San Mateo, perched on a cliff overlooking Crystal Springs Reservoir and the San Andreas fault zone. I'd taught introductory geology and oceanography classes at the college years ago. That experience had helped me land the teaching job in Tucson.

Another switchback, and the college was lost to view. As we crested the ridge, crosswinds buffeted the car. Far below, to the east, whitecaps dotted the bay, while fingers of fog invaded the western canyons. Heading deeper into the mountains, we entered a mysterious world where red-woods, digger pines, Douglas fir, and hemlock vied with deciduous trees to block out the sky. I felt like Theseus, wending my way to the heart of the Labyrinth.

The tires whispered on the roadbed. Underneath lay the ancient Franciscan Formation, rocks scraped from the seafloor as the denser oceanic crust of the Pacific Plate slid under the lighter crust of the North American Plate. *Subduction.* The rocks of the lower plate melted as they descended. The magma rose slowly through the crust until it crystallized as massive plutons or found release through volcanic events. Lenses of the volcanic material interfingered with younger marine sandstone in these coastal hills.

But when the North American and Pacific plates became locked at the surface, stresses shifted. Subduction ceased. The driving cells resolved the pressure by morphing into a transform fault, two tectonic plates sliding past each other. The San Andreas fault zone was born—along with faults like the Pilarcitos, the Hayward, and the San Gregorio.

Movement on the San Andreas had created the long, linear valleys on our left, while its sister, the extinct Pilarcitos fault, traversed forested ridges to our right. The wedge of Franciscan Formation beneath us—the only Franciscan rocks lying west of the San Andreas—was a relict, caught in a geologic no-man's-land between active and extinct fault traces. It was a reminder of how the unseen forces driving those deep mantle cells can change the way even massive plates interact . . .

Unseen forces effecting change. Whether hard rocks or fragile humans, nothing and no one escaped.

We turned west off Skyline Boulevard onto Los Osos Canyon Road. One lane, winding through the forest primeval. Ten miles per hour. I felt like a sitting target, a sage grouse during hunting season. But Philo, I noticed, was smiling. He thrived on the chase.

The mossy-backed trees blotted out the sky. I rolled down the window, breathing in scents of damp earth, clay, pine, fir, and eucalyptus. Last night's storm had deposited leaf litter and branches on the road. Soon we came to a side road barred by tall metal gates. Michael parked the Malibu on the dirt verge, grabbed an old hunting vest Alana had loaned him, and climbed into the back seat of the Honda. Philo pulled ahead to the keypad and punched in the number Margaret had given him. The gates groaned open, then closed behind us with a decisive clang. There was no place to turn around. We were committed.

The road climbed steeply for perhaps a quarter mile before the forest abruptly ended at the top of a hill. We halted just below the summit, pulling as far to the right as we could without sliding off into the dense undergrowth. We climbed out, walked the remaining distance, and lay down in the shadows at the edge of the road.

The single ribbon of asphalt followed the crest of hillsides long ago stripped of trees to make pastureland for livestock. I heard cattle lowing in the distance, out of sight. Half a mile away, a screen of cypress and pines hid the bottom of a two-story rectangular farmhouse with cylindrical rock towers at each side. Another American-style castle—this one, at the moment, in full sun instead of shrouded in mist. And much, much larger than Alana's.

"Welcome to Foggy Gulch Ranch," Philo said, taking binoculars from his pack. I followed suit.

I couldn't see another house or barn from where we lay. I said, "This is where the Hendersons live?"

"No, they run the ranch from the manager's place at the bottom of the hill." Philo waved toward the grassy slopes on our right, crisscrossed by cattle tracks. A truck, driving up Los Osos Canyon, was suddenly hidden from sight as the road dipped into a fold of the hills. "You can't see the house or outbuildings from here. You reach them by going back through the gate and continuing down the road a mile or so."

Michael was using the gun sight from one of Alana's rifles to study Derek's house. "Not bad," he said. "Nouveau riche, but rather quirky."

"My grandparents added the towers. Quarried the basalt on site." Philo stopped and stared at a massive wooden sculpture on a ridge in the middle distance. "I'd forgotten. Derek and Margaret brought me here one time," he said. "Just for a night."

"When?" I said.

"After my parents were killed." Philo paused, remembering. "That visit was a blur. I slept or stared out the window on the drive from Bishop . . . Derek drove a yellow truck. I rode in the car with Margaret. We got here after dark. Margaret heated me some chicken noodle soup and then sent me to bed. But I couldn't sleep. I watched them from my bedroom window. They unloaded furniture and boxes. There was an air of secrecy about it. They whispered to each other. Didn't use the outside lights. And we left before dawn."

"Did you ask Margaret about the furniture?"

"Later, when we got to Tucson. She said they were antiques that belonged to my grandparents, and that they'd *come home*."

He lifted the binoculars to his eyes. So did I. A metal-roofed barn was the closest structure. It had been painted recently. Behind it, I could see right through the house. The curtains weren't drawn. No lights were on. No one moved.

Philo passed me a Google Earth satellite image of the area. The asphalt road continued for about a mile past the pale drive leading to the house. The road wound between hills before descending in a great zigzag to a couple of buildings. "That's an artists' retreat," Philo said. "Googled their site last night."

"Does that mean traffic?" I said.

"Not much. Only eight residents at a time, plus a few staff members. And I doubt the international artists will have vehicles. We'll just have to play it by ear."

To our left, or south, the forest edge crowded a fence line that curved down and around the pasture. Parallel tracks showed where an old dirt road broke free from the forest, cut up through the pasture, and crossed the asphalt road. This track led directly to the wooden π-shaped sculpture. It reminded me of the entrance to a Japanese temple. Or a gallows.

"The paved road is too open," I said.

"Good," Philo said. "Heather can't leave without our seeing her. The only other road in or out is a dirt trail, a little farther along, connecting the house with the manager's place. Needs a four-wheel-drive vehicle. I doubt Heather rented one."

"So all I have to do, if she bolts, is pull the car across the road by the entrance gate. She won't be able to get around me. She'll be stuck."

"And hopping mad." Philo touched my cheek and smiled. "Be careful."

"Don't worry. I'll get out of sight once I move the car."

Michael had been scanning the terrain. "I can work my way around, through the trees to here," Michael said, pointing to where the faint track left the woods, "and follow the road up to the ridge. Anyone in the house will think I'm one of the artists." Michael squinted at the track. "Do you think it continues into the forest?"

"Haven't a clue," Philo said. "It was dark, as I said, during the second visit, and it rained every day but one during the first."

"The day your dad took that photograph," I said. "The windows were open, and the sun was shining on the ocean."

Philo nodded. "I think it was the day after Christmas. Santa'd given me a bike with training wheels. I learned to ride on this road. Grandpa took the training wheels off just before we went inside for dinner . . . They're probably still here somewhere." His words were matter-of-fact, but an echo of loss colored his tone.

Michael must have heard it, too. "I learned to ride during a holiday in San Sebastian," he said. "It was a day like today—a storm had just passed through, and a stiff wind was blowing off the sea. It was the first time I remember feeling proud of myself."

"Me, too." Philo cleared his throat and let the binoculars fall against his chest. Holding up the satellite image again, he touched the side of the house, just behind the southern tower. "I think the kitchen door's about here. And Grandpa's den was next to the kitchen. There was a back stairway leading from the kitchen to the second floor.

That's where my bedroom was, in the old part of the house. They said it had been the teacher's quarters. They used to hire a teacher for the school year. I found school-books in the cupboards when I was playing hide-and-seek with . . . Shit."

"Heather?" I said.

"And Gwen. Gabrielle must have been here, too. And Russell. I'd forgotten."

"I wonder if Heather remembers?"

"With luck, we'll soon find out."

Michael had been watching the house as we talked. "Still no movement. I cannot tell if there is a car parked between the barn and house."

"What do they use the barn for?" I said to Philo.

"A garage and workshop, I think. One of Derek's wives had a quilting business."

"What's in this third building?" I could see an A-frame metal roof in the distance.

"Grandpa called it the bunkhouse. That's where Derek and Margaret stored my parents' things that night."

Michael tucked his rifle sight into one of his vest pockets, eased back below the summit, and stood. "I had better be going. It will take time to circle around. Once I am on the road, I will walk past the house to this windmill." He pointed to the image. "Then I will cut into these trees and work my way back to the house."

"Good," said Philo. "If anyone's there, they'll be so focused on me driving through the gate and up to the front door that they won't pay any attention to an artist out for a hike."

"Don't worry—if anyone stops me I'll lapse into Spanish or Arabic." Michael touched Philo's shoulder, then mine. Humor brightened his dark eyes. "Thank you both. I have not had this much fun in months."

"Watch out for the poison oak," I said, but he was already gone. I heard a faint rustle of leaves as he entered the forest, then nothing.

"I called the ranch manager, Robbie Henderson, last night, while you were in the shower," Philo said. "He hadn't heard from Heather."

"And the lights aren't on," I said. "Which means either we missed her, or she's hiding from whoever's after Derek's treasure."

"And killed Gwen for it."

Sensing something behind his words, I touched his shoulder, needing to see his face, read his eyes. I nodded slowly, and said, "You think there's a good chance Heather's dead."

36

Driving the Pacific Coast Highway always reminded Theo Aristides of Eratini, the Greek fishing village where he'd spent the first six years of his life. For Theo, those were happy years—until he'd started school and learned what the word *nothos* meant. Natural child. Bastard. But by then Theo's mother had begged, borrowed, and saved enough money to pay for two plane fares to America. She'd prayed that life would be different in Chicago. It was, for a while.

Theo hated thinking about the time after his mother married Robert Herrod. What would have happened to Theo if Uncle Plato hadn't taken him in? There would have been no quiet chess games at night while looking out over the lake. No after-school jobs on construction sites. No one teaching him the ins and outs of smuggling. Uncle Plato had given him everything, including an inheritance.

Theo had risked it all in California. And lost. But he could still salvage his development—and possess the chess set. All he had to do was kill Derek Dain and his nephew. And the girlfriend, if she was there. Rico could have done it easily. Now it was up to Theo.

Theo Aristides left the ocean behind, turning inland on La Honda Road. He was prepared for what lay ahead. There would be four deaths, not the three Heather expected. He'd sensed days ago that Heather was planning to cross him. Big mistake.

He'd deal with her last.

37

The temperature and humidity rose as the sun warmed the grassy hills. I folded my braid up off my neck, secured it with a large barrette, and replaced my hat. The forecast predicted rain by noon, but until then it would be hot and steamy.

While Philo kept watch, waiting for Michael to make his way through the forest, I studied the satellite image. A memory stirred, triggered by the smell and feel of the place. "I was here once, too," I said. When Philo looked at me as if I'd lost my marbles, I added, "Thirteen years ago, for a geology exercise. We were looking at road cuts in the forest."

"You're just now remembering?"

"It was my freshman year. I'd played in a basketball game the night before. UCSB. A home game. We won, but I was bushed. So I slept all the way here and all the way back. I never did get properly oriented. We parked by an odd twelve-sided barn that had been converted to art studios."

"This one?" He pointed to the nearly circular structure on the map.

"I'm sure of it. See the road leading down from it into the forest?" Philo nodded. "There's a whole damn sculpture garden in that forest. We drove through it on an old logging road, stopping to examine and map the rocks. Butano Sandstone, mostly, just like we drove through on the road in. And some basalt. We must have come out through that grove," I said, pointing to where Michael would emerge at any moment. "Just inside the fence are huge geometric sculptures, concrete—all points and angles, held upright by oaks and madrone. The instructor told us the sculptor's name. An Italian . . ." Philo didn't interrupt the retrieval process. I smiled and said, "Staccioli. Not that it's important."

"It must have been important to you, or you wouldn't have noted it."

"That was the day I realized I had to choose between science and athletics. Some students can do both. I couldn't. I missed too much geologic context by sleeping on the way here and back. So, I gave up my athletic scholarship at the end of the year."

"Any regrets?"

"None. I was a good athlete, but not a great one."

Below us, there was a flicker of movement at the edge of the trees. Michael strolled out of the dappled shadows. Somewhere he'd found or fashioned a walking stick. He was whistling Bach's Air on a G String.

"Cute," I said.

The whistling tapered off when Michael's trail met the forty-degree slope of the hillside. He needed all his breath just to climb. When he reached the asphalt road he paused for a minute, staring towards the wooden π-sculpture and presumably catching his breath. When he turned and started walking west, still at a leisurely pace, Philo and I eased back to the Honda.

"Don't come to the house unless I call you," he said. "If Heather's alive, I don't want you anywhere near her. She's poison. If she's dead, well, someone might still be around."

"Okay," I said. I even meant it, then. "Ready?"

We turned our cell phones to vibrate. Kissed. "Time to go sleuthing," Philo said, closing the car door. Seconds later the Honda disappeared over the crest.

I looked down. My phone had lost its signal. If I went back to wait by the Malibu, I'd have no chance of seeing or hearing if problems developed. I was loath to cut off two of my senses, sight and hearing, by retreating farther down the hill. But Philo was counting on me to do just that.

Wanting to think this through, I climbed back to the summit and lay again in the shadows. My phone searched and found a signal. I had a decision to make.

Michael was even with the windbreak of cypress and

pine screening the house. Philo turned off the road, got out to open the fancy metal gate near the base of the driveway, and drove through and up a curving lane to the castle on the hill. He left the gate open.

Even after the Honda and Michael were out of sight, I lingered. In the distance, rain squalls had already come ashore. The storm was moving fast, the wind picking up. Soon the weather might interfere with cell signals here, as well.

An uneasiness spiked from some spot deep within my brain, primal as the fight-or-flight impulse, and just as potent. I felt the ground beneath my belly lurch, as if I'd been carrying a kicking fetus. A small quake, like the one Gabrielle mentioned yesterday. Or the one Philo and I felt in Tucson, just before we entered Derek's house and saw Gwen. Looking back, both tremors seemed like omens. Bad moon rising.

I called Michael. His phone rolled over to voicemail. He'd either lost signal, or turned off his cell. Damn. I refused to call Philo. He didn't need any distractions right now. I felt as if my lifelines had been cut. Nothing for it but to take up my post by the gate.

Jogging downhill, I smelled the rain, though sun still poured down on this side of the ridge. When I was close to the gate, I left the road to find a good observation post. A hidden place, screened from the road. Preferably a spot free of poison oak.

I found a massive sugar pine festooned with Spanish moss. Good cover. Perfect overlook. Close enough to run down and move the Malibu if Heather came over the hill. Plus, the spot would provide a good view of the driver's side of any car that passed up the road.

The ground under the tree sloped away from the road cut into a shallow swale littered with pine duff—enough to stuff a mattress. And I'd stay dry even in the rain. I pushed aside one of the lower branches and crawled in. I'd barely gotten settled—belly on duff cushion, binoculars in hand—when a muddy green Hummer rounded the corner . . . I started breathing again when he swept past the turnoff.

Note to self: You can't hear them coming.

38

Philo drove past the front door of what had been his grandparents' house and pulled into a space on the far side of the old bunkhouse. The outbuilding would screen him and the car if anyone happened to be watching from the castle. They'd begin to wonder, maybe even worry, about what Philo was doing. Good. He'd take his time, keep them off balance as long as possible. And if Heather wasn't here—or her body lay inside—that revelation, too, could wait a few more minutes.

The wind caught him squarely on the face when he opened the car door. Rain now obscured the ocean. Hands on hips, he inhaled the salty air, laden with the scents of Coast Ranges vegetation. Familiar scents. He realized he'd loved this place once. Loved it now. It represented a time when his family had been whole. His roots were here.

What was it about Foggy Gulch Ranch that had sent Derek down one path, KC down another? Cain and Abel. His father had preferred open spaces, limitless views of mountains and canyons that made the soul swell. He'd tried to capture those places on film. Ann had been the people person. But she was just as happy in rough country. They were a good match—loving their time together, loving their son, but welcoming solitude. They mirrored this setting. Derek didn't. Philo wondered why his uncle had kept the ranch, even after KC and Ann were—

Philo heard a curve-billed thrasher's call from the fir thicket behind him. A southwestern bird. A foreign sound. Philo leaned into the car and pulled the Glock from his daypack. Put a couple of extra magazines in his pockets. Tucked the sidearm under his waistband at the small of his back, hiding the gun with the tails of his shirt. Strapped his hunting knife to his ankle. *Time to throw out the first pitch.*

He dropped the keys by the gas pedal and walked into the shelter of the nearest fir. The thin copse would continue to hide him from the house windows as long as he didn't move around too much or too quickly.

Michael's dark clothes and camouflage vest blended with the bole of a tree. It took Philo's eyes a moment to adjust to the half-light and locate him. If Michael had been an enemy, Philo'd be dead.

"Nice," Philo said.

"I thought so." Michael grinned. "You took your time."

"Enjoyed watching you puff up the hill."

"I'm a little out of shape. Too much teaching, not enough dancing." Michael sat on the fir litter under the tree. When Philo had followed suit, Michael said, "I called my father while I waited. He and Derek are in the same line of business. They worked together on several projects."

"Of course. I should have thought of that. Did Cézar have any news? Any insight?"

"Everyone's talking about Derek's disappearance. And Gwen's death. Her picture made the morning paper, along with news that the killer's body had been identified. Common view is that Derek ran because he thinks he'll be next."

"He might even be right."

"Papa said to tell you that 'the wolf loses his teeth, but not his inclinations.'"

"In other words," Philo said, "age won't have slowed Derek down."

"If he is dangerous when cornered and fighting for his business life, how much more dangerous is he when his own life is at stake?" said Michael. "According to my father, Derek believes morals are for the weak—which, coming from my ethically challenged father, is pretty funny."

"I thought the old rascal'd mended his ways?"

Michael shrugged. "He tries to live up to his new heart. I think he is successful about 60 percent of the time."

"An improvement."

"As you say."

Philo stood. "Guess I'd better get on with it."

Michael looked up at him. "I picked the lock on the back door of the bunkhouse." He waved a hand toward the building next to them.

"Considerate of you. What's inside?"

"Old furniture and boxes. The tape on the boxes is yellow and dry."

"So Derek kept my parents' things. I wonder why." Philo thought back to the black time after his parents died. He had stayed at a friend's house for a few days while Derek and Margaret were cleaning out the house. "When they picked me up on the way out of town, they said they'd given everything but a few antiques away. That a clean break would be healthier for me."

"Your uncle has a lot to answer for, if you ever find him."

"We'll find him . . . Did you happen to check the barn while you were twiddling your thumbs?"

"Twiddling?" When Philo moved his thumbs to demonstrate, Michael said, "Ah, I see. Wasting time. Yes, I entered the barn through the workshop door—on the east there." He pointed. "Tables and counters and cupboards, all bare. I found a Hertz car in the other half, a sand-colored Ford rented at SFO. Heather's name is on the paperwork."

"Anything else?"

"I was watching the house when you drove up. Saw movement in an upstairs window." Michael pointed to the southeast corner, above the kitchen.

"The old schoolroom," Philo said. "Has views in three directions. Could you tell if the watcher was male or female?"

"Just that it was someone with light hair."

Michael walked to the bunkhouse and slid a padlock out of the iron staple that secured the back door. When the hasp popped free, Michael stepped aside, as if to say, this was Philo's journey, not his.

Philo rested his hand on the rusty old knob, turned it gently, and pulled. The wind caught the door and would have slammed it shut if Michael hadn't grabbed it. He used his body to prop open the door so Philo would have light.

The bunkhouse had one long main room with a wood-burning stove in the corner for heating and cooking. A dingy bathroom was on Philo's right. The curtains hung in tattered strips. A curving aisle, free of furniture and boxes, led from the front door to this rear area. Starting near the front door and working into the room, boxes had been opened at random, things pulled out and stuffed haphazardly back in, as if someone had been searching for a specific item. The last box opened had contained games. They lay on the floor where they'd been left—Scrabble and Boggle, decks of cards, and a leather game set containing chess and checkers, dominos and backgammon . . .

The memories came rushing back—those games, and others, in the hall closet of the house in Bishop. And up on the top shelf of the closet, tucked in a corner, was a black wooden box, simple, yet elegant. *The chess set,* Philo thought. *It was here all along. Derek didn't play chess. KC must have taken it home after my grandparents' estate was settled.*

Philo remembered asking about the box one time. "I'll show you on your fourteenth birthday," his father had said. But he'd died a year before that birthday.

Heather couldn't have known about the chess set. Only Derek knew. That meant Derek had searched for the chess set and taken the photos Heather had left in Gwen's safe, or he'd told Heather about the chess set and she'd rummaged around till she found it. But why was it important?

Bait. One of them must have thought Philo would remember the chess set once he'd seen the photos, that he'd want to recover what was rightfully his. They couldn't have known that Philo's only memory of the set came from that Christmas visit to this place. He felt no sense of ownership. He'd started this journey for different reasons. He'd come because a woman had been killed, and Derek had needed him—or needed to get the coins back.

Well, mission accomplished, except for that gold Double Eagle. And, if it exists, I'm betting it's in the house right now.

Philo was standing by a kidney-shaped dressing table. His mother had sat before it to do her hair each morning.

The trifold mirrors were spotted with age. Photos had once been stuck in the edges of the large central mirror. He opened the middle drawer, pulled out a small stack of photos. His school pictures. He stepped back to the door, where the light was better. He remembered the shirts he was wearing in each one, remembered choosing them with his mother. In the photos he was smiling, happy. It was like being given back his history.

"You were not a bad-looking child, apart from the ears," Michael said, peering over his shoulder. "What happened?"

Philo didn't answer. Under the school photos he'd found some three by fives his mother had taken in the Sierras. The upper one showed a twelve-year-old boy sitting on a large granite boulder next to his father. Sawtooth Glacier was a distant blur lit by the rising sun. Their fishing poles angled out over sapphire water. Their faces, nearly identical profiles, bore contented looks. Words had been unnecessary.

Philo remembered that camping trip. It was his last with his parents. They were dead a few months later.

Michael put a hand on Philo's shoulder, bringing him out of his trance. "I heard something," he whispered. "A door, I think."

Good. The watcher's been drawn outside. My territory. Philo put the photos in his breast pocket and zipped it closed, saying, "I need you to do something for me."

There was a gleam in Michael's eye. This was the fun part. "Name it."

"When you see me engage whoever's been hiding inside, I want you to go into the kitchen, up the back stairs, and find the old schoolroom. The chess set should be there, in one of the cupboards."

"And if it's not?"

"Try the den, the room in my father's photo. Next to the kitchen. You'll recognize the view, even if the decor's been changed."

"And then?"

"Hide the set somewhere safe. We'll play the rest by ear."

"You don't need to know where it is?"

"It's . . . safer if I don't. If something happens to me, see that it gets to Frankie. She'll know what to do with it."

Michael's eyes acknowledged what Philo didn't say—that he was here, in this place, so someone could kill him. Or try. "You think Frankie will stay by the entrance gate?"

"Probably not. Keep an eye out for her, will you?"

"Always." Michael clasped Philo's hand. "Be careful, my friend." With quick glances to left and right, Michael crossed the strip of bare ground and into the trees.

Philo set the hasp in place, looped the padlock over the staple, and closed the door to his past.

39

The dead-end mountain road below me had no traffic. I passed the time in my hiding place by mulling over what I'd learned about the chess set. What part did it play in all this?

The carefully crafted visage of Childeric the First harked back to a time before the game of chess was brought to Europe by the Moors. In the Dark Ages, when writing and learning and recordkeeping were left to silent monks in their abbeys, the tribes at the fringes of the old Roman Empire were constantly at war, facing foes both within and without. Childeric had managed to survive and unite the Frankish tribes long enough to found a dynasty. His son and successor, Clovis, must have been responsible for seeing to it that his father was interred with honor, ceremony, and riches. But why bury a king with a swarm of gold-headed, garnet-winged bees?

I remembered Michael's downloaded images of the two bees recovered from the Seine. They were all that remained of roughly three hundred found with Childeric's grave goods in Tournai. Aside from the crosshatched lines, the bloodred garnets bore no other clues to their origin. They could have been the spoils of war, brought back from one of Childeric's campaigns, or tribute paid by an underlord. Light and easy to transport, they might have been hidden in the lining of a cloak.

What struck me was how small and rich and fine they were. More like a woman's treasure. A dowry. Had the bees, in fact, belonged to Basine, mother of Clovis? Were they *her* grave goods? Michael had said two human skulls were found in the grave, one smaller than the other. Clovis might have buried his parents together. Or not. Basine's death was shrouded in mystery, the evidence long gone.

And the early histories, written by men of the cloth, had more to do with propagating myth and swaying public opinion than with recording fact.

I wondered what had happened to the rest of the bees. If the gold was melted down, as one source reported, where were the garnets?

Garnet crystallizes—or melts—at a higher temperature than gold. If most of the stolen gold was melted down and recovered, was a pile of garnet wings left behind in the foundry? Were they recut and reset into another piece of jewelry? It hardly seemed likely. But the post-theft tales were both contradictory and farfetched. With the trial records destroyed—

A dusty black Cadillac SRX whispered around the bend in the road, slowing as it passed the turnoff to Derek's ranch, but continuing down the road. A few yards farther on, it halted, backed up, and made the turn. Paused a moment by the Malibu, then pulled up to the gate. The tinted driver's-side window came down. A man's arm reached out to punch in the number. Short-sleeved checked shirt. Forearm hairier and more muscular than Derek's. Stubby-fingered hand.

Must be someone visiting the artist's place beyond Derek's house. Maybe the director. Most artists drive less expensive cars.

The man rolled through the open gate. The car window stayed down. Courteous of him. As he drove by me I saw black hair, receding hairline, heavy jaw. Scar crossing his left eyebrow. Thick neck and shoulders. A bull of a man— a sculptor, perhaps. Bringing stone to life could develop those arms and shoulders.

I watched the car disappear over the crest. Stretching, I settled in, keeping an eye on the hill above in case Heather tried to exit. It would help if I knew what kind of car she was driving . . .

A little tan pickup truck, bruised and faded, rounded the corner slowly. A starving-artist's mode of transportation. The driver paused at the unnamed Y-juncture, then made the turn, parking next to the Malibu. A man got out, closed the truck door, didn't lock it. He was about my height, with short, curly brown hair. His khaki-colored pants and long-sleeved work shirt fit a muscular body—the kind of physique derived from military training. He carried himself as if he still wore a uniform. Maybe he was a police officer or firefighter out hiking on his day off.

He checked out the Malibu. Peered in the windows and tested the door handle. It wasn't locked. I'd left the keys in the ignition, ready to go. He eased open the passenger door, checked the glove box. All he'd find would be . . . what? Registration and insurance. In the name of the charter company.

The man didn't look like a thief, but what if he were? I couldn't do anything without revealing myself, and I wasn't ready to do that. Even if he took the Malibu, he'd have to leave his truck behind. Philo or Michael would know how to hot-wire it.

The man straightened, closed the door with a soft click, and turned in a full circle. He took his time. When his back was to me, I shrank down still farther. Seemingly reassured by the quiet, the man reached into the truck and pulled out a backpack, a khaki field vest, and a gun belt. He strapped on the latter, slid his arms into the vest. It was long enough to hide the gun, and had an insignia above the left breast. I couldn't make out words, but it looked like a Fish and Game or Forest Service badge. He picked up a pair of binoculars and slung them around his neck. Then donned a weathered baseball cap. Same insignia.

From the backpack the man took another holstered handgun and a scabbard with a hunting knife. He attached them to his lower legs. A lot of weapons, I thought, unless he was expecting trouble. Maybe he was a government wildlife specialist chasing poachers. But if so, why didn't his truck have a matching insignia? Once he was gone, I'd check to see if he had a state or federal license plate. In the meantime, I'd stay hidden. I had Philo's Beretta, but unless the stranger made a move toward me, I wasn't going to use it.

He left the truck unlocked, put two hands on the top bar of the low fence abutting the gate, and vaulted over as lightly as a gymnast mounting a pommel horse. I'd seen the same move in a documentary of Marine basic training. He set off up the road at a run. As he passed by me, I noted he was clean-shaven. Nice, even features. Square jaw. Nothing memorable, but no one to mess with. And the insignia was a BLM badge. In my years as a government geologist, and in the years since, I'd never met a BLM-er who ran up hills in his or her field boots. Unless there was an emergency. What was this man's hurry? Was he late for an appointment and hadn't counted on the gate being closed? Did he want to finish his business before the storm hit?

His smooth easy gait ate up the ground. He was over the rise before I could blink. I still didn't move. He might stop and watch his back trail. Philo and Michael would. So would I.

I began counting to three hundred, my eyes on the spot he disappeared. At eighty-seven, I saw a flicker of movement off to the right. A woodpecker exploded out of the forest, complaining. I remained as still as the old sandstone beneath me until I sensed the forest return to its normal state. Then I took out my phone to alert Michael that a car and an armed runner were headed his direction.

No signal.

I climbed the sugar pine that had hidden me. Even ten feet up, there was no damn signal.

40

"Hello, Philo," said Heather Dain, as Philo rounded the wall of the bunkhouse. Her figure, clothed in black, seemed to focus all the energy and light in the courtyard. Triumph made her blue eyes glitter for a moment before she lowered her lids. "Glad you could make it."

Philo walked slowly to meet her, his senses alert to signs of danger. She'd changed since the last time he'd seen her, though not in overt ways. Still had the shoulder-length blonde hair, finely sculpted nose and cheekbones, full breasts, small waist, long legs. But, thanks to plastic surgery, her lips were fuller, her chin less pointed, the lines erased from her face.

"I assume Derek's here someplace?" Philo watched her eyes. He'd interrogated enough enemy combatants to recognize a liar's tells in body language, eye movements, gestures, and speech.

"He'll be along shortly. At the moment, it's just the two of us."

She was playing it straight, Philo decided. He smiled. "Will Derek be in for a surprise?"

"What do you mean?" Confusion. Her right hand lifted to touch a large silver spider clinging to the shoulder of her sweater. Philo recognized Navajo craftwork. This was Spider Woman, who spun the world into being. On Heather, the symbol reminded Philo of a black widow.

Philo took a step closer. "I imagine whoever arranged for Gwen's death is waiting in the wings."

She held her ground, but her eyes slid away from his. "I had nothing to do with that."

"You and Derek have been converting your assets to cash." Philo took another step, invading her personal space. "His death wouldn't negate the prenup, but one person could live a long time on the money set aside for two."

"I'm not a killer." Her left hand came up in protest, finger bones and tendons sharp under their covering of skin. Diamond rings caught and refracted the shifting light.

"You mean you wouldn't get your hands dirty. You'd hire it done. And you aren't above trying to lure me back here with my grandmother's chess set."

"Ah, you do remember it." Satisfaction again. "Derek wasn't sure it would work, even with your father's photo of the house to give you a hint."

So Heather had never left Derek. Philo still wasn't sure what their end game was, but they were in it together. And getting Philo here was the key.

"I'd forgotten all about it," he said. "A picture of the house would have worked just as well."

She laughed. "Not for us."

"You mean the chess set has other uses."

Heather lowered her hand, glancing at her wristwatch.

"Is it so valuable that someone would kill for it?" Philo prodded.

She shrugged. "Depends on the someone. It's not always about money, you know. There's obsession."

She can't be talking about Derek. He doesn't play board games.

"And revenge," she added, "something you wouldn't understand."

Philo flashed on a limestone mountain, riddled with caves. Nasrullah's killer was somewhere in the labyrinth, surrounded by his followers. Philo gave the order that brought in the airstrike and blew all the entrances, simultaneously. Guerrilla fighters, some no older than the boy who loved to read, had been entombed alive. No trial. No jury.

Revenge. I know it well. And at night I hear the voices of those lost boys.

"Where's that girl you're traveling with?" said Heather.

Alarm bells went off in Philo's head. "I put her on a plane back to Tucson this morning. She has to work tomorrow."

"But she knew you were coming here?"

"No. I sent her home with Derek's coins—to fulfill my contract."

Philo had expected this to bother Heather, but relief eased the taut lines of her neck. She smiled and said, "Playing by the rules, as always."

Not always, Heather. And not this time. He said, "You don't mind, then, about the coins?"

"They served their purpose."

Was she working *with* Derek or against him? Philo couldn't tell. "And you still have the Double Eagle."

"Not for long." The wind gusted, whipping her hair. She grabbed it and twisted it around her right hand. Dreamcatcher earrings—or were they silver spiderwebs?—danced along her neck. "I'd only be arrested if I tried to sell it."

Truth again, Philo noted. "Ah, a bargaining chip—but for Derek or for someone else?"

She ignored the question. Tilting her head, she tried to read his eyes. "If your job was done, and you didn't care about the chess set, why bother to come here?"

"To see the ranch one last time. I assume you'll be selling the place?"

"That's it? That's the only reason?"

"And to find you. Gabrielle needs you."

"She's not an invalid, Philo."

Anger bubbled up from a pool deep in his gut. He forced himself to cap it. Later, he could vent. But his voice was clipped as he said, "She's lost a daughter. You've lost a sister. Aren't you at least going to help Gabrielle with the funeral arrangements?"

"Don't worry. I'll play the dutiful daughter for a few weeks—help her sell the house and find an assisted-living facility. I'll even help her move in." She looked up. "Sky's going to open any minute. Shall we continue this inside?"

Said the Spider to the Fly.

Behind Heather, Philo saw Michael run lightly and quickly over the concrete drive from the house to the barn. No noise. Just his shadow blending with the darker shadows inside the barn. But he'd been holding something.

Philo smiled. "After you, Auntie Heather."

Heather led Philo through the country-size kitchen. One of Derek's wives had remodeled it perhaps twenty years earlier, judging by the outdated refrigerator and stove. He followed her past the back stairs and into what had once been his grandfather's den.

The stately old furniture, solidly built of oak and leather and meant to last generations, had been replaced by chintz-covered armchairs and sofa in a pattern of pink cabbage roses. Accent pillows with appliquéd roses continued the floral theme. The built-in bookcases had been painted antique white, and cherubs looked down from niches around the room.

"Welcome to my bower," Heather said.

"Not your thing, " Philo said.

"What *is* my thing?"

"Hard-edged. Chrome and glass and steel. Black and white, with red accents." Like you're wearing now, he wanted to say, noting the crimson lipstick and nail polish. "What happened to my grandparents' furniture?"

Heather shrugged. "Derek said Deirdre put it in the north tower when she had her go at the place. It's probably still there. I wouldn't know."

Heather was giving off vibes—whether from nervousness, excitement, or anticipation, he couldn't tell. Her back was to him. She stared out the window, the same one his father had photographed. But now the rolling green hills were obscured by clouds and rain.

Philo sensed Heather was stalling for time. He could simply leave. He'd found her, recovered the chess set and most of the coin collection, said his piece about Gabrielle. But there was still the Double Eagle.

"Do you remember that Christmas visit?" she said, without turning around.

"You, Gwen, and I played hide-and-seek upstairs. Gwen cried when she was It."

"And because she couldn't open the cupboard where you were hiding. She was only three."

"She couldn't open it because you'd put a wooden ruler through the handles to lock me in," Philo said. "And then you left me there."

Heather turned. "I wondered if you'd remember that

part." She ran the tip of a finger over her brow, as if smoothing away lines. "You didn't scream or yell or cry when we left. You just reappeared down here a few minutes later. And you didn't tell on me."

"No."

"I hated you for that." She turned back to the window. "Later, when you were outside riding your bike, I checked the cupboard. I wanted to see how you'd done it. I found the two halves of the ruler in a drawer. They looked like they'd been cut."

"Santa gave me a penknife in my stocking. It had a little saw blade."

"Just my luck."

Philo didn't know what she meant by that. But then, he'd never understood Heather. Philo doubted if even Derek did.

"When you came back from that mishap in Colombia," she said, "and I saw the cuts and burns on your body, your leg in the cast, I was glad you'd been hurt."

"Why?"

"Because you got away that Christmas day, and were too goody-good to tattle . . . And because you didn't think I was beautiful, I suppose."

"You're wrong. I thought you and Gwen were the most beautiful creatures I'd ever seen."

"You still don't get it, Philo. It couldn't be both of us—it had to be me. Just me. At least Derek gave me that . . ."

Philo noticed the use of past tense. Wondered what it meant. Didn't ask. Instead, he said, "If you'll just give me the Double Eagle, I'll be on my way."

Outside, a car pulled into the front drive and parked. A black Cadillac SRX. Derek's kind of car. Philo watched the driver pop a black umbrella before getting out.

"I don't—" Heather began.

But Philo was gone before she finished the sentence.

41

A wet wind swept through the open kitchen door and into the den. Heather ran to the front door and wrenched it open, yelling, "Theo, you *idiot*. I told you to park in back. Now you've spooked him."

Theo Aristides paused midstride. "Who, Derek?"

"Philo."

"Did he take the coins?" The rain cascaded off the lip of the umbrella, soaking Theo's brown pants below the knee and his leather shoes.

Heather ignored the plural. Theo couldn't know, at least not yet, that Philo had recovered the bulk of the coin collection. Later, it wouldn't matter.

"No," she said.

"The chess set?"

"No."

"Then stop worrying. He'll be back." He stepped into the house, left his umbrella open and dripping on the varnished plank floor of the entrance hall. "Now, show me the chess set."

"It's upstairs. This way."

42

I stared down at the entrance gate and pondered my dilemma as rain began to fall on the forest around me. *To wait or not to wait? That was the question.*

Philo had said my job was to block the gate if Heather tried to run before he had a chance to talk with her. Wouldn't I be just as effective if I blocked the castle driveway instead of the entrance gate? Yes. Besides, I hated being this far away from the action.

Decision made, I stowed my binoculars in my daypack and started to rise. Just then, a white car rounded the corner. I eased back into my former position. The white Mustang turned in without pausing and nosed up to the keypad. The driver's window hummed as it slid down. An arm poked out. Derek Dain's long fingers touched the numbers. The gates swung open and he punched the Mustang's gas pedal. Now I really did have to reach Philo.

I crawled out of my hiding place and climbed down to the road. Derek was out of sight. The Malibu keys were still in the ignition. Luckily, I remembered the gate code Philo had used. *Open sesame.*

I didn't want to drive into any traps, so I pulled the Malibu to the side just below the summit. The car stuck out into the road. I hoped no vehicles would come barreling over the crest.

I climbed to our earlier vantage point and lay down. Rain pelted my body. Without tree cover, I was soaked in seconds. I pulled out my phone. Still no signal. *Shit.*

To block the driveway and get to Philo, I'd have to cross that neck of no-man's-land. I'd be vulnerable. But without my information, so was Philo. And Michael.

I had weapons. Philo's Beretta was in my backpack in the car. I felt for the leather thong that held the sheath for my knife, a gift from Michael's Tía Miranda. The sheath hung between my shoulder blades where I could reach it in an emergency. To help counterbalance the knife in front, I'd looped the leather thong through a polished labradorite circle. It looked like I was wearing a necklace. A lethal necklace. I was as ready as I'd ever be.

No humans moved about. I felt as if I were alone with the earth and the storm. The rain was now a wall between me and the house. Wind whipped the trees. A branch cracked and tumbled. The storm offered some protection—my invisibility cloak. I hoofed it to the car, threw it into drive, and crossed the summit.

Once I was free of the trees, the horizontal wind hit with full force, nearly pushing the car off the road. I drove slowly. The wipers couldn't keep up with the onslaught. At the base of the driveway I made a clunky Y-turn, backing up until the Malibu's rear end was even with the gateposts. After sliding out, I found a drift boulder of basalt, and used it to prop open the iron gate. Didn't want the wind to slam it against the car.

I reached back into the car for my backpack. I couldn't see the house, so they couldn't see me. Closing the car door, I ducked into the trees along the perimeter fence. Maybe, if I were lucky, I'd intercept Michael.

43

Philo Dain, crouching halfway up the back stairs, listened to Heather and the stranger. *Theo,* she called him. Now Philo had a face and a name to go with Heather's partner.

Philo knew that all hell was going to break loose in a minute, just as soon as Theo and Heather discovered the chess set was missing from the old schoolroom.

The sound of footsteps came closer, passed his father's old bedroom, the room where Philo had stayed during that Christmas visit and again after his parents' deaths. He remembered the old maple bedroom set, the National Geographic photos tacked to the wall . . . The footsteps continued down the hall, stopped, entered the schoolroom. Philo eased up two steps, staying close to the wall to avoid creaks.

Heather said, *"Shit."*

"What's the matter?" Theo said.

"It's gone."

"Gone?"

"Philo must have taken it. I don't know how or when, but he must have."

Philo heard the flat crack of palm against skin. Heather cried out.

Theo said, "You know what happened to the last person who scammed me? I fed pieces of him to the Great Whites off Monterey."

Ah, so that's *why Heather didn't tell him about the coin collection being en route to Tucson. The party would be over before it started.*

"Fuck you, Theo."

"Skip the drama. Just help me find your nephew."

"He's out there, somewhere. In the rain."

"Then we'll just have to find a way to bring him back . . . Who's that?"

"Must be Derek."

Philo heard the swish of tires circling the front drive. He moved, softly, silently, quickly. By the time the Mustang passed the open kitchen door, he was down the stairs and searching for another hiding place.

Then he remembered Frankie. She'd have seen Derek down at the gate. She'd have tried to call Philo, to warn him. And when she didn't reach him, she'd head for the house.

Michael. Michael will be watching for her. Michael will keep her away.

In the corner of the den, a round pedestal table was draped with a pale pink quilt crowded with appliquéd roses. The cloth, anchored by a brass table lamp, brushed the floor. Philo ducked under the quilt, sat cross-legged behind the pedestal, and put his back to the wall. Taking out his pocketknife, he cut the center out of one of the roses, finishing just as Derek walked into the kitchen and called, "Heather?"

"Be right down," she said.

44

I moved through the trees, skirting the fence line on one side, the outbuildings on the other. Rain drummed on the barn roof, pattered on dirt and gravel, swished down branches. A wild rain, washing the world clean . . . and probably closing the road.

I thought about being stranded on this hilltop. Found I didn't care. Derek could hardly refuse to offer us shelter till the road was cleared. We'd recovered his coins—all but the gold Double Eagle. He should be grateful.

Then why hadn't I revealed myself when Derek paused at the entrance gate? Why had my instincts been to stay hidden?

Because I didn't trust Derek any more than Philo did. Derek shouldn't be here. He should be on his way to Mexico or Costa Rica, not detouring to meet Heather at this isolated ranch.

Worry made me increase my pace. I left the trees to peer in a rear window of the barn. Two vehicles. One was Derek's Mustang. Was the other Heather's? Probably. Another window, farther along, showed an empty workshop. No Philo. No Michael.

I slipped back into the trees. Between the barn and the bunkhouse was a wide expanse of nothingness. But a light was now on in the room next to the kitchen. Must be the den. I could see movement inside.

I took out my field glasses. The mist and my breath condensed on them. I tried to dry them with my shirt, but it just moved the water around. My thumb worked a bit better. Through the now-greasy lenses and the gray veil of the rain, I saw a blonde woman and a man. Heather, I presumed, and Derek. Where were Philo and Michael? I'd heard no screams, shouts, or shots, so chances were good that they weren't dead. They must be hiding. But inside or out?

I couldn't call their names. This wasn't a game. I'd have to narrow it down by searching the outbuildings, starting with the old bunkhouse. It was the farthest from the house. Couldn't be seen from the den. But first, I'd find Gwen's Honda. Philo might be waiting in the car until the rain let up.

I zigzagged through the windbreak trees, stopping now and then in a dry patch to listen and look over the terrain. In the southwest, thunder rumbled. The wind and rain covered all other sound.

I finished my circuit at the bunkhouse. The Honda was snuggled in a space between the building and the trees. The car was empty. Philo had left the keys on the floor.

I ran from the car to the side of the bunkhouse, following the wall around to the back. The door was open a crack, the padlock dangling from the rusty staple. *Philo or Michael?* Philo should be closer to the action in the house. But Michael might have holed up in this dry spot to keep an eye on the car.

Opening the door I called, "Michael?" softly. No answer. I wedged the door open with a rock to allow a rectangle of daylight into the building. Rain spattered the footprints on the dusty floor. Two sets—Philo's running shoes and Michael's boots. The boots stayed by the door. The running shoes followed an aisle between cardboard cartons, stopping halfway to the front door. I saw games on the floor, packing paper scattered about. My mind made the leap to the chess set, just as Philo's must have done.

The return tracks paused at a woman's dressing table. It had an eyelet curtain tacked to the edge, scalloped border touching the floor. The material was yellowed with age. Were these his parents' things or his grandparents'? Or were they castoffs from Derek's failed marriages?

Only one way to find out. I stepped inside. "Michael?" I called again, a little louder.

Again no answer. I made my way down the dusty aisle to the front door. Windows with open muslin curtains framed the door and let in muted light. I peered through the window on my right. Saw rain sheeting down, and beyond, the curved stone wall of the north tower. Two stories. No, three. The conical roof, gently angled, had at least one window.

The front door of the bunkhouse had an old-fashioned deadbolt for security. The outside would be keyed, but here, inside, there was a small knob. I turned it, just to see if it was frozen shut. It slid smoothly back with a click. My mind eased. I avoided places with only one entrance.

I relocked the deadbolt and retraced my steps, stopping, as the tracks had done, at the dressing table. I opened drawers. Makeup, travel bottles of shampoo, spare combs and brushes and hair bands, a letter addressed to Ann Dain. It was from Gabrielle. Derek and Margaret hadn't bothered to clean out the furniture. They must have been in a hurry to empty Philo's parents' home.

Arms came around me from behind. A hand covered my mouth. I could barely breathe.

A man's voice whispered in my ear, "Who's Michael?"

45

Philo wanted to sneeze in the worst way. Dust bunnies the size of hamsters had collected under the table. He pressed his left index finger under his nose. His right hand held the Glock.

He could see little of his grandfather's den through the hole he'd made in the table cover. But two pairs of shoes faced each other—Heather's black slingbacks and Derek's loafers. "Where's Aristides?" said Derek. "His car's out front."

Aristides. Philo now had the last name of the man who'd set Gwen's death in motion.

"He's checking to make sure no one's hiding upstairs," Heather said.

Philo heard footsteps overhead, doors opening and closing, sounds moving away.

"I thought he was sending his man?" Derek said.

"He was. I didn't have a chance to ask him about it. Philo was here."

"Was?"

"He ran out when Theo arrived." Heather's feet shifted nervously. "Ummm, Philo's got the chess set—"

"He *what?*"

"It's gone. Theo and I just checked. Philo must have come in last night, or while I was in the shower this morning." Heather paused. "He didn't mention finding the chess set, but he told me he found the coins at Mother's house—sent them back to Tucson with his girlfriend this morning."

"Including the Double Eagle?"

"No. That's here. You're almost standing on it."

Philo saw Derek's shoe twitch the edge of the Kirman rug under the little writing desk. The desk stood by the front window, where his grandparents' game table had been . . . the game table he now sat under, he realized, recognizing the carved lion's feet with their brass claws.

Philo rested his forehead against the smooth turned wood of the pedestal. Fragments of memory seemed to flow from the wood into his mind . . . The table wasn't round at all. It was an enchanted table, with thick leaves that folded down like a flower to reveal the edges of a square chessboard. Sliding bolts locked the four leaves in place. He'd found the bolts that Christmas day when he was playing with a toy dump truck at his grandmother's feet. He'd asked about them.

"Can you keep a confidence?" she'd said. She'd pronounced it *con-fee-DONS*, but he'd known what she meant. A secret. He'd nodded.

"You have to say it," she'd said, her green eyes serious.

"Yes, Grandmama, I can keep a secret."

"I trust you."

Powerful words. They'd made Philo feel important.

"Your Grandpapa Kenneth made the table for me. He's very good with wood."

His grandmother had shown him how to slide the bolts back and drop the leaves. Then she'd pressed on one side of the thick chessboard. A drawer slid out. The drawer was lined with red felt. A lumpy square of blue velvet lay across the bottom. On it was a faded envelope, with writing on it. Just two words. Philo remembered feeling a sense of disappointment. He'd expected a magic drawer to have treasure in it, or at least a model car or two.

"Only you and I and your Grandpapa Kenneth know the secret, Philo," his grandmother said, as he helped her close the drawer and lift the leaves. "I couldn't tell your father without telling your Uncle Derek. He . . . well, someday you'll understand. And when you're older, I'll read you the letter."

But that had been their last time together.

Philo lifted his forehead away from the pedestal and looked up. He touched the sliding bolts. *Derek stole that "someday."*

At that moment Philo hated his uncle with a rage so visceral that it set the blood pounding in his ears, deafening him. He lifted the Glock. His finger tightened on the trigger . . .

He took a couple of deep breaths to calm his pulse. The red tide receded. Footsteps sounded on the front stairs, followed by the hollow sound of metal brushing the foyer floor. Aristides, picking up his umbrella. The front door opened and Philo heard the drum of rain and wind, louder now. Then the door closed firmly, authoritatively. Aristides was a man on a mission. He hadn't uttered a word to the two in the den.

Philo lowered the Glock. It wouldn't be long before Aristides returned. Philo hoped Frankie had stayed in position by the road and that Michael was hidden away. Aristides meant business. He was a killer.

Philo settled down to listen. He wanted to know who had conspired with whom. And why. And how he fitted into their plan. He wanted to know everything.

He might, after all, have to kill one of these people. Or more.

46

"Who's Michael?" the stranger repeated softly in my ear.

He'd trapped my arms against my sides and covered my mouth with one hand. I didn't struggle, but every muscle tensed.

"Um-hmmm-um-mmm," I mumbled.

He spread his fingers. "Say again?"

I gulped in air, hesitated, then said, "Michael's an artist—a musician."

"Staying here? At this house?" His voice was a soft baritone.

"No. There's a place down the road." I sucked in another breath. "An artists' retreat. We were out walking and got caught in the rain. Michael was a little ahead. I thought he'd holed up in here." I was trying to give the impression I'd stumbled into this building. Would he buy it?

"I've never intentionally hurt a woman," he said, leaving the rest to my imagination.

When I still didn't move or acknowledge his threat, he said, "If I take my hand away will you scream?"

I shook my head.

He loosened his grip enough to strip away my backpack with one hand. As he tossed the backpack aside, I leaned forward, slumping a bit. I wouldn't have a second chance.

I slammed my right elbow into his solar plexus. When he dropped his arms, I stomped on his right foot. He hissed and hopped backward as I spun around and aimed a kick at his knee. He blocked it, grabbed my left arm, and twisted. Instead of resisting, I leaned into him and slammed the heel of my hand at his nose. He turned his head at the last second. The blow connected with his jaw. He dropped my arm.

I jumped back, and dodged around him. Tried to snatch the gun from his holster. Missed. He stuck out his foot. I pitched forward, landing half inside, half out, my hands breaking the fall.

The stranger yanked me up, and held me by both wrists. Blood oozed from cuts on my palms. I struggled to breathe.

"Who *are* you?" said the man in the BLM uniform. His tone was raspy as a steel file.

I stood with my weight evenly distributed on both feet, eyes fixed on his. I didn't answer.

"Why are you here?"

I silently contemplated my options. There weren't any. He still had his guns and knife. He'd handled my limited martial arts moves easily enough. He'd give me no more opportunities to surprise him.

"Well?" he said.

If he wanted to kill me, he wouldn't be talking. I switched tacks. "Who are *you?*" I said. "And why are you here?"

He nodded, thinking it over.

I saw movement behind him. Michael. My eyes must have warned him because he released my hands, spun around and dropped to a crouch, gun pointed out the door. But Michael wasn't outside. He'd slipped into the room. His camouflage vest and black clothes blended with the shadows. He kicked the stranger's hand. The gun flew outside, into the rain. The gun had a honking big silencer on it.

Michael's knife blade, thin and wickedly sharp, pressed into the flesh of the man's neck just over the carotid artery. The slightest movement, and the stranger would be dead.

He looked at me. I'd pulled my own stiletto from its sheath. I pointed it at his heart. Twin blades. I could tell from his eyes that he didn't doubt I'd use mine.

"You couldn't have come in a few minutes earlier?" I said to Michael.

"I wanted to see how you handled it. You stole those moves from a Sandra Bullock movie."

"*Miss Congeniality.*" I smiled. Michael chuckled softly. The stranger didn't look amused.

"He's fast," I said.

"I noticed."

"And he's got a backup gun and a hunting knife strapped to his shins."

The stranger's eyes held mine. "You were hidden near the gate?" I nodded. "My mistake," he said.

"Answer the lady's question, *por favor,*" Michael said. "Who are you, and why are you here?"

"You're Michael, the artist?" the man said.

"Most certainly." The knife didn't move.

"My mother called me Rico."

"Why are you here?" I repeated.

"To kill a man."

I said, "He's honest, anyway."

Michael nodded. "What man?"

Rico didn't answer. Michael pressed his blade into his flesh. I saw blood trickle down.

"Theo Aristides," said Rico.

"What kind of vehicle does Aristides drive?" I said.

"A black Cadillac SRX."

The puzzle was coming together, albeit with a few missing pieces. I said, "You followed him here."

"Yes."

"Does Aristides play chess?"

"Obsessively, but not well."

"And he collects chess sets?"

"Yes. How did you know?" When I didn't answer, he added, "He's responsible for many deaths."

It was the first information he'd volunteered. We were getting someplace.

"I don't doubt it," Michael said.

I bent and picked up something from the floor. "You dropped this," I said, extending my hand. In the palm lay a blue-paper bird, a heron. "You're the Origami Man. You killed Arnulfo Sánchez in Tucson."

"Sánchez tortured and killed a woman." Gingerly, without moving his head, Rico reached for the heron and tucked it into his vest pocket. "Aristides wanted me to kill you, too, I think. He said there were four."

"You turned him down?" Michael said.

"I'm out of the business."

"Yet here you are."

"And your origami bird's all folded and ready," I said.

"One bird. One man. I came here to stop him."

A gust of wind and rain shook the old bunkhouse. Outside, a tree branch cracked and crashed down. Rico grabbed Michael's knife arm, pulled it away from his neck, and head-butted Michael.

"Run!" Michael hissed, as they began to wrestle, dragging each other outside. Either the wind caught the door, or one of them kicked it, because it slammed shut, plunging the bunkhouse into a gloomy half light.

I ran, threading my way between the boxes on the floor. I stumbled over a game. Chinese Checkers. Plastic marbles rolled everywhere. I kicked them out of the way as wind buffeted the building. Thunder boomed. Simultaneous lightning drove out the shadows for a moment. The center of the storm was overhead.

My left hand grasped the doorknob. My right, still holding the knife, reached for the deadbolt. The doorknob turned in my hand. Someone outside pushed against the door. The deadbolt held.

I flattened my body against the door. Just in time. The shadow of a face, framed by two hands, peered into the window on my left.

In my hurry to get away, I'd forgotten my backpack. I dearly wanted that Beretta now. But it lay where Rico had tossed it, beside the back door. I'd have to make do with what I had.

I eased to the right, hugging the door, tightening my grip on the knife. My knuckles touched something smooth and hard—an old hiking stick, leaning against the edge of the doorframe. I transferred the knife to my left hand, grabbed the stick with my right. It was the length and thickness of a Japanese fighting stick and fit my hand perfectly. I now had two weapons.

The shadow disappeared from the window. I pressed my ear to the door. Felt the vibrations of footsteps crossing the porch. Counted to twenty before running back to grab my daypack. I took out the Beretta, slid the knife back into its scabbard, and shrugged into the backpack. I couldn't handle both the walking stick and the gun, so I left the stick. Retracing my steps, I slid the deadbolt and eased the door open an inch . . . two inches. Saw a blurry figure of a man disappearing around the north tower wall, heading toward the front of the house.

That brief glimpse of black hair, thick neck, and powerful shoulders was all I needed. The man in the Cadillac, Theo Aristides, was here—and he was heading toward the front of the house. I had to find Philo, warn him. It meant leaving Michael to deal with Rico, but Michael had faced mano a mano situations before and come through unscathed. I had to trust that he would again.

I went out, closing the door behind me and holding it while I checked the yard from the relative dryness of the porch. The rain was a billowing, eddying curtain, cascading from the eaves. But there was no one in sight. Clutching the gun, I dashed to the house. The tower wall provided a windbreak, but the basalt rock chilled my skin.

Where was Philo? He'd be in the den with Derek and Heather, or somewhere nearby. I was sure of it. But did Philo know Aristides was around? If not, I needed to find Philo, warn him, and even the odds a bit—without getting captured or injured myself.

I knew of two entrances to the house—the kitchen and the front door. I couldn't use either of those. I hadn't seen a door on the back of the house, but there must be at least one, if only in case of fire. There should also be doors in each tower.

Soaking wet and shivering, I followed in Aristides' footsteps, hugging the curving wall. I became aware of the pain in my palms where they'd scraped gravel when I fell. I wiped the scored skin on my pants, clutched the gun again, and went on till I found a door set in the western arc of the tower. Locked with a deadbolt.

I turned around. No sign of Michael or Rico in the yard. As I worked my way back along the wall of the house, I reviewed what Rico had told us in the bunkhouse. Rico admitted killing Sánchez, presumably for Theo Aristides. Aristides had also tried to hire him to kill four others, people Aristides knew—or thought he knew—

would be here today . . . Philo, Heather, and Derek . . . and me.

Rico claimed he'd turned Aristides down. But had he? Could I trust what a man said when he had a knife at his throat and another pointed at his heart? Of course not.

I moved as quickly as I could, but my pace was slowed by caution. I had to peer into windows before I crossed them. Heather and Derek might have left the den. Aristides could be anywhere. Halfway to the den, I found a living room. Lots of couches. The large chimney had screened my view of the French doors on the far side.

The door handle was simple and long, extending horizontally. It didn't move when I tried it. I put the Beretta in my pocket and slid the tip of my stiletto into the thin crack between the doors. Lifted. Nothing. Pushed against the lock. It didn't budge.

Shooting at the lock would tell everyone where I was. I had to work quietly. I looked at my engagement ring, wishing it had a fat diamond, one large enough to score glass. Garnet is harder than glass, but the stones in my ring were rimmed in soft gold. Nothing to do but smash the pane.

The storm swirled about me as I wrapped the haft of my stiletto in my shirttail. I waited, hand poised to strike. Lightning crackled almost overhead. *One-one thousand* . . . Thunder boomed and I punched the glass. Pieces rained onto the Oriental rug inside the room.

I reached in, fumbled with the handle. It had an inset button lock. I pressed it and turned the handle. Nothing happened. I felt around the inside handle. Found a horizontal bolt. Tugged hard, harder. It was frozen, rough with rust.

I tried jerking the knob on the bolt up and down, hurrying, knowing that someone could come into the living room. I pulled on the bolt again. It gave way. But the wood of the two doors had swollen together. I wanted to kick the door down.

Leaning back, I looked around the chimney toward the bunkhouse. Saw a hand, then a forearm. Someone was coming carefully around the rear corner of the building. It wasn't Michael. Different shirt. Rico's shirt.

Lightning flashed. This time, thunder was three seconds behind it. The storm cell was moving away. Soon I'd lose my covering noise.

I put one foot against the left door, two hands on the handle, and yanked. The door gave way with a grunting sound.

I took out the Beretta and moved quietly into the house. Taking off my shoes, I tiptoed across the thick rug to the closed double doors on the other side. I hoped they'd lead to a hall. I hoped the hall would lead to the den. What I'd do once I got there, I had no idea.

I listened at the doors. Chose one. Turned the handle. Heard a click behind me.

The man called Rico stood just inside the French doors. Blood seeped from a cut on his cheek. He brushed the blood away with his left arm before a drop could fall on the carpet. The gun in his right hand was pointed at the floor.

He was younger than I'd thought. No more than twenty-five or -six. His eyes went to the Beretta held in both my hands. It was pointed at his chest.

"Where's Michael?" My voice, no louder than a whisper, shook with anger. Or fear.

"We decided it was pointless to kill or hurt each other. We're on the same side."

"Are we?"

"We both want to stop Theo Aristides."

The Beretta felt heavy. My hands began to shake, as if I had palsy. "Then why isn't Michael with you?"

47

No more than five minutes passed before Philo heard shoes scrape on the front porch. The opening door let in a gust of wind and rain and smells of grassy hills and damp earth. He heard the umbrella bounce, rock, and settle in the hall. Aristides was back. Philo lifted the Glock again.

Brown driving mocs joined the two pairs of shoes beyond Philo's peephole. "No sign of your nephew," Aristides said. "But his car's parked beside one of the outbuildings. He's around somewhere."

"Did you check the barn?" Heather said.

"Yeah. It was empty. But I know how to draw him out. And when he comes, the odds will be in my favor."

Philo expected Derek and Heather to ask for details, but Theo's statement was met with silence. Philo guessed that they wanted to maintain at least a verbal distance from Theo's plan in case someone stumbled on the scene before they could get away. Someone like Robbie Henderson, the manager. Philo could almost hear Heather saying, "How could we have stopped what we didn't know was going to happen?"

Plausible deniability. The concept rarely worked in practice.

The tension in the room grew until finally Derek broke the stalemate. "So, what do you want us to do?"

"Well, you could start by paying me to kill your nephew."

"Hold on," Derek said. His tone was hard and brittle as flint. "We agreed we'd pay the first half before, second half after."

There went the plausible deniability.

"I'm not a moron, Dain. I remember our agreement—

chess set first, coins later. But since you don't have the chess set at the moment, I'll take the coins."

Derek and Heather said nothing. Philo could imagine the what-do-we-do-now? looks they must be exchanging. Or maybe they were carefully avoiding each other's eyes.

Theo took a noiseless step toward them and said, "What the fuck, Heather? You told me you had the coins."

Heather cleared her throat. Philo knew she couldn't tell Aristides that truth—that she'd left the coins in Daly City. She'd be confessing that she tried to double-cross him. And Theo had already warned her what would happen if she did. "They were, um, with the chess set. But we still have the Double Eagle, and it's worth forty times more than the rest of the coins, put together."

"I don't know. Let me think."

Philo felt oddly detached from the negotiation of his death price. His mind was stuck on one thought—Derek and Heather had liquidated their holdings and transferred them out of the country. Presumably, Derek had torched the mansion, the one property they couldn't sell. Their plan must be to flee and not come back. *But what does that have to do with me?*

Nothing, as far as he knew. Even if Philo died, Derek wouldn't receive anything from his estate. Though Derek hadn't seen Philo's updated will, he'd received a copy of the predeployment one. So why did Derek and Heather need to kill him? And how did they plan to benefit from his death?

The Dain Trust. The words floated up from his subconscious. He heard Derek's voice again, explaining that the coins were entailed by the trust. So was Foggy Gulch Ranch, hundreds of acres of prime Bay Area real estate. The property must be worth millions. More, if it were subdivided. Derek and KC would have inherited it jointly from their parents. Perhaps that's why Derek hadn't sold it, even after KC and Ann died. He couldn't sell it because Philo, their heir, was co-owner under the Dain Trust.

Philo smiled. What Derek and Heather didn't know was that there was another blood heir to the trust—Nasrullah's son, Azim. And Ziba might someday have a son. Killing Philo wouldn't stop the bloodline.

Had Derek hoped that Philo would die while on active duty? Of course. Derek had almost said as much after Colombia. And his feelings hadn't changed when Philo went off to Afghanistan. Philo thought back to the months he'd been out of touch with Frankie and her family, with Killeen. That coincided with when Derek and Heather had started quietly liquidating their assets. It must have been a shock when Philo had turned up again, healthy and whole.

Derek's solution to any financial obstacle had always been to destroy the obstacle. The only reason Philo had lived to reach adulthood, he realized, was that Derek had had free use of Philo's inheritance—as long as he was a minor. What would have happened if Philo hadn't washed his hands of his uncle, if he'd brought a lawsuit to investigate his uncle's misuse of funds?

A car accident like the one that killed my grandparents. Or a plane crash like the one that killed my parents.

Instead, Derek had left Philo alone until the need to sell this property became a priority. Only then had Derek reverted to his old habits.

The very fact Derek was here, calmly discussing Philo's death price, made it likely that he'd been responsible for all the tragedies in Philo's early life. The only problem would be proving it after all these years.

"Here's what we're gonna do," Theo Aristides said. "You give me the Double Eagle up front, like you said. I get your nephew in here, and he gives up the chess set and other coins before I kill him."

Philo smiled. Heather and Derek were in a pickle. They believed the coins were en route to Tucson with Frankie, not with Philo. What would they do now?

"Sounds good to me," Heather said. "Well, what are you waiting for, Derek?"

"Nothing." The black loafers stepped toward the desk under the window. Derek went down on one knee. He was reaching for the edge of the rug when Heather said to Aristides, "So, what's your great plan for luring Philo into the house?"

Damp brown pant legs, creased at the knees, moved next to Derek. Metal caught the light for a moment as a plastic envelope changed hands. The Double Eagle.

Aristides said, "My plan? This."

48

Rico hadn't answered my question, so I tried again, in a voice soft as a whisper. "Where's Michael?"

"On his way to the kitchen."

"Why?"

"We don't know where your Philo is, but everyone else is in the den. Michael will give a signal, then create a diversion near the kitchen door," Rico said. "He'll draw their attention while I come in from the hallway."

"While *we* come in from the hallway," I said. "It's a good plan, except that I have no reason to trust you. I have only your word that Michael's not dead or dying right now."

Rico took a step toward me. He was watching my eyes, not the Beretta.

"Don't," I said.

"I'm going to put down my sidearm."

I watched him set the handgun gently on the rug. "Your backup weapon and knife, too, please."

He shrugged and bent down. Seconds later, a smaller handgun and hunting knife joined the first gun on the floor. He held up his empty hands. "Satisfied?"

If I turned my back on him, he could get to all the weapons in a flash. "Go outside and close the door." I waggled the Beretta.

Without taking his eyes off me, Rico did as I asked. He was just closing the door when I heard a shot from the other end of the house.

I lowered my gun, turned, and yanked open the hall door.

49

The gunshot reverberated in the small den. Derek toppled left. Heather screamed. Theo Aristides slapped her and said, "Your turn."

Philo fired through the quilt, aiming for Theo's knees. Planting his hands on the underside of the table, Philo shoved it up and out, following it with his body. His dilated pupils took a moment to contract. Derek was face-down, in front of the desk. He'd been shot in the right temple.

Aristides had pushed the table to the side, but he still struggled under the folds of the quilt, his movements punctuated by muffled yells and curses.

"Go ahead, finish him," Heather said. "Or I will." Her face bore the marks of Theo's fingers. She stared at Philo, mouth a thin, angry line. She was holding a SIG-Sauer. Aristides must have dropped it as he fell.

Philo stepped to the side, grabbed her wrist, and twisted. The SIG fell to the floor next to the Double Eagle, its plastic case splattered with Derek's blood. Philo kicked the SIG out of the way. Taking out a handkerchief, he retrieved the gun with his left hand and pocketed it.

Keeping his eyes and the Glock on Heather, Philo patted down Aristides, looking for other weapons. He'd stopped moving and cursing. He was either dead or unconscious. Blood stained the pink quilt. And the stain was growing. The bullet must have nicked an artery.

Philo lifted the quilt from Aristides' face. His eyes were closed, his skin pale.

A noise in the corridor. Philo turned, ready to fire.

Frankie stood in the doorway, holding Philo's Beretta. Behind her was a man, a stranger. He held a Browning Pro-9, with a silencer.

50

I looked at Philo, at the Glock in his hand, the two bodies on the floor. One was Derek Dain. The other, the man from the black Caddy.

"Did you . . ." I couldn't finish the question.

Philo smiled grimly. "Only this one." He tilted his head toward the man half under the quilt. "His name's Theo Aristides."

"I know," I said, as something moved in the shadows beyond the kitchen doorway. Michael. "You're late," I said.

Michael shrugged and said, "Aristides killed Derek?"

"Yes." Philo leaned forward, put his left hand on the dark center of the bloodstain, and pressed. "He's in bad shape."

"Let me help." I slid the Beretta into my pocket and knelt on the other side of Theo's motionless form. I took over from Philo, using two hands to apply pressure.

Philo took in the bloody faces, arms, and clothes of Michael and Rico, and then looked back to me, waiting for an explanation. Michael grinned and disappeared into the kitchen. I heard water running. Rico's gun was pointed at Heather. "BLM to save the day?" Philo prompted.

"Not exactly," I said. "His name's Rico."

"Rico?" said Heather Dain.

She'd been standing like a statue in a corner of the room. Now she stepped close to the desk. His name must mean something to her.

When Philo made no move to lower his Glock, I added, "He's the Origami Man."

"That's supposed to reassure me?" he said.

"He's here to prevent Theo Aristides from killing four people. I presume that included us."

"And me," said Heather. "The double-crossing son of a bitch." Absently rubbing her wrist, she stared at the blood-stained quilt that had hidden Philo and now covered Theo. Her face reflected the efforts of her mind to find a way out.

"It's no use, Heather. I heard everything," Philo said. "I'm sure the police will be interested."

Without comment she leaned down, snatched the Double Eagle from the rug, grabbed an oversized leather purse from an armchair in the corner, and ran toward the kitchen.

"Want me to go after her?" Rico said, holstering his gun.

"I'll go," I said.

Philo finally lowered the Glock. "Don't bother, Frankie," he said. "The police will catch her."

"Yes, well, the Malibu's blocking the ranch gate, and I don't want to have to explain to the sheriff why I planned ahead to stop anyone leaving."

Philo nodded. "And I can't claim to have stumbled onto a murder in progress if I anticipated problems might take place."

A car engine started up in the distance. "There she goes," I said. "Rico, would you . . . ?"

Rico knelt and took over the pressure on Theo's wound. I jumped to my feet and headed for the back door, thinking, as I ran, how ironic it was that Rico was now trying to save the life of the man he came to kill.

Heather drove by the door, going fast. I saw Michael at the kitchen sink, washing blood off his shirtfront. "She won't get far," he said. "I punctured her oil pan."

"Good job," I said, but didn't stop.

"Wait," Michael called, "your shoes."

I stopped, looked down. My shoes were back in the living room. There wasn't time to get them. I ran in my socks.

Outside, the rain had slowed to a fine drizzle, and blue sky showed through patchy clouds. But runoff made the concrete drive slippery.

Michael caught up with me and matched me stride for stride. He'd washed his face and hands, but both were beginning to show bruises. His wet shirt clung to his torso. "Why are we—"

"You'll see."

We rounded a curve in the drive and saw Heather parked behind the Malibu. She was thinking clearly enough to realize that she couldn't ram the Malibu or the rental car's airbags would deploy. She did the next best thing, at least for her. She put the car into Low and stepped gently on the gas. Bumpers crunched and buckled. The Malibu lurched forward—one foot . . . two . . .

Michael and I reached her car. While he pounded on the driver's window, I ran for the Malibu and wrenched the door open. The car leaped forward. Sheetwash had reduced the friction on the driveway. The Malibu skidded clear of the gate.

Michael had given up pounding on the window. He had his knife out. I saw him lean down and puncture the treads of her left rear tire. He ran around the back of the car as Heather gave the Malibu enough of a nudge to move it out of the way. I jumped back just in time to avoid having my feet flattened. Her grinning face turned toward me as she swept by.

Michael was smiling, too. "Given the slashed tire, no oil, and the trees that are no doubt blocking the road, we should have no trouble catching—"

The ground jumped and he stumbled into me. We both went down. "What the hell?" he said.

"Earthquake." I could feel the earth thrum under my hands and chest. Was this an isolated temblor or another foreshock?

We watched Heather drive rapidly along the paved road. As she approached the point where the dirt track to the sculpture grove met the main road, the ground trembled again. This shock was longer and stronger than the first. I could see the waves undulating across the hillside. Trees swayed. Heather braked. The car slewed to the right, the flat tire losing purchase on the slick road. She fishtailed, overcorrected. The car disappeared over the edge of the steep slope.

51

The first shock hit as Philo picked up the phone to dial 911. He stumbled back, pulling the phone from the desk. It bounced off Derek's back and landed on the floor.

Philo calmly retrieved the phone and tried again. The emergency lines were jammed. He said, "How are you at field dressing, Rico?"

"Lots of practice in Iraq. You?"

"Afghanistan—and assorted postings before that."

Aristides shifted under Rico's hands. "Richard?" Theo's voice was little more than a thread of sound. A frown creased his forehead, pale as wood putty. "What are you doing here?"

"Trying to save your life."

"Rico called you?"

"What did they do, that you wanted them dead?" Rico spoke with a soft, Spanish accent.

"What di—" Theo's moan was half frustration, half pain. "Fuck me."

"I came to stop you. Someone had to."

"Then you failed. I got Derek Dain." Theo's smile faded. He was silent for maybe five seconds. "Your last move—bishop to g2—again you left the center open. Why?"

"To warn you to watch your flanks."

Aristides sighed. "I wasn't smart enough to get it . . . I'll miss our chess games."

"No you won't."

Aristides seemed not to hear him. His eyes closed. "I feel so cold," he said.

Philo dropped the phone and felt for the pulse at Theo's neck. Nothing. He grabbed a framed photo of Heather from the desk and held it to Theo's lips. The glass didn't fog. Philo listened to Theo's chest, then sat back on his heels and looked at Rico.

"Nothing you could do," Rico said. "He lost too much blood."

"Aristides called you 'Richard.'" Philo waited, not sure Rico would answer.

"I was his personal trainer . . . and the Origami Man, like your Frankie said."

"Why?"

"Because there are some evils no one should fight alone." Rico took an origami bird from his vest pocket, looked at Aristides' body and said, "I promised my mother I'd retire today, after I stopped him." He carefully unfolded the blue heron, saying, "I won't be needing this now."

Philo watched him tear the paper into tiny pieces and tuck them into his pocket. Just then, the main shock hit. The old house rocked and creaked. The men ran to the kitchen table and dove under.

"I'd prefer not to be here when the police come," Rico said.

"Fine. This is my mess to clean up."

Rico thought for a moment. "Heather Dain might be a problem."

Philo shrugged. "That's out of our control."

The waves receded and they crawled out. Philo hoped Frankie and Michael had fared as well. But he wasn't worried—being outside had advantages.

"Before you go," Philo said, "just what was Theo Aristides' relationship to my uncle?"

"They were partners in a development down near Monterey. When the economy tanked, Dain left Theo to fend for himself . . . And Theo and your aunt were, you know."

"I guessed."

"Anyway, it made for bad blood."

"I understand. Thanks." Philo held out his hand. Rico took it. Both hands were still covered in blood.

"I don't suppose you play chess?" Rico said.

Philo smiled. "My father taught me. My grandmother was very good."

Rico glanced at the bodies on the floor. "I'd call their game a draw."

Philo righted the game table that had been lying on its edge. His hand smoothed the marble squares at the center. "I'd call it justice."

Rico hesitated, then said, "If the roads are blocked—trees or slides—I'll see what I can do to clear them. In my official capacity, of course." He pointed to the badge on his sleeve. "I'm betting they won't turn down free government help."

Just as Rico took a step, an aftershock hit.

52

A car horn blared in the distance. Probably Heather, I thought, signaling for help.

"She'll never make it back up that hill," I said to Michael.

We ran the half mile to the intersection. Just as we reached it the ground shook again, less forcefully this time. We hit the dirt anyway and waited for the earth to settle down. I heard a roaring, as if a freight train were bearing down. Behind us, the end of the jutting ridge broke away and slid into the canyon, carrying the wooden π-sculpture with it.

Air and ground reverberated with the shock waves of the landslide. Michael and I lay flat, not knowing if more of the hill would go, not knowing which way to run. He was swearing or praying in Spanish too rapid for me to follow. The car horn went silent.

I looked over my shoulder at Philo's grandparents' castle on the hilltop. The tower walls were of basalt. Philo's grandfather had built with care. The house seemed intact—though, from this distance, I couldn't tell how much structural damage it had sustained. But were Philo and Rico okay? Had Aristides survived the shocks? And what about the ranch manager's house at the bottom of the canyon?

"If you promise not to think about Philo, I promise not to think about Alana," Michael said.

"Right. First things first. Heather."

When we agreed it was safe to stand, we walked far enough to look over the steep hillside down which Heather and her car had disappeared. A mist had enveloped the glen. I called Heather's name. The mist swallowed the sound. She didn't reply.

"After you," said Michael. His clothes were covered with grass stains, as if he'd just fought the Green Knight.

We slipped and slid down the drenched hillside, entering that gray mist. Heather had made it through the open gate of the fence and into the sculpture grove I remembered from that long-ago field trip. But she'd hit the base of the closest monolith, a vast concrete slab that once must have stood on the point of an acute angle. The oak tree that had supported the sculpture had toppled. The pale-gray monolith had fallen lengthwise across the car. Heather's hand and wrist jutted through the space where the driver's window had been. I felt for a pulse. Not a flicker.

Michael picked up something from the leaf litter and glass below that white hand. The Double Eagle, still in its plastic sheath. *"Quien mal anda, mal acaba,"* he said softly.

"He who walks badly, ends badly?"

"Exactly."

Return

[T]he hero re-emerges from the kingdom of dread . . .
The boon that he brings restores the world . . .

—Joseph Campbell, *The Hero with a Thousand Faces* (1949)

53

The next twelve hours were an endurance test.

Michael and I met Philo and Rico as we finished scrambling up the slippery slope down which Heather's car had plunged. They'd come looking for us, worried that we might have been injured in the quake. Philo said, "Heather?"

I pointed to the car tracks that led down into the mist and described what had happened.

Philo shook his head, his face bleak. "Shitty way to go."

"Poor Gabrielle," I said, wrapping an arm around Philo's waist.

He took a deep breath and called Gabrielle with the news—an accident during the quake, was how he put it. He gave her an abbreviated version of the Aristides/Derek shootings. If Gabrielle read between the lines, she didn't let on. And instead of breaking down, she told Philo not to worry about her. She was in good hands with Bea.

"There will be funeral arrangements to make for both Gwen and Heather," Philo said. "I'll be there—I won't leave you, Gabrielle."

"I know, *chéri. Merci.* Your grandparents and parents would be proud of you. Call me when you can."

Philo's eyelashes were wet when he ended the call. He handed the cell to Michael so that he could check on Alana, then wrapped his arms around me. We stood like that, not talking. Words and images swirled in my brain. Too many words, too many images—most involving death.

From the corner of my eye I saw Rico nod and turn away. He broke into the fast, smooth jog I'd seen before. In moments he'd reached the point where the road emerged from the woods. He stopped there and tossed a dark tube—his silencer?—into the thick undergrowth. Turning, Rico lifted his hand in farewell before disappearing over the crest.

Michael was smiling when he handed back the phone. "Alana and her castle are fine, except for cracks in the garden wall, books and art supplies littering the floor, and a power outage." He dug something out of his pants pocket and held it out to Philo. The Double Eagle.

Philo let me go and took the coin in its blood-spattered plastic envelope. "Such a little thing to cause so much death. I'll be glad to see the end of it." He gave it back to Michael. "Once the power's back on at Alana's, would you ask her to lock it away till I get there, please? Or, if she doesn't want to touch it, you're welcome to toss it into the ocean."

"I will give her the choice. You wish me to take the chess set, too?"

"And the table. I don't want them here when the police arrive."

He nodded. "Honda or Malibu?"

"Malibu. That way, I won't have to explain the damage to the rear bumper."

We all understood, without saying it, that Philo would have a ton of explaining to do as it was. And there was an even chance he might be arrested.

"Do you want to go with Michael?" Philo said to me. "I can cover for you."

"I'm sticking to you like cactus spines, remember? Besides, if they arrest you, someone's got to drive the Honda back."

"And bail him out," said Michael.

"That, too."

"Then, thanks," Philo said. "I'd like the company."

We turned back toward the house, but detoured to a point overlooking the canyon. Philo wanted to check on the Hendersons, down at the ranch manager's house. He'd tried to reach them but couldn't get through.

From the point we had a clear view of the damage below us. A lobe of the landslide had come within two hundred feet of the barn, but a low ridge had protected it.

The ranch house and other outbuildings appeared to be okay. The main road, however, lay under tons of rock and mud.

We spotted four figures moving in the ranch yard. All the Hendersons were accounted for. Philo raised his arms to try and get Robbie's attention, but I stopped him. "Let's wait till Michael's back at the house. One more thing you don't want to explain, even to Robbie."

Michael had been sitting on the grass, cleaning his knife. He slid it back in its scabbard, stood, and said, "Good plan. While you finish here, I will remove the chess set from the Honda, disassemble the game table, and stow everything in the Malibu."

While we waited for Michael to get out of sight, Philo called Killeen. After giving him the bare details, Philo ask him to get through to the sheriff's office via whatever channels he could. I fished my Brunton compass from my daypack, which still clung to my back like a limpet. When Philo disconnected from Killeen, I offered him the mirror to get Robbie's attention. It worked, and we gave him thumbs up to let him know we were okay.

"He'll be up here to look at the main house as soon as he checks out everything down below," Philo said, as we turned back to the house.

"How much time does that give us?"

"Hard to tell, but at least an hour, I'd say."

I called my parents as we walked, then logged onto the USGS seismic Web site. The quake had been on the San Gregorio fault, eleven miles west of us. The San Gregorio was the southern extension of the Seal Cove fault, which ran near Alana's house. Neither had ruptured in historic time. This had been a magnitude 5.9—not large, but the epicenter was shallow. Highway 1 was closed at Devils Slide and other points north of Monterey. Luckily, the quake hadn't generated any tsunamis near Half Moon Bay or Moss Landing, low-lying areas that would have suffered from a seismic sea wave.

Killeen called back to say he'd reached local authorities. They didn't know how soon they'd get here. There were live people to save. Dead ones could wait.

Back at the house kitchen, I started to make coffee, but

the water lines were down. That meant the bathrooms were out of order, too. I tried the lights. Nada. Philo found a wrench and shut off the water and gas. We were marooned on an island with three bodies.

The good news about the lag time was that we could do damage control and get our stories straight. Philo, Michael, and I held our powwow by the Malibu. Philo told us the whole story and decided to stick to the truth as closely as he could without mentioning Michael and Rico.

Decision made, I added the Beretta and my knife to the pile in the trunk and said, "Wait. Shouldn't Michael take the quilt, too? You can explain shooting Aristides from a crouch—after he'd just shot your uncle—but that quilt has gunshot residue on it. The law might take a dim view of firing from a blind."

"I knew there was a reason I hired you," Philo said.

"Only one?"

"I'll count the ways later, after I deal with this mess," he said, and ran back to get the quilt.

When he returned a minute later, Michael stuffed the quilt in the trunk, saying, "I'll burn it when I get to Alana's."

I grabbed my handbag from under the seat, kissed his cheek, and watched him drive off, feeling deflated. Philo focused on business. There was no longer any reason to sequester Margaret. But he wanted a word with her before Cinna drove her home.

Although I heard only one side of the conversation, I gathered that Margaret took the news of Derek's death philosophically. She was more concerned with whether or not she'd still receive alimony payments on time. She didn't break down until Philo asked whether Derek had been involved in his parents' and grandparents' deaths. He spent the next five minutes trying to quiet her. What came out, eventually, was that Margaret had begun to suspect Derek after the second accident. He'd been away from Tucson on both occasions.

"If Derek knew you suspected him, why didn't he take care of you, too?" Philo said.

I stepped close enough to hear Margaret's response.

"Because my lawyer has an envelope, to be opened if I die from anything other than natural causes. Derek was willing to pay alimony to keep that letter from coming out. Even if I couldn't prove anything, the allegations would have ruined him."

Philo ended the call and looked off across the wrinkled hills toward the ocean. The clean wind flattened the clothes against our bodies. Mine were still damp. When I shivered, he put his arms around me, saying, "Margaret started drinking heavily a month after I moved in with them. It was the beginning of the end of their marriage . . . Funny, I always thought *I* was the trigger. But drinking was Margaret's way of coping with the knowledge that her husband was a murderer."

"Judging by what's happened the last few days," I said, "Derek and Heather were a better match, anyway."

"A match made in hell."

Hand in hand, we walked up the drive. When we reached the kitchen door, I said, "I'll see if I can find a table to fit where the game table was."

"You might retrieve your shoes from wherever you left them."

I looked down. My shredded socks revealed feet as bare and filthy as my scraped hands. They told a story all by themselves. "They're in the living room," I said, removing the remnants of cotton from my feet.

"That's where you broke in?"

"Seemed a better choice than ringing the front doorbell. You had Margaret's key."

Surprise touched Philo's eyes. He'd forgotten all about it. "I'll stash it in the car," he said. "Better than trying to explain why we broke in when we had a key."

"Good thinking. And if you could find a first-aid kit somewhere, I'd appreciate your help cleaning my cuts. I fell getting away from Rico."

He took my hands gently, turned them palm up, and examined the damage. "My new hire definitely got her feet wet today," he said, kissing each palm, dirt and all.

"I think I deserve a raise."

"What am I paying you now?"

"We said we'd settle it later. At this moment, I'd go for clean socks, bandaged hands, and food."

"I can do that."

"You're a prince among men, Philo Dain."

When I was patched up and wearing socks and shoes, I searched for and found a pedestal table in the north tower. The table matched the dimensions and style of the game table, and I wondered if Kenneth Dain had used this one as the model for the piece he built for Claudine. Philo accompanied me back to the tower, which was stuffed to the gills with old furniture. Derek hadn't gotten rid of anything. Because Philo was part owner? Odd that Derek would have had this one scruple.

Philo carried the table down so that my fingerprints wouldn't be on it. I watched from the kitchen while he installed it in the corner and placed the lamp on top.

Other than the tower, I didn't explore the house. There would be time enough to do that later. I was afraid I'd leave tracks where they shouldn't be.

Robbie Henderson still hadn't arrived by the time we'd done as much as we could to support our stories, including relocking the bunkhouse and blurring any tracks inside and out. Though it meant leaving the crime scene, we decided on a quick trip down to the ranch house via the steep, muddy fenceline track. Our excuse was that we were two people who'd just witnessed a horrible event. We needed support. And hot food. And coffee—lots of coffee.

Robbie Henderson turned out to be a droll Scotsman who hadn't lost his burr, though he'd been in the States for thirty years. He shook his head over the news, grabbed the keys to the ranch Hummer, and drove us back up to the main house. Lorraine would make us a hot meal as soon as he could get the backup generator running.

The Hummer went up the muddy track without problem. Robbie took a quick look in the den and then went off to check Heather's crash scene. Philo went with him in the Hummer, obliterating any traces Michael and I had left. I waited at the bottom of the driveway. I'd already seen the site. Once was enough.

A car went by from the direction of the artists' retreat down the road. A man and a woman. I stopped them and asked if they had power. No, they replied, but we can always grill outside. They were on a wine run, and hoped the roads were open.

Robbie, still shaking his head, dropped Philo off beside me. Robbie said, "Philo told me the news—about your engagement. I trust you'll still have him, after this."

Philo took my hand and said, "She's got sand."

I couldn't speak, so I just nodded. It was perhaps the nicest thing he'd ever said to me.

While we were waiting for Robbie to return with food, we sat on the hillside in front of the house. Miles away, waves broke on a bit of shore. The storm had passed and the mist had cleared. The Coast Ranges looked green and deceptively serene in the afternoon light, as if no destruction had recently taken place.

Philo told me about what he'd overheard in the den—details he hadn't shared while Michael was there—and about the memories they'd triggered. I listened and let him talk. He moved on to tell me more about the boy he'd killed, about how he'd used the map the boy had left in a book to locate all the entrances to the caves where the man he hunted was holed up. The man who'd strapped the vest to the boy. The man who'd killed Philo's brother, Nasrullah.

I said, "So you have dreams about Nasrullah, and the boy, and the boys who might have been in that cave?"

"And occasionally about the time in Colombia. But those are fewer these days."

"Will you have nightmares about today, do you think?"

Philo plucked a scarlet pimpernel from the grass and brushed a finger over the tiny coral petals. "I'll sleep like a baby."

Deputies finally arrived at six that evening. Philo and I were questioned several times. So were the Hendersons. Philo's Glock was taken into evidence, but the detectives didn't arrest him on the spot. They reserved the right to question him again once the evidence was collected and analyzed. They took our contact information, but neglected to ask us to stay in the county. A stroke of luck at the end of a disastrous day.

The bodies of Derek and Theo Aristides were removed around ten that night. Before driving down to his house in the canyon, Robbie Henderson volunteered to have the house cleaned once the scene was released. He and Philo could go over other paperwork later, when Philo returned to deal with the remains of Heather and Derek.

When we left the hilltop, power had been restored to the area and all the lights were on in the Dain castle. Crime scene experts were going over both it and Heather's crash site. They were still trying to free her body from its monolithic headstone. The problem was that the necessary equipment had been co-opted to clear slides along all the mountain and shore roads. The director of the artists' retreat stopped us as we drove by the crash site, worried that there would be a lawsuit over the sculpture. Philo assured him no one would sue. We heard later that Heather's remains hadn't been freed till noon the next day. I shed no tears over her. Or Derek or Aristides, either.

Philo and I arrived at Alana's just before 2:00 a.m. She and Michael had cleaned up the quake's mess and everything looked normal. We showered, covered my hands with antibacterial ointment, rebandaged them, and fell into the huge four-poster bed.

Philo was up at his usual dawn time, but I rolled over and lapsed back into dreams of a disturbed, shifting landscape full of angular gray slabs, rocking and sighing as they rubbed against the supporting bloodred madrones.

The smell of waffles and fresh coffee woke me at noon. Philo set a tray on my lap. The plate held four squares of cinnamon–whole wheat waffles covered in a mound of crushed strawberries. "My idea of heaven is breakfast in bed," I said, taking a bite. "I'd marry you just for your cooking."

"I accept," he said, setting a small ceramic pot filled with beach sand next to my coffee mug.

"What's that for?"

"I figured you might have lost some of yours yesterday."

I smiled up at him. "Not so's you'd notice. But I appreciate the gesture."

"Good. Eat quickly. The children are anxious to open their Christmas presents."

I'd forgotten about the chess set. "I'll eat in the other room. Tell them I'll just be a minute."

Philo grinned back as he retrieved the tray. "Thought you'd say that." He stopped and turned at the door. "If you don't mind, I'd prefer not to discuss yesterday in front of Alana—no reason to make her an accessory after the fact."

"Not that I care a fig," Alana said, peering around his arm.

"Did you look at the chess set?" I said.

"Just to check for a smith's mark." She came in and sat on the bed while I pulled on clean pants and T-shirt. I'd brought only a couple of changes with me, but she'd apparently washed them while we were out.

"And?"

"If you'll hurry up, I'll show you. Philo's afraid the detectives might arrive with more questions."

Alana linked her arm through mine and half-dragged me to the kitchen. The ebony case sat, like a boxy black centerpiece, squarely in the middle of the table. My plate of waffles occupied the same placemat I'd used yesterday morning . . . an eon ago. The game table, reassembled, stood between Philo's chair and mine.

I lifted my fork, waved it in the air, and said, "You may proceed."

Instead of opening the box, Philo unbolted the leaves of the game table. They folded down, leaving the chessboard—or, more accurately, game box—sitting alone. The sides were of ebony, matching the box that held the pieces. Philo pressed one side and a drawer slid silently out. We all leaned forward. The drawer, lined with red felt, contained a square blue-velvet pouch and a cream-colored envelope.

I picked up the pouch, which looked as if the faded drawstring cords hadn't been tightened in a long time. But the hummocky surface of the velvet suggested that the material had once conformed to whatever it was designed to carry—perhaps loose gemstones or small pieces of jewelry. But it was empty now.

Philo was holding the envelope. *Claudine Marie* was written across it in script. No address. No last name, unless Marie *was* her family name. I didn't know Claudine's maiden name.

Philo opened the letter, skimmed it, and said to the room in general, "It's in French, of course."

"Mine's schoolgirl French," I said. "But Alana's pretty fluent, and Michael worked for an auction house in Paris."

Philo handed the letter to Alana, who passed it to Michael. He perused it for a moment and then said, "It is dated 1 May, 1940, and appears to have been written by your Grandmama Claudine's father." He read the letter aloud.

My precious Daughter,

When the Germans come, Tournai will be directly in their path. I send you these for safe-keeping. I believe that France is too great to fall, but if it does, please keep these hidden. You were told the story of the grave goods of Childeric I when you were small. All Tournai knows the story. I was waiting for you to finish your studies before telling you the rest, about how some of the treasure made it home to Tournai. In short, it is this:

Your Uncle Philippe, many generations past, was a younger son, without property. He apprenticed himself to a silversmith in Paris and opened a shop there. He was a fine craftsman, with an interest in antiquities. He survived the Revolution only to see the rise and fall of Napoleon.

During Napoleon's time he did restoration work at the Bibliothèque Nationale, helping them repair objects that had been damaged. During the Time of Troubles that followed, he became worried that the bees and signet ring, artifacts from Childeric's grave and therefore linked to the early days of the Frankish kingdom, would be lost. His solution was to steal the bees and ring and hide them till peace once again reigned in France.

Your uncle was apparently a very complex man. He

loved chess, and he loved his adopted country. But perhaps he was not a good man. He stole gold and silver coins from the grave goods, all but forgotten in the vault. When he had enough of the coins, he melted them down and crafted a chess set. The pieces were hollow so that they could contain the bees and the signet ring. Only the king had a visage—the face and bust of Childeric I, copied from the ring.

When the set was made, Philippe began to steal the bees, a few at a time. Only the ring and two bees were left when the thing he feared most came to pass. Thieves broke in and stole the richest of the grave goods. A few items were recovered from the Seine, including two bees—or so the story goes. The records were lost.

Philippe smuggled the chess set, with its precious cargo, home to Tournai. He was an old man, then, and near death. The family agreed to protect the treasure till France was peaceful again.

But France has known little rest in the past century. War is again on the horizon. This time, Tournai will not escape. The treasure is safer with you.

Please, child, guard and protect this with your life, and only share the secret with those in the family who can be trusted.

May God guard and protect you always. I love you,
Papa.

Michael passed the letter back to Philo who folded it and carefully placed it in the envelope.

I looked at Alana. Her blue eyes were bright, excited. "It fits with what I was able to find out," she said. "Please, Philo, open the box."

He swung the brass-colored hook away from its knob and lifted the lid. These were the pieces from the photographs. Alana lifted one of the kings from its velvet bed, and showed us a simple *P. de T.* stamped into the golden base. She handed it to Philo.

"Philippe de Tournai," Alana said, "was, as the letter said, a metalsmith in Paris. He's believed to have been born around 1760. He died in 1833. Not all of his work survived the French Revolution. But he continued to produce fine pieces during the Napoleonic era, including assignments from England. That's why I thought his work looked familiar—though, as far as I know, he made only one other chess set. It was a scale model of this one, out of brass and pewter. It's in the British Museum."

I lifted out the silver king. It was around ten inches tall, tarnished, and heavy. I handed it to Michael and picked up a golden castle—smaller, but equally heavy—and set it on the chessboard. The base just fit within the marble square of the board. The same was true of all the pieces.

We were silent, absorbing the exquisite workmanship of chess set and board. I looked at the rook I held. I shook it and thought I felt the faintest shifting inside its core. I ran my finger carefully along its length. Like the other pieces, even the kings, it had three decorative, incised rings about an inch above the base. I slid my fingernail into the upper one. It was smooth, no breaks. In the middle circle I felt a fine join. I twisted the bottom below the join and unscrewed the golden threads. Inside was a roll of royal blue silk. I paused and looked at Philo.

"Go on," he said. "You found it."

"It's *your* treasure."

"It was never mine or my family's. We were just caretakers."

Michael and Alana got up and came to stand behind my chair. Philo removed my empty plate, coffee cup, and placemat. "Wait," Alana said. She ran upstairs and came down with cloth gloves for all of us and a soft black cloth, which she placed in front of me.

I worked the gloves over my fingers and bandaged palms. "Okay?" I said. Everyone nodded. I pulled out the blue silk, and unrolled it on the black cloth, revealing eleven gold-and-garnet bees.

"Oh, my," said Alana. "I didn't really believe it till now." She went into the living room, returning with the magnifying glass.

I took off the left glove and laid it on the mat. "May I carry one into the garden?" I said to Philo.

He nodded absently. The three of them, wearing gloves,

were unscrewing the bases of all the pieces. Lumpy rolls of blue silk were placed beside each open piece.

The sunlight picked out the fine crosshatching on the garnet wings, and there was a trace of white thread caught around the head . . . from where it had been sewn onto an emperor's robe?

My engagement ring flashed as I turned to go back inside. It had been Claudine Dain's, Philo said, when he put it on my finger. *Garnets and gold.*

Setting the bee back with its mates, I rolled up the silk. Then I slipped off my ring and went back outside. Inside the band I found a faint stamp: *P. de T.*

I stood there, looking out over the nature reserve. The tide was down, exposing the syncline, black against blue. The fault that had moved yesterday ran just beyond the rocks. I felt emotionally jolted, as if the energy of the fractured earth permeated the air I breathed.

Michael and Alana joined me. She was holding the blue velvet pouch. "Two hundred and eighty-eight bees in all," she said. "They would have fit nicely in this, don't you think?"

I smiled. "Mystery solved."

"Not quite," Michael said. "Two bees were recovered in Paris, but at least ten are still missing."

"For all we know, Napoleon lost some off his robe," Alana said.

"Or some of the garnets were broken over the years," I said, handing her Claudine's ring. There was the one large stone, which could have been recut from a bee's wing, and nineteen smaller stones ringing it. Twenty stones in all. Twenty wings. Ten missing bees.

"Dear God," she said, and passed it to Michael.

He repeated her sentiments in Spanish, adding, "There's no way to prove the origin of these garnets now."

"Not without testing them against the bees," I said.

"Wouldn't that damage the stones?" Alana said.

"Possibly. Probably."

"Then I say wear it in good health," said Michael.

Alana said, "Wear it for Claudine."

"It's up to Philo," I said.

He had joined us moments before, but had made no comment. We all looked at him. He was holding something. A gold signet ring.

"Is that what I think it is?" Alana said.

Philo held it up to the light and shook his head. "I found it in the gold king," he said.

I stood and moved close enough to get a good look at the ring. "Surely, it's not the original?"

Smiling, he showed me Philippe's initials, engraved within the band. "No, but it's an exact copy." Taking my left hand, he said, "With this ring—"

I snatched my hand back, saying, "Don't even think it, Philo Dain."

"Then you'll just have to make do with garnets and gold."

Back inside, as we replaced the bees and signet ring in their hiding places, it struck me that Philo's grandparents had created a modern castle to house these treasures, legacy of an ancient king, until such time as they could be rightfully returned to their homeland.

To the world they would be Childeric's bees. But to me, they'd always be a woman's treasure. Basine's dowry.

Epilogue

Before we left the Bay Area, Philo quietly contacted a friend and former colleague, now in the Secret Service. She met him in San Francisco to retrieve the gold Double Eagle and its story, then returned with it to Washington. We never heard of it again, though a document no doubt exists somewhere that records the history of the Dain possession.

We rented a car for the journey home. Philo had asked Killeen to go to my house and retrieve the ginger jar containing KC and Ann's ashes. Justin flew the urn to the Bay Area, and Philo and I picked it up on our way out of town. We crossed the Sierras via Tioga Pass, and spent the night in Bishop, California. We scattered their ashes early the next morning at a lake where Philo's family often camped and fished.

The house where Philo and his parents lived had been torn down to make room for a chain motel. But we toured the gallery where his parents once sold their photographs of remote places. The proprietor remembered them. He had written to Derek Dain after the plane crash, asking what should be done with the remaining photographs. Derek never replied, so the man boxed them up and stored them in the back room.

"I couldn't sell them, or give them away," he said. "Not in good conscience. And I couldn't bring myself to destroy them, either. KC and Ann were good friends. Their work deserves to be remembered." He rustled around in the back and came out with a large box, handing it to Philo. "I was so sorry about what happened. Glad to see you're okay."

Philo thanked him, and we took the unopened box with

us to Tucson. Philo hung the photos at his house—all except two. He gave my parents a photo of the ruins at Chaco Canyon, where my father once excavated. The second, a photo of the Grand Canyon at sunset, he gave to me as an engagement gift—and a promise of the trip we had yet to take.

Derek's coin collection was assessed as part of the Dain estate. They're worth, at present market value, an estimated quarter of a million dollars. They will reside in Philo's vault in Tucson until we take a trip to Switzerland this fall. Philo plans to give them to Nasrullah's children, Azim and Ziba, as a legacy from their paternal grandfather. They'll each be one-third owners of Foggy Gulch Ranch, as well.

Derek and Heather's joint estate will be in probate for as long as it takes the executor to track down their offshore accounts and sell their remaining properties. Years, no doubt. Whatever remains after settling with the creditors, taxes, and Heather's beneficiary, Gabrielle, will be divided between Philo and his niece and nephew.

The chess set turned out to be the easiest issue to solve. It had belonged to Philo's father, and had been inherited outright by Philo at the time of his parents' deaths. Although theoretically Nasrullah's children had a share in its assessed value, the antiquities had not been obtained legally by their however-many-times-great-uncle Philippe. The chess set and its secrets would be returned to France. Azim and Ziba asked only that they be allowed to view the set first.

Michael and Alana acted as delivery agents. They knew all the players, and Michael knew how to move the artifacts secretly. They flew to Geneva, met with Azim and Ziba for a Skyped teleconference with Philo and me, then drove south into France.

The news of the return of Childeric's bees and the chess set dominated the French news for a day or two. They were stored in the Louvre vaults until they could be authenticated by comparing them to the two bees still in the archives—and until a display could be built.

The donor was listed as "Anonymous."

Acknowledgments

I gratefully acknowledge Dennis O'Leary and the staff of the Djerassi Resident Artists Program, Woodside, California, for a "gift of time" to work on *Fracture* during a 2008 winter residency. During my first sojourn at Djerassi, in 2002, I was privileged to meet Diane Wood Middlebrook, cofounder with her husband, Carl Djerassi, of the DRAP. Diane was a gifted biographer, poet, and Stanford educator. She and I discussed the joys and difficulties of writing biographies of women writers and poets. Though I was looking forward to continuing our conversation at a later date, Diane died in December 2007, a few weeks before I returned to visit the Bay Area. The work she left behind continues to inspire me, as Djerassi inspired one of the settings in *Fracture*.

Molcie Lou Halsell Rodenberger—professor emerita, McMurry University, regent of Texas Woman's University, and Fellow of the Texas State Historical Association and the Texas Folklore Society—published books, articles, and essays on Texas women writers and Texas history. More personally, she served as my mentor and as first reader for the Frankie MacFarlane novels. She told me she was looking forward to reading *Fracture,* but I wasn't able to finish it before her death in 2009. I will miss her insight, knowledge, guidance, and delicious sense of humor.

For their constructive comments on all or part of the manuscript, my heartfelt thanks go to writing compadres

Wynne Brown, Margaret Falk, Elizabeth Gunn, J. M. Hayes, and William K. Hartmann, and to University of Arizona SIROW Scholars Elena Diaz Bjorkquist, Fran Buss, Mary Driscoll, Corey Knox, Nancy Mairs, Pat Manning, Senzil Nawid, and Sally Stevens. Senzil also advised me on Afghan history and culture.

In addition, I am grateful to choreographer Sara Shelton Mann, who introduced me to qigong during two sojourns at Djerassi; to Detective Daniel Barajas, Pima County Sheriff's Department Economic Crime Unit, who answered questions concerning law enforcement; to Clark Lohr, who reviewed my use of firearms in the book; to Michael Floyd and Julian Lozos, Department of Earth Sciences, University of California, Riverside, and James E. Conrad, U.S. Geological Survey, who discussed the San Gregorio/Seal Cove fault system; to Diana C. Kamilli, who reviewed the geology; to Lynda Gibson, who shared her knowledge of origami; to Charlene Taylor, who served as first reader for the manuscript; and to Lewis H. Cohen, professor of geology, emeritus, University of California, Riverside, who assigned the "garnet problem" to my optical mineralogy class long ago.

Lastly, I'm indebted to Judith Keeling, editor in chief, and the staff of Texas Tech University Press, to John Mulvihill, copyeditor, and to Jonathan, Jordan, and Logan Matti, for their continued support, understanding, humor, and patience.

About the Author

Susan Cummins Miller received degrees in history, anthropology, and geology from the University of California, Riverside. After working as a field geologist with the U.S. Geological Survey and teaching geology and oceanography, she turned to writing fiction, nonfiction, and poetry. She is a research affiliate and SIROW Scholar with the University of Arizona's Southwest Institute for Research on Women, and the editor of *A Sweet, Separate Intimacy—Women Writers of the American Frontier, 1800–1922*. *Fracture*, the fifth Frankie MacFarlane, geologist, mystery, follows *Death Assemblage, Detachment Fault, Quarry*, and *Hoodoo*.